D1065095

The Slow Natives

Also by Thea Astley

THE
SLOW
NATIVES

Thea Astley

G. P. PUTNAM'S SONS   NEW YORK

G. P. Putnam's Sons
Publishers Since 1838
200 Madison Avenue
New York, NY 10016

First G. P. Putnam's Sons edition 1993
Published in October 1967 by M. Evans and Company, Inc.

Library of Congress Cataloging-in-Publication Data

Astley, Thea.
      The slow natives / Thea Astley.—1st G. P. Putnam's Sons ed.
            p.   cm.
      ISBN 0-399-13875-7
      I. Title.
PR9619.3.A75S57   1993   93-12168   CIP
823—dc20

Printed in the United States of America
1 2 3 4 5 6 7 8 9 10

Sir Walt, being so strangely surpprised and putt
out of his countenance at so great a Table,
gives his son a damned blow over the face;
his son, as rude as he was, would not strike
his father, but strikes over the face of the
Gentleman that sate next to him, and sayed,
Box about, 'twill come to my Father anon.

—JOHN AUBREY
Brief Lives: Sir Walter Raleigh

"What is the black stuff between elephants' toes?"
"Slow natives!"
—*Juvenilia*

1

He'd first begun to steal when he was eleven.

No, they had both said, surprisingly in agreement, no, you may not have a cricket ball.

He'd got a bit sick of arguing that October. The heat was terrible. The Terrace was a dried-up strip of sticky tar-paper. Okay, he had said. And he had gone into town and taken one from a city counter. It was so easy there wasn't even much fun in it. And of course he couldn't even use the ball but had to keep it hidden at the bottom of his playbox. Fondling it in bed after his light was out, once he had dropped off to sleep with it against the pillow and when it had been discovered in the morning he became involved in a series of lies he was unable to sustain. They kept on hoping for a long time that he had borrowed it from a schoolmate as he had insisted, but each knew that glossy red globe was bright with its own guilt, and he became so tired of their upset and accusing eyes he had walked down to the park near the ferry one afternoon and chucked it straight back into the river where it went bobbing off down the tide. "I gave it back," he announced at tea. "Satisfied?"

There was a lull for a while, largely because they gave in rather than provoke another crisis, and in any case it was something he had done mainly for amusement. If he had

7

really lived up to his intelligence quotient he would have exchanged the ball for cash or a more anonymous article; but then and afterward his actions were motivated solely by the longing to protest against his home.

There were various ways of doing this.

Last year, for some crystalline weeks in his late fourteenth summer, he had been in love, not shockingly so that days melted in atomic illumination of the phase; nor with the sadness that demanded *schmalz*—canned music and stars shattering out of course in the molecular fission created by tenors. Any intensity he felt was only cultivated in order to prove he was in love; he knew it would madden his mother and he envisioned himself as another Vronsky. Slouching on a garden chair in a private place created by a mango tree, Keith would swing one sandaled foot and examine his pudgy square-nailed toes with the beginnings of self-discovery a baby might have envied. This must be the ideal state, he pondered, youngness and love at one ringety-ding-ding swoop—aware all the time of his shorts too small for him and sun-warmed, of his hair bleaching, of guiltlessness and a good breakfast one hour earlier. There was, too, a tooth whose chipped enamel laid open another kind of tenderness.

Her name was Brenda. For three months they had waited together for the Edward Street ferry and he was interested by her finely carved arrogant profile, her private-school voice, and her quite incredibly red plaits that dissolved or caught fire in the sun as it struck her pale cheeks and closely set ears. In the pre-conversation days she had always been carrying adult novels whose jackets provided talking points that he did not early pluck up the strength to use. But later . . . later they would meet by casual cautious pre-arrangement at the top of the ferry path where it dropped down to the sodden green of the river and the mirrored park. She was not pretty but her enormous self-containment atoned.

"My parents are frightfully rich," she told him unemphatically, not finding it necessary to pull her silk cuff back from the heavy gold watch she wore on her thin wrist. "It disgusts me."

"Why?"

"Oh, I don't know. Perhaps because they're bores. I've never had to fight for a thing. It's made me horrible inside. I simply don't know what it is to enjoy the things the way you would."

"No?"

"No." She turned her gray eyes on his smiling, sulky face. "I intend to give everything away."

"You'll be sorry afterward."

"You're very young," she said in a way that fascinated and infuriated him at once. "You must believe in faith helping me do this." Beyond them the river was carved into a silver V by the ferry. "Strength, you know, and faith. Even healing. You can do anything at all if you believe." Her own muddled words trailed a V of dubiousness that tempted Keith to say "bosh"; but then, trapped no doubt beneath sun cascades that flowed from her head under the regulation panama, he agreed, "Perhaps."

She took him to Christian Science gatherings in the city for a couple of Saturdays ("Changing my library books, Dad!") and the amalgam of sincerity and phoniness had them embedded like two new sharp teeth. Once, moved by weather, springtime buildings in the lists with clouds, the sensuous apparatus of a Brisbane summer, she had taken his hands as they came jangling on the tram's hell-box through the Brisbane suburb known as Gabba and for just those few seconds Keith had wondered why there should be anything beyond this moment but her hand, flat, warm, firm—and only that—impressing all the season on his own palm with such unexpected generosity he heard himself say, as if he had extracted the words from her own pale mouth, "I wish I could give you today."

And from that uneasy ledge of utterance he viewed promised lands he had uneasily awaited.

"Tomorrow will do very nicely," she had said.

"But school?"

"School nothing."

"I can't ask you home," he said.

"Why?"

"Oh, my parents. They're . . ."

"They're what?"

"I don't know. If you met Bernard you'd know what I mean."

"What's wrong with him?"

"Nothing's wrong, I suppose. Oh God, yes. Everything is. He's sloppy and middle-aged and going bald and red and gets full."

"All the time?"

"No. Not all the time. But enough."

"Doesn't he like you?"

"Yes, of course he does. That's what's so ghastly. He loves me and I'm ashamed of him. He lets Mum wear the pants because he simply isn't sufficiently interested to care. He repeats his jokes and forgets things a kid would know and makes feeble puns and stops talking about sex when I come into the room. And now—now he doesn't even play the piano particularly well."

"But does that matter?"

"Oh, I guess not. But I used to be rather proud of him once and now I feel such a crumb when people know he does it for a crust—teaches, I mean—and he still mucks about with corny bits of things. Never finishes a movement. 'That's how it goes,' he says. 'Afraid I'm terribly out of practice.' And he dishes up one of those Chopin instant waltzes."

Brenda got it and shrieked. Mischievously she tied the ends of her plaits in a half reef-knot and pulled them up toward her chin.

"What about your mother, then?"

"You've seen Iris on the ferry and things."

"Yes. But only smiles and social hellos. What's she like actually?"

"A nice dull ordinary mum. No. Not so nice really, the way she pushes the old boy around."

"Why doesn't he stand up for himself?"

"Oh, he's not that sort. He's too gentle. Wishy-washy, I guess you'd call it. After all, he does have a brain. Maybe one of these days he'll run away with a blond stenographer. Fancy letting himself be shoved around by a bird-brain!"

"Oh, Keith!"

"Well, she is, really. Bedroom stacked up with digests and crummy magazines."

"But so is mine."

"Well . . . there you are!"

He took her to the pictures one Saturday night and afterward, instead of going home, they wandered along the Terrace, sports coat clutching polished cotton, out of step in more than one way, to the small creek that ran down near the end of the links. Despite the invitation of house shadow, tree shadow, and finally the isolation of the haunted links, he could not find the courage to kiss her. His ardor was modified by certain pressing physical needs that he was far too shy to mention; though if he had only known it, she was suffering also, regretting the orange squash at interval and the double capuccino afterward.

They crossed the footbridge and finally he said, "Could you walk on for a bit, Brenda?"

She knew at once what he wanted and hated him because she could not similarly take advantage of his absence. Female, she was trained to endure. She walked slowly, deliberately away along the path, not nearly quickly enough for Keith, who paused by the bridgerail and waited impatiently for her to move ahead. She was still visible but a white lost shape in the granulated dusk when he relieved himself into the stream.

And then the ashamed agony of his relief.

From below in the darkness an empty can drummed back tinny reduplication of the act. Frozen, he could do nothing in this deafening silence where his private desperation tattooed the landscape with tin notes.

He knew she had heard because he was aware of her moving faster, and although he was not sufficiently brave to call out, when he did attempt to follow she was far ahead and running up the hill toward the road.

Sulking furiously, he dawdled along behind hoping she would be forced to find her own way home, but near the bus stop where the park met its match with blocks of flats he came straight on her, and all they could do was exchange stiffly clad politeness to cover his shame until they reached her gate when she knew and he knew it was finished and they could never again giggle freely together without being conscious of that moment by the bridge. Romantic love did not suffer the body.

So afterward whenever he saw Brenda they would nod almost like strangers, only strangers with an intimacy that prevented their ever corresponding in a normal way; so terrible is the strangeness between two who have touched souls, but not hands.

For kicks, he would say to himself, when he wilfully moved out on an unexplained evening. For kicks. He developed a habit of loitering about the coaching college he attended, hanging around Valley Junction with blank eyes that took in every detail of the summer night crowds packing the joy-racks of trams as they crashed in toward Queen Street, dawdling just a shade too long so that traffic cops moved across not quite kindly and asked him this or that while his sulky baby face tightened over a knot of lies. By and by he became more cunning, could dandle a coffeecup refill for sixty minutes that caused frantic parents to phone up neighbors or to peer down the bland flat-lined Terrace above the river, longing for the sight of him returning.

So he sat now, cool as ice cubes, measuring up this evening spent with the folks. Moron bores, he decided bitterly. Morons. He stroked one tightly panted leg. A series of sensuous impressions seemed to have created him spontaneously at fourteen. Before that—*rien*—as he used to say in a mocking pansy parody of Louis Seize's post-nuptial diary entry. There was the cluttered living room, and by peering between the red-hot pokers and agapanthus whose color-lost shapes made phrenetic splotches in one velvet corner he could see Leo Varga's amused coarse face quiver behind the palpitating fan. Or vibrate to it.

That voice above the slides! That voice! As each rectangular reminiscence joggled into position, Mrs. Coady, who was tortured also by tight shoes and falsifying undergarments, worried her memory. "Here's a street in Dublin. No, not

Dublin. Belfast. Was that Belfast, Poppie?" The eaves had pointed straight to the antipodes. "Sorry, everyone!" she had cried gaily. "Upside down. Just a minute. There. There we are. Now you can see—ooh, that man! He was drunk. Poppie would never have taken the snap if he'd known he was drunk. Now here . . ." Her bust throbbed and Keith began to laugh quietly into his handkerchief. "Here's a little Australian tea-room we came across in Cairo. Isn't that fun? Such nice people. From Coogee, I think."

Mr. Varga turned and gave Keith an enormous unsmiling wink that bounced back like a beam. If there be, thought Keith, a beam in thine eye, cast it out so others may get lit. He fanned his fingers on his plump knees in the dim drawing room and sensed himself warm, be-jeaned, inhaling teacake and someone's after-shave lotion and a faintly disgusting smell when Mrs. Coady moved and worshipfully fed another culture biscuit into the projector. My face, my rudimentary blond moustache, Keith pondered. Everything beginning. And he ran exploratory fingers across his chin and eased one pointed side-laced suede against the other.

Everyone stared obediently at the hideous little shop.

Mrs. Coady laughed tentatively and eased her corset furtively in the darkness. "Poppie nearly got gypped here. Some dreadful camel drivers. They had him right on a cliff-edge and refused to go on unless he paid more, but Dad stood firm, didn't you, dear?" She had glanced hopelessly at her absorbed husband stroking the thigh of a younger guest.

Released, Keith unstoppered a cackle and latched onto Leo's ready eye, which continually investigated an artist's perspective that he used as a please-excuse-me-but for what others might consider an impertinence.

"And there. That was a funny little laneway in Port Said. Dad simply loved it. He went back and took a couple of night shots. They seem a bit blurred though." She had fumbled them into the machine. The filthy brothels hung suspended on the spotless living-room wall. "Aren't those little windows quaint?" she had cried. And they all goggled, hearing the supper-time rattle, longingly, lustily, enduring until they could talk about their jobs and each other and those not present and certain furtive arrangements that required skill and strategic communications. Like Leo. Or like Keith. Or Mr. Coady greasing a trail of some significance toward an autumnal debutante who worked havoc in the summer months, aided by Bermudas and brown limbs and witty beach shirts that invited: "Ring me. I'm waiting!"

From across the room Mr. Leverson watched the back of his son's head, Mr. Leverson who did not like parties, who was thick-set and bored by the fools and who suffered Coady's desperate off-color jokes only because he did not listen. "I can always flush out a room in four minutes flat with a little chamber music," he used to say. And longed to be able to pull the cultural chain at that very moment. A grog, a grog, he prayed. Let there be grog. Yet there was the prospect of coffee only and incidental cocktail music from a scaled-down laminated stereo set while he scratched his thin brown hair and prayed social litanies of despair and supplication that he had not now for years imagined could be answered. His despair, Bernard knew, was scrawled all over his face. It must be the biggest vine in the business. The genuine home-product of leaf gone wild, small bitter fruit fecund as all-get-out, and tendrils gone mad.

A snapping passing summer rain bounced on the roof, nailing them inside, into a stuffy over-House-and-Gardened room junked-up with cultural symbols: a small and well-toned grand ("I haven't practiced for years!"); a guitar ("One of the strings has gone, hasn't it, Poppie?"); a clarinet in pieces; and half a dozen people who would loathe being wrecked together. "Think of an island," Iris had said sentimentally one evening over a pre-Yuletide brandy. "Think of the most gem-like exotically gleaming island you can, Bernard. All pandanus and banana palms. Who would you most hate to be wrecked with?"

"Well," he had replied consideringly, "I can think of six Viennese instantly."

Yet there he was with not one lurking in the yellowing beam of his fifty-year-old eye which found, nevertheless, enemy islanders snoozing behind rubber plants and wall-dividers, the marooned of a suburban evening. Bernard stirred his coffee lingeringly and measured them up. Mrs. Coady, widow to what? . . . Mr. Seabrook, aerodynamics . . . Iris Leverson, wife? mother? . . . Mr. Varga, private coaching . . . Miss Lumley, secretary, sex . . . gallant Mrs. Seabrook . . . Keith . . . Dr. Geoghegan, late menopause . . . Professor Geoghegan, medieval Latin poets and other people's gossip . . . Killer Coady, girls . . . If forced, Bernard mused, staring absently across the coffee bar, to emerge from this banana-thatch fortification, then toward whom, all things being equal, risk of tropical infection at a minimum and so on, would this old boy move? Miss Lumley was so much the obvious choice he recoiled, for he took much pleasure in being an original; and despite crudely pneumatic attractions that would wear thin with time, she was pea-brained, tone-deaf (said Bernard) and afflicted with a long and determined jaw. He hid behind a palmetto and spied on Dr. Geoghegan. A teeny bit old for wrecks at fifty? fifty-two? -three? Although, Bernard decided, her handsome Semitic head would remain so graven despite the mutilations to flesh through the next ten years. In two copper bracelets, half a dozen rings and nothing else beyond the comb that slicked back her oily charcoal hair, he could envision her controlling with governing poise a mothers' school auxiliary or a horde of cannibals. On no account, he imagined her saying—and he began to laugh—must you boil the bracelets! They're a rather dangerous tin and copper alloy. Now quickly, where is the cauldron?

Or maybe Iris? Would he move automatically to his wife? Bernard drank quickly to hide something he wanted to shout. Or Keith? he hoped. Would it be Keith? His wife's neat housing-estate face and Vogue-couturier-clad figure obtruded themselves like conscience and Bernard fled into the coast jungle and out on to the lighted uplands where he found Mr. Coady bumbling for the swanlike curves of Miss Lumley's shoulders beneath the veil of hair. This she would move in forward-flung concealing motions, fluidly hiding her eyes or her intentions that Mr. Coady believed riveted on him but which had a general hunger. Bernard raised his eyes and found his son watching, too. A Father and Son night, he conceded. Embarrassingly progressive.

During supper Keith had observed his father and Mr. Varga come together above the dip, contiguous only physically, although Leverson, had the boy known, was wishing that somewhere he might touch openly the source of his son's restlessness that for half a year had disrupted living, had bleached his hair, had squeezed him into the forcing-tubes of epidermis jeans, had brought him too early to smoking, superciliousness, sick jokes (Bernard, *I* am the slow natives!), and a tendency to take a nip for spite, on the side. Remember, remember . . . that time he had vanished immediately before dinner for nearly an hour and they had found him exhausted and frantic on his bed after a fantastic struggle to climb out of the tapered pants he had bought against their wishes. He had lain with his silly white behind sticking up while Bernard tried bracing himself against the wall and tugging the garment by the ankles. Finally Iris angrily slit the pants up each leg with scissors. This is father-dumb, Leverson thought mournfully, the back answers, the resentments, the secret comings and goings to which I make no protest. (Protest! Protest! his son was crying silently.) It's not my idea of it, Iris had objected, missing the point and ironing all the same her son's fourth clean shirt for the weekend. What he needs is a father who will take him fishing or camping or rock-climbing or out to the cricket matches. What, me! exclaimed hilarious Bernard, flexing his long double-jointed fingers and playing a chromatic protest that made his listening son smile. A no-hoper arty like me! Oh come, Iris! The neighbors are starting to affect you, if they haven't done so already.

And what I need, pondered Keith, resenting him from across the room, is a strong hand. I could respect that. I'm tired tired tired of all this pals-with-the-parents crap. I would like—and he grinned—a good strong hand across the seat of my pants.

Mr. Leverson had so wanted to be friends with his son and

had been investigating the wisdom of saying to him, "Call me Bernard," when the boy, on the thought, so it seemed now, had said not more than a week later, "Bernard, I badly need five pounds."

"Girls?" his father had asked. But the wary fish of his son's apprehending eyes glided away past him.

"Not exactly."

"Well, you can't expect me to lend you a sum like that without knowing why, can you?"

Keith had shoved his hands into his denim pants, pulling them like paper over his plump bottom. He shrugged.

"Well, can you?" silly Bernard persisted, his curiosity alone giving the boy the victory.

"Forget it," Keith had said indifferently, staring out at the back garden—hibiscus, crotons, umbrella trees—and beginning to hum irritatingly.

His father fidgeted with a pile of sheet music, shifting it from a record sleeve that he held up as an introduction to revelation.

"I wish to God you had tidy habits, boy. What's this? 'Surfer Stomp'? Is it more of this stuff you're after?"

"No."

But he went on as if he hadn't really heard. "I wouldn't care, you know, if just occasionally, mind you, only once in a while, Keith, you left this muck alone and bought something decent. Anything but this bawling from the guts. Those clotted howls you kids go for. You don't owe anyone anything, do you?"

Keith said, "Hey bop a re bop. Forget it, Bernard!" And waggled his shoulders and snapped his fingers, his eyes distant and away.

Being disloyal to Bernard by liking Mr. Varga gave him a semi-adult adulterous thrill.

Leo Varga was an artist of sorts. He fashioned Japanese gardens with intricate terraces of falling water and chapters of pebbles. He water-skied. He had built himself a shack at Surfers. He slept, if all his bragging were true, with a variety of not beautiful but fascinating mistresses who allowed him to cook for them. He was an inspired cook! Them with their *bas bleus* and him with his *cordon bleu*, witty Bernard would groan. *Kyrie eleison!* He painted carelessly and facilely in oils, tempera, water-color, house-paint, screen dyes and pigments he ground himself with a great deal of carry-on, applying his colors with quills, brushes made from his latest sweetie's hair (Of course not, Bernard! It's far too curly!), leather strips, toothbrushes (marvelous whipped smartly against a wire!) and bits of cardboard that he tore inspiredly from old shoe-boxes. In whimsical moods he wore national costumes that he had collected in half a dozen aimless wanderings around central Europe and Mexico. Tonight he had come to the party in nattily side-laced *Leder-Hosen* which ended at his knotted knees and were supported by a bib and braces. "God!" Iris had whispered to Bernard. "I wouldn't dress a child in those!" His long socks had a fancy design in primary colors around the band and his white silk shirt was just that merest bit soiled at the collar. He was very sad.

"In Mexico," Keith overheard him saying to Bernard, "I did a whole series based on the sombrero. Everything was sombrero-shaped. Buildings, pools, cacti, breasts, the lot. Marvelous people—simple, superstitious, fanatical, Catholic or Communist. It didn't seem to matter about extremes in a climate like that. Even the landscape was extreme."

As he munched teacake he breathed heavily, not always closing his mouth, exposing strong yellow teeth and a thick busy tongue that flicked rapidly after lost crumbs. His mind's like that, Bernard thought, listening to him investigate a memory evoked by a memory, and inside that penultimate box another even smaller—and in that . . . atrocious.

"More dip?" he asked, watching Keith sideways watching both of them. "How's my boy getting along with his French?" Keith looked away as he listened for the answer, and Mr. Varga paused to wipe his mouth vigorously on a week-old handkerchief that he wore tucked into the cuff-opening of his gleaming sleeve before he gazed across the room at Keith's too-large head now bent over a sandwich tray he inspected with flicking finger.

"Reasonably, reasonably. He responds well to coaching, you know. It's never for the dull pupil." He had smiled. That was the face, the attitude he reserved for interested parents, a kind of testudo to shield against questions that might pry him open like an oyster and reveal his pearl-less state. Someone joggled a coffeecup into his balancing hand and self-defensively Mr. Varga caught Harry Geoghegan's eye and rearranged the group while Dr. Geoghegan, who had been shuffling records in a corner, distracted Keith in an appeal for advice.

The doctor, Keith mused. He almost admired, despite his adolescent arrogance that forbade overt admiration of the adult.

"Do you stomp?" she was asking his bitter baby face and not waiting for an answer. "Keith, dear, have you ever thought of using vast slabs of iambics when you've run out of records? Chanted fast, heroic couplets are devastating for the twist, and stomping needs the same two-stress beat!" She was really way out, that zany, so far it was on the point of embarrassing. "Know *then* thy*self*, pre*sume* not *God* to *scan*, the *prop*er *study of* man*kind* is *man!*" she intoned rapidly, swishing her wide thighs. Keith had wanted to laugh, but was uncertain, for she coddled his genius. Years later, people referring to him and evoking the absurdly babyish face with its thin curly mouth, would dismiss him as one of Julia Geoghegan's mistakes. But now it was hard to tell who was whose disciple. "My dear," continued Dr. Geoghegan, still gyrating, "I made my two biddies learn the whole of the *Essay on Man* this way. Ruined the poem of course, but then that's what it deserved. Here we are—'Pipeline Stomp!' " She slid the record on to the turntable and, guiding Keith to a recess formed by a bamboo wall-screen, locked her hands behind her back and began bumping from one foot to the other. Soon the Seabrooks came over.

"What I like about it," Dr. Geoghegan panted, "is that only one need play."

Gerald Seabrook grinned in the accommodating way that made him popular ("Let's ask Gerald Seabrook. He's always so nice!") and, facing her, made more or less rhythmic duplicating patterns. For that moment, observing their turtlenecks, lined cheeks and awkward bodies, Keith could not smile, the inward grimace showing through.

"Conformist!" heaved out perceptive Julia Geoghegan between polished lips, a stinger that urged him, unbearably tight pants and all, into their group.

"Darkness after light," Kathleen Seabrook said apologetically to Mrs. Coady, who did not hear as she watched her husband bend over Miss Lumley. Oddly enough, Miss Lumley's pancake face was disapproving, her displeasure aimed at the stompers, primitively tribalistic, waving sandwiches in a free hand and snapping with the other. But not, not at coarse-pored, heavy-pawed baboon Gus.

By eleven the bored guests regrouped themselves in the dining-nook and bright Kathleen Seabrook with her wide charming smile and incredulous eyes talked musical shop with Bernard. Professor Geoghegan was listlessly turning the pages of an anthropological work that should never have been allowed through the Customs ("It's been done before," he yawned, pursing a critical mouth) while beside him Gerald Seabrook and Bernice Coady and Dr. Geoghegan were losing their tempers over state aid for schools. Mr. Coady and Miss Lumley were no longer in the room but had unobtrusively moved to a darkened lobby or laundry where he pressed her somewhat harshly against the gleaming corner of the chrome tubs, accepting her agony as ecstasy. Meanwhile Leo Varga, cozily knowledgable, demonstrated yoga positions to Keith in as nearly an unobtrusive corner by the wall-divider, sitting at the moment oddly mute in lotus position, concentrating on an enviable nothing.

The room dizzied with pattern. The adolescent ear missed nothing.

"I saw exorcism practiced in the country once," Professor Geoghegan was saying, "strangely reminiscent of this, for instance." He flourished a not quite indecent picture at Iris Leverson, who was wedged between him and his wife. "Two seasonal pineapple-pickers up in the Wollum. He did it by loud prayers and rolling with his pal in an old tin lean-to on the boss's property. As they rolled they screamed together."

"It sounds disgusting," Iris said, taking a prophylactic sip of black coffee and leaning across to pat Mrs. Coady's knee with a comforting hand as she fought and fought the impulse to go out through the kitchen.

"No, no," Geoghegan assured her. "It was most intriguing. Most intriguing." He was seized with a terrible coughing fit. "Anyone who cared could join and roll with them. Most cathartic. Afterward the fellow being exorcized claimed he felt free of his incubus at last. The physical work-out, that's the thing."

"What is that roareth thus, can it be an incubus?" parodied Bernard softly. "It must have been invented for tired married couples."

"What's that?" Iris asked who had not quite heard. "What's that about tired married couples?"

Keith smiled, watching them, observing how they sprouted out of their chairs like a lot of tired old fungi, yellowed, browned, spotted. You were always a tired married couple, he accused, from way back. Way back when we went each year for a beach fortnight and you wrestled with sand and surf and kerosene stoves and trailed around the merry-go-rounds and the beach-garden competitions and the roller-skating rinks and the hamburger stalls—all, to keep me happy. Your feet ached, Iris, and Bernard's sensitivities when the speaker-crowned life-savers' tower at Kirra used to spew pop tunes all over the bathers and both of you used to moan; because I remember and would run off to the rocks and lie with my nose over a pool, not wanting a conducted joy-tour. I didn't need you and I didn't know how to tell you then. Hot dogs eaten solo were twice as good as hot dogs paid for by you, consumed with you. Once I put a handful of raw peanuts in the pockets of my shorts. I wore a clean white shirt and my sunburn had settled into tan and I felt brave and strong and free and I sneaked off for an hour across the dunes under the twisted salty scrub and watched the twisty salty breakers eat away at the beach while two lovers coiled in a hollow fifty yards away. You never knew. I never told you. And I was eight that year and Bernard used to sing on the seat-beaten glassed-in veranda in the after-bed dark, "Me father kept a boarding-house hullabaloo-belay," and only last week I discovered how he'd guarded me even then from a word.

"Excuse me?" the boy asked Varga. "Excuse me, Leo. I won't be a minute."

As soon as he rose to edge across the living room he felt his mother's eyes swivel with inquiry that probed his new adult anger. Even if I told her I only wanted to go to the john, he thought, she'd still be curious. He went out to the kitchen where he found the remainder of the savory tray resting on top of the refrigerator. Swiftly he scooped up some biscuits and then pushed back the laundry door behind which his host was most terribly engrossed.

They did not hear him at once and then, after that paralyzed moment, wrenched themselves apart under the confrontation of his knowingly innocent face.

"Sorry," Keith mumbled through savory.

He sidled past them, past the lavatory and around the side of the house into the maze of privet and japonica. All of a sudden his sophistication had gone where? He could not support the flimsy child who began walking groggily to the gate but who still did not look back once at the lighted windows behind which adults talked and corrupted each other, slandered, hated, betrayed, remained pathetically loyal and pretended—above all, that was it—pretended self-containment, assurance, all the adult virtues he had regarded himself as having.

The slopes down to the river were sticky with moonlight that fawned all over the posh houses and the blocks of flats between which he then strode, not looking really, not seeing the wet moonlight or the tiger gardens crouched across the river. Curled tight as a fist he went smashing, punching darkness that syruped out thinly to the ferry hill, below which the river, seen suddenly, its swoop and the deep grooving of it, and the boat hulks, was black as lusting Coady, lusting for the sea. It was so still that behind the chug-chug of the ferry dripping drunk across on its cables, drunk as Coady and as purposefully finding the shortest distance from A to B, Keith could track the rattle of a Queen Street tram.

As he waited in the ferry-shed his thumb smoothed over the impersonal face of his watch and in the half-dark he rested on the sweep of the hands that now, greenly luminous, moved up on midnight. Later, he decided, later he would go home. But some time before that, his parents would be anxiously pestering Mr. Coady's embarrassed ear, a Martian projection that caught up the delicate sound-waves created by girls' skirts.

Rattling his small change, he stepped aboard the rocking ferry. Ten minutes to walk up town. Another thirty to circumnavigate the shoppers' coasts. Perhaps twenty for a coffee. Ideally absorbed, Keith had watched the minute hand move steadily up the dial. It seemed to become slower, sweeping across the moon's face, bridging craters of sixty seconds deep down which Keith plunged again, again. Soon, he told himself. Soon. The river quivered. Fish-tail lights flickered. The town's big gold teeth grinned. Soon they would be home.

Prowling downtown, all-absorbing, he slipped into an arcade cellar, where he huddled on a late-night-diner stool, prodding the nerve spots of the last two hours.

Lay me down baby blues . . . bawled a crooner, canned, from a corner microphone, moaned loudly and dreadfully above the chairs and tables and the three other patrons. Keith watched the electric wall-clock creep down the next day, sensing his smile brazen as a jukebox, as the machine now whimpering . . .

> *Pay me down baby,*
> *Never say maybe,*
> *I've got the want you blues.*

There they would be. The old folks at home. They would call "Keith," then "Keith" again, with interest and increasing urgency, and while Bernard looked hopelessly at the smooth bed Iris would pick up the receiver and start dialing.

He kicked the chrome legs of the stool and nodded sadly to the music beat . . .

> *Lay me down baby,*
> *Pay me down baby,*
> *I've got the want you blues . . .*

Sometimes in spring Iris Leverson, who normally lived her life in the contrived activity of organized theater groups, diet charts, weekly "sets," and shopping at what her circle was pleased to call the "village," had thought it might be pleasant to take a lover. All pipe and tweeds, she imagined, influenced by some replays of old films on the telly where engineers ran off with girls who simply had to play Rachmaninoff concertos at Carnegie Hall, forgetting that thereby she would more or less duplicate Bernard. When this first adulterous thought tipped her with tentative finger, she sought back for what might have been the incitement and saw only that last holiday, that last season, the snoozing beach town with its skirt of bitter blue surf, the dangerous green river and beat-up stores with sharks' teeth for sale and last year's hats like hollyhocks or everlastings growing out of magazine mulch and views of the town. There had been long evenings, lavender-stippled air floating over the sea and beach in that terrible nostalgia that comes with sundown and the porpoise shoals cruising and curving fifty yards out in the cold threatening desert of water. And in this romantic ambience, Bernard's mild voice saying amusedly, "You know, Iris, after twenty years of marriage you feel as if you're the same sex."

Her initial reaction was laughter, standing there seeing the mellow gold cliffs reflecting some reluctant glory in the west and everywhere else bottle-green and silver and weed-purple darkness of the sea, the headlands and beach that rhymed with a hundred other eastern coves, gobbled out by wind and surf. That was her initial reaction, and she clutched his elbow, laughing boisterously, and told him he was a funny old thing and then, as she leaned against him with her well-cared-for hand tucking itself under the warm flabbiness of his arm, she was conscious of terrible shock and thought. Yes, indeedie, we're standing here like a couple of middle-aged ladies, comfortable enough together, with nothing much at all to say to each other. She removed her hand, but Bernard did not notice and continued smoking and gazing out to sea. So, with the finicky calculation she might have given to the intention to have a permanent, or a tooth jacket-crowned, she made her decision, just as carefully, as deliberately, though moral implications did not come into those matters certainly. Nor did she imagine for the moment that infidelity would be hard to achieve.

She took vague-mirrored stock of her forty-one, forty-two years. Fair—but not tartily so. Thickened, of course, but reasonably shapely. There were one or two lines she didn't like about her eyes, but the general effect was youthful with straight bob and blond-brown skin pulled tight over her cheek bones. She peered at herself in half-lights, by shaded bed lamps, and in late spring evening rooms before the lights were on—and she felt sufficiently confident. She would justify her casuistry! I'll be working in lights like this, she told herself, and with cool-cookie brazenness, some of her resentment of Bernard evaporated. I am a courtesan at heart, she hoped as she bought herself unfrockery of a frivolous kind with the attention one might give to preparation for an exam. Was it not? Yet she was not yet certain she might sit for this one. There had to be an examiner. Who? Who?

Bernard was so spaniel kind she was half tempted flippantly to ask him as she mentally listed the possibilities of approach. It would have been quicker and cleaner, she knew, had she gone to the city and simply picked up a stranger marooned on the desert isle of an espresso stool, but would-be arty Iris, who was as conventional as they come, even in sinning, selected instead the one possible out of their social group, a man who had once flirted unsensationally with her the Christmas party before last.

It took Gerald Seabrook by surprise, too.

Nevertheless, elderly Gerald and calculating Iris did eventually achieve rather unspectacular adultery in a tizzy motel on the Sandgate Road, and, once the first cliché had been accepted, they settled into a humdrum routine of deceiving their partners, not out of love but from boredom.

You're getting to be a habit and you make me feel so young I'm in love, I'm in love . . . caroled Iris, flogging it along, as hair in dust scarf, Hoover in hand, she set her house in order, in some aspects at least. Gerald was conscious first of obligation, then of tenderness and pity, and then a tenderness and pity that became emotional enough to make him feel susceptibly guilty when he met Bernard and accepted a cigarette from a flipped pack, hopeless when he was with his own wife whom he loved but had been with too constantly, and eager when he was with Iris to placate her self-deception. Too fleshy and pale to be the field and stream man of her dream but tweedy enough in self-shaped sports coat with leather elbow patches, he was, however, downily bald, the pleasant dome of his head fuzzed over with a reticent whitish growth. He had two chins and a very pleasant mouth which Iris had to recall in those moments when passion sputtered like a bulb nearing the end of its lifetime, for at her dangerous age sentiment achieved more than lust.

Perhaps if Bernard had known at the beginning there might have been the impetus of her guilt. It was not until the affair was trailing through *longueurs* like some creeper which has outlasted the fertility of the soil that he discovered she was deceiving him, easy as smiles.

Feeling sad for Gerald and tinnily amused, his initial concern was only that Keith should not uncover the situation and suffer further the domestic punches that winded his ego daily; for he was convinced of the boy's peculiar pain in growing. He nodded and nodded over examination papers and said indeed go darling it will do you good why don't you get someone to go with you being a bit of a bastard as he said that but not too much. "That's what I loathe most about him," sour Iris complained to Gerald, who was not actually listening. "He's completely unconcerned about me. I could be going out to pick up a sailor or squat in the park and all he does is rush home to baby-sit so I can get out to do it."

When the conversation reached this stage Gerald knew he was expected to say that Bernard failed to appreciate her, and to comfort and fertilize the sparse vine that trailed all over his days, hungry tendrils finding him out in the office, sneaking into domestic crevices. But he could only squeeze her hand as if it were a moist little hanky, grubby with tears, and hope to God his own wife did not know.

This, Bernard told himself, told his strumming fingers that, enraptured with technique, dissipated the faintest annoyance in a musical work-out, will peter out by Christmas and probably do Iris a lot of good. His tolerance produced fruit bulbs of self-congratulation for both of them to munch. And he was surprised, as well, that he didn't care more.

"I'll never forget," Iris said to Gerald, straining to remember, "the time Bernard saw us out together."

He had been away examining on the north coast, but an unexpected mumps outbreak in a country town had halved the number of his examinees and he was able to get away twelve hours earlier than he expected, crawling in on the Sunshine line in a mixed goods train that took eight hours to pick its way through the Wollum flats and cuttings, shunting like a tic douloureux in and out of sidings. At one stage they forgot the guard and had to pull back half a mile to pick him up, waving him out of the local pub still with his schooner clutched in his hand. If this slowness had endured only two hours more, perhaps Bernard might have been spared the knowledge that his wife was unfaithful; but just outside Eagle Junction the engine picked up amazingly. Bernard crawled out at Brunswick Street, soot outlined and exhausted, in time to catch a bus from the Valley corner, a gay jouncing bus onto which, as he focused his bloodshot four-o'clock eye, he saw Gerald Seabrook, running late, propel his leaping, panting wife, who collapsed four seats in front of him with giggles of thanksgiving a shade too gay.

He was not surprised. They lived two streets apart. But he was too tired to force out the soggy phrases he knew they would expect; so he shrank behind a summer hat and watched the glass reflection of his own concern. Unnecessarily—for they had not spied him, the lurker, and he returned to good-natured prying, shaping in his mind a genial Clementi sonatina whose first movement had been played indifferently by twenty-five girls and six boys in the last three days. He hummed softly under the bus vibrations and inspected the glossy back of his wife's bright hair with the impersonal evaluation he might have for a stranger. There she is, he thought, and we have known each other in romantic, disgusting, and boring attitudes for twenty years and it is only now that my special lenses are penetrating the image—the nose a little too thick at the tip, the chin a shade too recessive. Profiled toward Gerald, she was talking with that extra animation she reserved for parties, and, without actually seeing it, Bernard sensed her tucking a naked brown arm in Gerald's and squeezing some dregs of affection out. What have we? inquired Bernard's quickening mind, and was answered by a swift loving wing-brush imposition of wifely cheek to Gerald's jaw-line. So swift, a shadow, a not-seen-at-all.

For the first time in years his interest was piqued.

He lit a cigarette and settled back into the bleachers, noting the expression on Iris's face equate itself with that hostessly one which accompanied her set dinner of chicken and almonds and the unnatural green of frozen peas.

Even this joy would trickle away like an inland river, the water-holes, the sand-patches, the lost artesian seas where his own marriage pumped a weak current.

"Good luck, old girl!" Bernard pronounced, the benedictus of the only too willing, and half a stop before Gerald was due to alight, he rocked, seat-clinging along the corridor between the drip-dry and the synthetics, and clapped a hearty hand on Gerald's shoulder. His guilt bounced three inches.

Smackety-smack—adultery's trampoline, Bernard mused, now gay as lollipops with a need to celebrate the severing of habit and boredom that had bound him to Iris through twenty Christmases whose green-treed candles shone less and less brightly.

They had all said oh and where did you get on and how is it you're back so soon. All the usual things. And Iris said he looked tired, darling, said it with that phony sympathy which could only mean a concerned attempt to conceal herself, and just for the metronomic spasm of a second he knew mad Othello, glaring from his eyes.

"Some plague of childhood," he said vaguely. "Convents stricken all along the coast. Come back with us for a drink, Gerald, and celebrate."

"Celebrate what?" Gerald asked, too sharply, too acidly.

"Oh, I don't know. My sudden release perhaps," Bernard smiled disarmingly, making his eyes twinkle behind his glasses that flashed no warnings.

Iris pretended to pick at a thread that nevertheless eluded, for anxiety tightened her clothing in the sunny afternoon of worn bus leather and crumpled tickets. So imagining a world of disaster she searched upward and discovered only charity on Bernard's square red face which turned an exact and similar gentleness upon Gerald. Cleverly brazen, she tucked a now innocent pally arm again into Gerald's and prodded his unwilling body.

"It won't be water," said knowing Bernard jocularly, and they went home together. Which one was blind? really blind? Bernard asked mentally as he poured beer. A good question, student, a good question.

2

Leo Varga stretched, flexed his shortish ape-shape in front of a wall mirror and watched muscular vee-clad Mr. Universe flex back, while, with uncompromising candor, lumbar muscles were inspected, as he winked awkwardly over one shoulder. He rubbed a little more olive oil into his shoulders and tensed.

"You're a bitta orl right," he assured himself nasally and humorously. "Woo!"

On his own he was almost likable, the vulgar charm of his honesty diminishing customary egotism. He did a few body-presses and leg-pedalings and then lay back, panting slightly, on the rattan-covered floor. Around him the walls closed in. There were just sufficient facile abstracts to establish his intelligence and skill; a dubious set of nudes whom he would claim to have known in the most realistic way, and an even stranger set of male studies about which he said nothing at all. Nothing at all except at the right time and in the right company. Doctor Varga, he called himself in the thick of the coaching-college junk sales. ("Late Hiroshima!" Bernard growled when he heard.) But he collected pupils scattered from all over the place and farmed them out to a few students and hungry teachers who could push them through matriculation while he hunched in his cubicle office adding the receipts up and then down to try to make them come out more. They never did. But he was adequately profitable.

Playing it casual, he stepped into houndstooth shorts and pulled a second-skin sweatshirt over his head. Although he was ugly within reason, his belief in his fascination was an article of faith, a dogma pronounced *ex cathedra*, despite or because of the fleshy nose, scrubbing-brush beard and brilliant eyes that he could use masterfully, nailing his victim with a charm dart. He played a rhythmic but not harmonically interesting type of tearoom music while looking like a bruiser whose deep cultured voice had all the greater impact—effete taste complemented by muscle-bulge as he casually tossed off a flamenco song with his own guitar accompaniment when the party became more informal, thereby establishing a quite delicious delicacy if the performance was achieved in his Tyrolean outfit.

He made coffee and watched Saturday morning slide across toward Surfers, lounging on his back *lanai* where he could see the long-haired cuties and the sand-boys amble north to the town and the clip joints. Too yellow, too blue. The coast was all of that. He'd just about had enough of its extremes. Too hot, too salt, too dear. Spearing a bottled oyster on a plastic pick, he dipped it into a sauce bowl and worried it for a while, almost failing to hear the questioning knock at the western door.

Entering new towns, establishing himself, answering telephones, opening doors had always for him inexplicable excitation.

He pulled it back and some reward smiled tentatively.

"I almost missed the bus," Keith was explaining. "They wanted me to say where I was going." (Come in conspirator, said the shrewdie. Be in it. Get trapped.) "And I had rather a job not." He smiled, diffident as goldfish with fins pocketed for support.

Leo observed this. He put on his crooked engaging smile and pushed the door wider.

"The chief difficulty at your age, Keith," he said, "is to grow up without offending those whose sole aim seems to be to prevent it. I know. I had all that. Painful biz—but more so for parents than for me. Ultimately we were divorced without fuss and I gave them reasonable access!"

He went back to the kitchen-nook and set out another coffeecup, put salt pretzels on a dish, leaned a confident hand on the redwood oiled bench he had made, and tendered Keith a look combining careful insolence and affection that he had found successful before.

"Oh, come in," he ordered benignly, as Keith remained awkward at the doorway. "Come in and relax. Of course I'm glad you could make it. I've just banished three startlingly seductive women to make room for you and your sensibilities. Don't get lost in your own adolescence, for God's sake."

Keith came over, took a pretzel and nibbled it slowly, bringing his front incisors together with a thoughtful tapping.

"There were two fairies coming down in the bus," he said reflectively, not looking at Varga. "One was a guy dressed up. Lush as could be. All lipstick and eye-stuff. None of us could take our eyes off them."

"How *about* that," Mr. Varga said noncommittally. "Coffee?"

"Please."

"And—?"

"Nothing, thanks. Nothing. I just wondered how the dressed-up one felt. When he first discovered he wanted to go on like that, I mean. Was it watching his big sister or some minute in the wings done up for the school play? Or would it just whack him suddenly as he came in on a wave? I mean, how would you discover?"

"Who knows?" Mr. Varga said. "Perhaps the spring had seduced him. He knew he'd look prettiest in pink. Boys, my dear Keith, should most definitely be boys." He patted the lad's shoulder in a father confessor way. "Come and have an oyster. They're marvelously self-contained, you know . . . you didn't know? My dear lad!"

"Like an old married couple. Like Mr. and Mrs. Leverson."

"Perhaps."

Leo was a bottomless man. When he turned away to get

more biscuits from a shelf his rear was a teeny bit pathetic. Even in Mr. Universe leopard-skin he would still not have got away with it.

"Your father asked about you, you know, last night at the party."

"I knew."

"How, may I ask?"

"I saw your face go tight and Dad's go bland. You know, it's easy when you've lived with him for years."

"He's not a bad old boy really," Mr. Varga mused. He held out the plate. "I like him."

"He embarrasses me," Keith explained, forgetting to take another. "He seems like a silly old fool alongside most of the fellows' fathers. Never says a thing unless it's about music. And long-hair stuff at that. But the worst thing of all. . . ."

"Yes?" prompted Leo, delicately looking away.

"Well, the worst thing of all is the way he lets Iris shove him around. In front of people, too. Only looks amused. It makes me want to curl up."

"Yes, he does that rather," agreed malicious Leo. "Did you know—?" He stopped.

"Know what?"

"Oh, nothing. Simply an unpleasant rumor."

"Come on, Leo. You can't start telling me something you're not prepared to tell in full. After all, they're my parents."

"True. But better a millstone, you know."

"I know. Just hang one around this neck." He remembered the biscuit.

"Sauce?" Leo, smiling Leo, inquired solicitously. Each baring of enamel was recorded by Keith as proof of success. He wanted to make Mr. Varga laugh more and more.

"Well," Leo enunciated slowly, pulling the sticky cover-all off. "It is rumored about the place—only the faint bruitings of bastards, you understand—that your mamma and Tommy Seabrook's papa are more than friends, as the film magazines put it."

Keith went white. He gripped the sink edge momentarily

and automatically, without even seeing what he was doing, filled a glass at the tap. Mr. Coady, Miss Lumley in the laundry dark.

"It's not true. It's not, is it?"

Mr. Varga shrugged. "You see. I didn't want to tell you. Now you're upset, silly boy."

Keith recovered himself by hauling both at metal and practicalities like blue water visible through a dune gap, while his mind, rocking as if it had been cuffed, refused and refused. "Don't be crazy," he said. "Of course I'm not." His mouth shook.

Leo observed this with deep satisfaction and their eyes seemed unable to shift from each other's face, so filled with triumph and disaster, the false sheen of pretended friendship and the dreadful high gloss of preliminary seduction. Keith picked up his coffeecup in a shaking hand, a small-boy hand that wanted to slog the patron and protector opposite but could not. Could only hold and quiver. Deny it, cried the voice within. Deny. Deny. But he hauled himself together, sucked in strength from an outside view of brassy wealth, and puckered his lips for the final betrayal.

"Of course not," he said. "Who'd look twice at Iris? Or Gerald, for that matter!"

Molding a canvas deck chair and keeping his straw hat well down over his face that Iris might not apprehend his sleeplessness, Bernard sorted through a great number of ancient photographs thinking perhaps there or there he had missed the clue: the three of them now, and the scene later when the boy finally did turn up as he must. There would have to be one of those disgusting hearts-on-the-table showdowns. Iris, exhausted from beside-herself telephoning half the night, lay drained away in her bedroom with witch-hazel pads on her eyes—or so he had left her, still plaintively insisting they should ring the police.

"Nonsense," Bernard had replied at once. "Keith would find that far too satisfying."

34

Iris then had increased the volume of her whimpering to a little shriek at his failure to exhibit parental frenzy, and uncontrollably her lover's name (a previously unclassified exotic!) flowered again and again. She would, she threatened, sweeping her striped and too-girlish brunch coat about her, she would ask him what to do. He was kinder, more sympathetic, had more keenly developed responsibilities as a father and so on, insisting until Bernard turned his back on her and tried a short phrase that had been interesting him on the piano.

He expected Iris to hit his hand in the James Mason manner—and she did. The keys clanged back at her.

"Ring Gerald," he said. "Ask him. But you are being completely silly. Keith is trying for an effect. Remember the other times he's tried us out. Iris"—his punished hand nevertheless took her gently by the shoulder—"calm down and remember when he couldn't have that bicycle. Remember how he hid all day at young Coady's and only emerged when hunger drove him out? And the time he couldn't go on the Cairns trip with all those kids? He's been vanishing off and on for years."

"But what have we done? What's he punishing us for?"

Bernard rubbed his hands over his gritty eyes. "God knows. Who knows? The whole system of his punishing us makes him sound like a disgusting little swine. Unless, of course, we deserve it. Or he thinks we do."

He regarded Iris steadily and could not help enjoying a natural pleasure when her eyes dropped.

"Perhaps I deserve it most," he could not avoid adding either. "You're right, Iris. I am a poor sort of father."

Turning away he briefly experienced the grief he normally could only wish for but not attain and determined his own punishment would extend its full term, for he felt no real concern for his son's safety but only a strange wish to suffer himself. Now and again he would examine matters of the evening before and wonder if some adult carelessness had tipped the balance. Iris and Gerald had barely spoken, let alone communed, so there could be nothing in that. Perhaps they were tiring of each other, he reflected regretfully. They would discover that the relationship they had rejected and the one they now enjoyed and the one each might enjoy later on all went the same way.

Bernard was genuinely provoked to pity and a sudden awareness of emptiness. I have no problems, he thought, not even this. Not even my marriage is endangered, for you can only endanger a happiness and it has hardly been that for a long time. My work does not absorb me and create spasms of pain within time. Nor yet does it lack all interest. I read. I play the piano—only a little—but still I do perform, if indifferently. I drink more than a little but do not womanize. I smoke to excess. I am punctual on the job. I play a record now and then and I am gentle, calm and completely civilized when my wife deceives me, my son leaves home.

Trellised and mesmerized leaves shuddered uneasily on their wooden rack near which mango trees, heavy with fruit and plummy shadows, hunched, sleepily aware of Bernard's sandaled feet stuck to the bole. Shadows loitered across the lawn to watch. And Bernard found himself time-watching while the black fingers under glass shifted no more quickly than the shadow of a croton to whose final destiny—the arm-rest of his chair—he had affixed a decision to go inside.

The phone was ringing like ice-cream bells—as vulgar, as insistent.

The enemy was there first, but her irony stood aside with eyes of glass, angrily transparent, and made him do his duty, focused in silence his hands picking up the receiver, explored him as he stood with the tiny unreal voice worming its way into his ear.

"Hello." Somber, deadly slow, funereal vowels. They were unmistakable.

"Yes. Leverson here."

"Geoghegan speaking."

"Oh."

"Is something the matter?" He had his ear always to the ground for domestic frenzies—not a sexual voyeur but one who squeezed joy out of whimsical infractions of the domestic rule. "I can always ring later."

"I'll bet," Bernard whispered.

"What? What's that?"

"I said not yet. There's nothing wrong yet."

"You sound rather distraught."

"Question or statement, Professor?"

"Oh, my dear Leverson. It's too hot. Too stinking hot. But you do sound rather screwed up like a bottle top to the point where the thread may snap."

"What nonsense!" Bernard attempted laughter. "You're imagining things. Or hoping for."

"Perhaps. Look, what I really rang for . . ." Liar, thought Bernard.

Iris had moved away (Ask him, you fool! Ask him!) and had begun a neurotic rearrangement of certain week-old fronds that projected from a jardinière in a manner she classed as Japanese. She had been an Ikebana cultist for a while. "She can work at them half an hour before she achieves a climax," Bernard used to say unkindly. "Everything seems to be all stamens and pistils and pollination processes."

Iris's rage was willing to explode like a wonderful flare that might finally illuminate the tundra of her marriage, for now words exposed this thing to her husband who would stolidly play out her passion in his favorite sonata and discover when he had finished that she had been forced to remove her knotted person to some deaf corner of the house where neither his music nor any projection of himself through it could possibly touch her.

She was given to drip-dry suits and wooden beads. Nun-like her fingers told strings of ochre pips or smoothed the guaranteed uncrushable primness of her skirt thinly down and down so that even she felt spinsterish and wondered what voluptuous spasm had engaged Gerald.

"I can only get the score on loan," Bernard was explaining patiently while Iris twitched with impatience. "And there is no proof anyway that the lyrics were written at the same time. He probably wrote the music long before the words were appended . . . What? . . . No, of course I can't tell by the Latin."

Iris began to cry quietly and steadily.

God in Heaven, thought Bernard watching those regular and deliberate pulsings.

"No," he said. "No. I'll get it for you. It was autographed if I remember rightly . . . what? Don't get excited, Harry. I can't hear you. There probably won't be anything on the lyrics at all. Come over, if you want, or go and have your siesta, do. Or de-tick the Labrador."

He hung up. "There's cultural zest for you," he said smiling with an effort at his wife. "Geoghegan on some imaginary trail of a medieval lyrist. He's like a cultural Mountie. Or do I mean mountebank? Tavern songs and some rather delicious little—"

"Shut up!" Iris said unexpectedly. "Shut up shut up shut up."

Because for years she had been afraid to explode the legend of for ever and ever, the durability of love within marriage, and had kept this lie alive along with a dozen other women with whom she took coffee breaks and who complained boastfully of their husband's incessant attentions, she was staggered now by her lapse into truth. For half a minute, perhaps, their denuded dislike glared across the hire-purchase jungle that bound them in a cocoon of habit and monthly payments. "Till final instalment do us part," witty Bernard had murmured provokingly, and then she took her frenzy with her into the back garden and started the car.

Since there is a divination that apprehends the hawk about to fall or the branch, or the shadow within shadow, the held breath behind the darkened door, Bernard was able now to recognize that, Gerald or no Gerald, they had separated across rivers and the bridges were crumbled years ago. At this point the leaves are almost counted by the stripped brain; an exaggerated interest notes droplets swell on faucet ends and tumble into sinks, gutter, swell, tumble; nostalgia melts at last and the soul hops about like a ticket-of-leave man. Observe this frond, the spores of velvet, or this, this anguished new green bursting its sheath, or that jean-clad bottom-bouncing cookie or this fragile amber of pre-storm luminescence that might crack and reveal some horrible normalcy of the sky.

Bernard could scarcely bear to look into the garden where thousands of shapes revealed piquancies he had not observed for fifteen years, could hardly withstand the blast of light let in by her repeated phrase. Groggily he raised the fly-screen and pushed the window out. Two incredibly beautiful, feather-soft, beak-sharp birds jazzed over the grass. The grass stabbed with millions of individual blades. Fence palings became identifiable with knots that rang chords, serrations that bit blue. His nothingness brimmed over and, still trapped by minutiae, he went out again to the canvas chair under the mango trees and sat down to wait for his son.

Yet neither flustered nor ashamed, Keith came in softly with his suede feet at eight fifteen. He did not like the look of the anxious illumination of the porch, the clearance-waiting garbage bin too early by half, the show-boat brightness of number twenty-three that blazed its dangerous festivity onto the side lawns of twenty-one and twenty-five. Keith trod rubber silences by the side bougainvillea and came up the one, two, three, four, five back steps into the accusations of refrigerator and gas hot water switching noisily on. Through the open kitchen door he could see in the dinette his parents not speaking over coffee.

"Hullo, Bernard. Iris." He was the jaunty attempter but his father told him to sit down in a tone he did not recall ever having heard before. Iris could not speak for relief. He counted the plastic canisters on top of the dresser and suddenly, idiotically became aware of Professor Geoghegan's pedagogic tones talking with persistent mania into the living-room telephone.

"Where have you been?" Bernard asked.

The terror-pleasure aspect of Mr. Varga's weekender blazed like cracker-night and the sight of his denounced mum slumped there beside deceived dad choked him for a moment while his father, with outward calm, waited. Sneakily Keith kept sliding his eyes toward his mother who had become the whiplash of the dirty joke.

"The beach," he replied, without looking.

"But *what* beach? Where? Did you go with anyone?"

"No."

"Are you sure?"

"Quite sure," he said, and gave the clear-eyed look that liars by omission can always give.

"Where were you then? I want to know exactly. Where did you spend last night?"

"I walked in to town. I mean I went over on the ferry and walked about a bit."

"That would hardly have taken all night. Where did you go in town? You're lucky the police didn't pick you up."

"Oh, be your age, Bernard." Keith smiled. In the other room sad Geoghegan replaced the phone and came somberly to the kitchen door where he unobtrusively and joyfully inspected the boy.

"He sat on a railway-station platform," he suggested. "The foolish lad. A filthy squalid urine-stinking station littered with trash bins and candy wrappers and dog pee. Ask him! He'll tell you. That was it exactly."

Keith reeled within. The pompous old windbag! Clued up, forsooth! He wanted to shock them.

"No. That wasn't it," he said. "It wasn't like that at all."

Geoghegan huffed and lit his pipe.

"I picked up a girl." Keith hesitated. "A woman," he said, trying not to look at his mother.

"I hate liars," Geoghegan stated abruptly, and blew smoke over the lot of them.

Bernard put one exhausted hand across his eyes. "You mean she picked you up?" he asked.

"Yes," Keith agreed, warming to it. "She asked me home."

Iris's gasp hissed out into the silence. Keith almost laughed and even this new hatred of his mother had its revenge.

"He's lying, of course," Geoghegan insisted. "The little fool had no money, had you? Had you? And what did she look like, anyway, this street woman of yours?"

"Just like anyone's mother," Keith said brilliantly.

"Oh, for God's sake!" Bernard had to shake his head to clear it, and instantly room detail magnified with the same sharp-edged clarity as the garden, cake bins with "cake" in black cursive; the stove revealed chips, stains, streaks, five ebony power keys studded with a sparkler of a screw. He said, "And today? You've been gone all day."

"I told you."

"Not really. I want to know where, please."

"Surfers," Keith said. "Oh, this was proper." His guilt raged. "Relax, everyone. I was with a responsible adult like yourselves."

"And who," Bernard asked, letting it ride, "was this?"

"It was Mister Varga."

"Had he asked you?"

"No."

"Did he mind your coming?"

No indeedie, he thought, and said, "I don't think so."

"You realize I can check on this."

"Check away."

"Is it the truth?" his mother asked. Keith did not, could not, answer.

"Answer your mother," Bernard ordered. The boy turned his head from the light and the light came at him still from behind and ripped.

"I'm tired," Keith said. "If you people don't mind, I'd like to go to bed."

"*Answer* her!" Bernard shouted.

"No," Keith said very firmly. "No." He pushed his chair back, having this quorum by the throat, and said to no one in particular, "Never again. Not once again. Neither her, nor your Professor Geoghegan, nor any adult."

"Don't!" Bernard said suddenly as Iris half opened her un-painted lips and went to him. "Leave him."

His arrogance lasted nicely to the side veranda where he slept in a glassed-in study, lasted until he stripped off his jeans and sweatshirt and burrowed his bewilderment beneath the blankets. He knew, and he could not bear to know, that at this moment his father was aware he would be howling like a baby.

41

"Saint Gretta is patron of the mentally disturbed," Bernard said mildly to old Bathgate of the Board as they creaked out of the conference room. "We need an icon." Bathgate gave his three-note guffaw, padding beside Leverson along the Terrace. Now and then he waved his stick hopelessly at passing cabs, but none paused, so he plodded on after the other man, his lumbering movements holding Bernard up. "Mad," he agreed. "Quite quite mad. Lord, I could do with a drink. Couldn't you, old fellow? After listening to all that nonsense for two hours. Blithering piffle. I say, what did you think of that chestnut Garnsey cracked, eh? Syncopation is an unsteady movement from bar to bar. Let's syncopate, Mr. Leverson. Let's."

"Sorry," Bernard flapped his free hand gull's-wing fashion. "I have to get home. We're being social this evening."

"Ah! Poor fellow!" Bathgate coughed violently for a few seconds. "By the bye, what did the great Clerihew want you for before the morning session, if one may be so impertinent?" He puffed and panted, looking downhill at the trolley cars.

Curious geezer, Bernard thought, but he humored him. "Candidate trouble. Teacher says there's been terrible domestic upheaval and so on and so on and could I possibly . . .? You know how it goes."

"Do I not? Don't want much, do they?"

"Ah well, I might pop back in a couple of weeks when things ease off here a bit. There were two others who missed out because of some transport let-down. The milk truck couldn't get them in on time. I'll do the lot. And, to tell you the truth, I'll be glad of the run back."

Bathgate pursed speculating lips, but said nothing. The unsaid hmmmmmmm.

"Blessings!" he chortled. "Blessings!"—as they parted at Edward Street in a tautened crowd swirl. Frantically his stick conducted some plea and a cab at last did slide to a stop. *Portamento, ritardando* . . .

Bernard pushed sweatily through peak hour toward the Valley where, in a coffee lounge at the bottom end of Queen Street he bumped into Professor Geoghegan before he had

time to conceal himself behind his paper. Cunningly Geoghegan allowed him to be seated first and then dropped into the
seat opposite with such surprised warmth (feigned, decided
bitter Bernard) he could only click his teeth bad-temperedly
and endure.

Geoghegan was having one of his days when he talked
zanily and engagingly about incredible and, Bernard suspected, mythical humans who peopled a Geoghegan Landscape, assembling antics and pranks of exquisite, detached
nonsense.

"I remember my aunts," he was saying dreamily as he
sugared his coffee. "They're dead, thank God, but they were
the most awesome pair. Used to drive a car, the dear old
things. A big Bentley, black, thirty feet long like an under-
taker's carriage."

"Lucky them."

"I suppose. Oh, I don't know, dear fellow. You see, they
couldn't manage it separately and one used to steer and the
other used to change gears. 'Are you ready, dear?' Zoe—that
was the older one, the one steering—used to say. 'Right!'
would say Hester. And zoom—off they'd go!"

"Who declutched?" Bernard asked, interested despite himself.

"Well, that I can't really say. The steerer, I imagine. Sometimes Hester couldn't get it into gear and Zoe would say,
'Not quite right, dear. Let's try again!' "

"It's all a fabrication!" Bernard laughed. His cheeks,
plumped by time, filled out with amusement, he could observe in the flashy mirror strips all around him. Fattening
Leversons smiled back cozily every way and he accused himself: False kindliness, but I'll be a lovable old daddy-oh of the
music world. I'll tell corny jokes to students. I'll totter ever
so slightly going in and out of examination rooms, will be
caught humming bits of Purcell and forget my overcoat. Jot
motifs on menus. Be Santa Clausish, Daddy Bach—and he
laughed again—wrong place this time, for Geoghegan looked
put out and said, "Well, I was only asking."

About what? Keith? Gerald? Not Keith, he hoped, gazing

into the sticky street where mums dragged toddlers who dragged cones and lollipops and crumpled toys. Desperate parenthood hauling its brats along, he thought, when it is the brats who really have them by the nose. Keith asleep, he remembered. Keith with closed eyes and a heavy curve of lash on a pink football cheek. Withdrawn, the head turned away on the pillow, the fists bunched in sleep, the mouth parted. Along the drooping lids the blood pulsed lavender, the shadows were delicately blue. "Little pet," he said softly, bending over, bending to kiss, to touch the down of skin. And there had followed a punching tiny fist, right on his throbbing nose, and a squeal of impish giggling that still managed to endear itself, to make him utter more foolishness, to nuzzle the struggling child.

"Everything," Bernard lied, "is all right. We are a clockwork home."

They parted with mutual reassurances at the bridge turn-off where Bernard eyed the broad sweep of hot bitumen, the tan river, the sleeping ships. He was not even emotional enough to dislike the suburbia that crowded the far point, but paced steadily over and up the hill past the state school and went bland as junket through his front garden back into the family circle.

"Saint Gretta," he said, repeating the fact for those who cared to listen, "is patron saint of the mentally disturbed."

Iris plunged right inside the apple pie she was creating— the word for Iris's activities, he thought—and did not even peek at him over the fluted edges; but Keith, who was scraping down a palette at the kitchen drainer, blinked with the first filial interest he had shown for weeks.

"Saint who?"

"Saint Gretta."

"We could have one alongside the dwarfs and the gnomes."

"We could," Bernard agreed somewhat wearily, playing along a worn family joke.

"Dinner," Iris said emerging, "is nearly ready if you're going to change."

"Oh, I don't think I'll bother."

He chose to be maddening and wandered into the living room where he turned on the wireless and burrowed into its furry blare. Much surprised, he found his son had followed him.

"I say, Bernard," the boy said, but speaking in a careful way that convinced the man Iris was not intended to hear. "Could I get a duffle coat?"

"Duffle coat? What's a duffle coat?"

"You know," Keith explained, speaking with difficulty and a great deal of urgency against the wireless. "A sort of short overcoat. A car-coat, man. Very sharp. The young Rimbaud. Way out."

"Oh, I don't think so," Bernard said. "I don't quite see you as the young Rimbaud. I can't see the need, anyway, in this climate."

"But all the fellows are getting them."

"I thought you were the keen nonconformist. What's up?"

"But that's it. All the keen nonconformists are getting them."

"Aren't they rather loutish?"

"Only slightly," Keith said with insolence he did not even try to repress, observing his father's face harden, and hating himself underneath the triumph, for these easy victories he had been scoring up for years at each little occasion made him just that much more unhappy.

"No," Bernard said. "No. Definitely not."

The Leversons munched a sulky dinner and through baked pumpkin the boy asked again. "But why can't I?"

Iris tossed one of her look clichés at her husband (despairing eyebrows up, shoulders hunched), a glance that claimed intimacy with this problem. Under the circumstances, reflected Bernard, she looked bloody arch, but he smiled wryly and went on eating lamb with mint sauce.

"I warned you," Iris said. "I told you no."

Keith would not look at her but, with the skill that had been playing it this way for years, proceeded to set parent against parent.

"You only say no because she says no, don't you?"

"Nonsense."

"No, it's not nonsense." He scowled. "It's true. A fundamental truth of life at the Leversons'."

"Dear me," Bernard said. "Sauce please, Iris."

"If she said yes, so would you. If she said anything at all so would you. Simon says. Simon says shit. Iris says shit. Bernard says shit."

"You know dirtier words than that, lad," said Bernard.

"Not dirty enough for this," Keith shouted at his father, control lost at last. "Not nearly dirty enough for this. Because she pushes you around you're afraid to have an opinion."

"Oh, for God's sake shut up! I said no no no because I mean no, do you understand? Because you don't need this stupid garment and because you are not damn well going to get one. And that is final. And kindly leave your mother out of it."

Keith shoveled beans and potato into a mound and laid his knife and fork beside them with superb, lingering care, seeming to measure distance for effect.

"You stupid blind cuckold," he said at last, deliberately and clearly, and stared straight into his father's eyes.

Plates bounced like disks as Bernard reached across and slapped him ringingly, smartingly, for immediate relief; and when Keith's crumpled face broke into tears, the humiliation erased the hatred, and essence of his antagonism seemed to present itself like the crucified Christ and he loved his father so much he wanted to die.

3

THESE DAYS, BERNARD decided during the few seconds a perfunctory wave to his wife took, we are in an armed neutrality. Keith had mumbled something farewelling through a mouthful of cereal and had not bothered to look, really look, at his old dad going off to earn the family livelihood. That should hurt me, Bernard worried a little, as he drove west to Ipswich which was forever to him the town of the burnt-up park and the slightly-off Windor-sausage sandwiches he had munched there once as a boy between his own rowing parents parked on the grass above the picnic lunch. But it did not, and today there was not even the apprehending quality of that early occasion last week when he had spun over the walls of freedom. The rain wept sadly and unforgivingly across his windscreen, whose two rhythmic lashes swept it back and forth in clean semi-circles through which he saw only the suburbs standing on tiptoe and the wet sheen asphalt.

There were no problems left because he no longer cared, huddled empty in his damp raincoat, his rain-spotted hat on the bucket-seat beside him. Behind was his bag—("Towel, Bernard? Toothpaste? Slippers?" But not—"Love, Bernard? Concern?") Yes, Iris believed in the marital symbols of comfort, all right, but those hidden things, the genuine tenderness that survived the solitariness when the last guest was gone, the cigarette-ends piled into the sink tray along with the olive stones and the bits of salami, and all the scummy glasses stood easy along the formica, then did she believe in love? Not even hot-paws with Gerald ("Poor old bastard!" he said aloud) could survive that, could beat the nakedness of two souls. Bodies weren't in it when it came to stripping!

He stopped at Helidon for a drink, glooming through the pub windows at a rain plastering the sky and the countryside as far as he could see. Hills had vanished. As he drank he thumbed down the list of examinees—fifteen convent pupils, six private, only three elementary, thank God. Some strays at Stanthorpe and Toowoomba. If he shot through that lot smartly he could polish off the rest in a day as he had planned and his little lie to Iris would bear fruit. He'd have a nothing-night away from home.

For a few vicious seconds he thought of wiring Gerald, but a vision of Iris, her curlers scarfed up from the dust, propelling a niftie-swiftie of a vacuum cleaner through the spiritless rooms, pumped away behind the bar with such domestic absorption he could have wept at the nonsense of it all and ate no lunch but drank another, and felt like cutting his throat.

He drove into the garden city through tender drizzling emotional trees.

It went as he had planned.

Hotel sheets embraced him that evening and in a dream of pianos and convent parlors, a never-ending line of pigtailed girls played a Grieg *Albumblatt* and stumbled in exactly the same spot until thanks to God the tea and thin bread-and-butter rolls and the gem scones were served. "I want the downlands tour," old Bathgate had badgered at the last staff examiners' meeting. "I want to go to that convent on the range where they make those marvelous gem scones." He had eaten four, and grinned all through his second and third cups of tea, thinking of Bathgate stuck up along the coast in the wet. "I've got it all plotted with flags," Bathgate had pronounced. "Drew it up for today!" And he had unrolled a crazy map of the state with all the centers marked with flags inscribed "pikelets" or "teacake" or "asparagus rolls" or "éclairs." "There's not much to choose," he said thoughtfully, "but I'd say the Ursuline convents have it every time. Flavor and lightness and size of helpings." The ten other men looked incredulously at the map on the table.

"What are those little multiplication signs for?" one wanted to know.

Bathgate had looked up innocently.

"My dear fellow," he explained carefully, "this is the result of enormous research and widespread but delicate questioning. I've done this solely for the benefit of all of us. Photostat copies will be issued. Those places marked with a cross are the ones without a gents!"

Soon after breakfast he went down to Condamine in sun patches between showers that lit up the wonderful greens of nearness and lilacs of distance, and as his car raced along the straights of the downlands he was conscious of nothing but speed and quick scenery, the comfort of having recently breakfasted and well, the pleasure of aloneness. Yet this was dissolved when he came downstairs two hours later in the Condamine Focus and found awaiting him in the lounge a handsome, gloomy cleric who had been meeting him in this manner for several years now. They smiled briefly.

"The good sisters?" Bernard asked.

"The good sisters indeed. Anxious as ever. I'm to drive you over."

"Have I time for a beer?" Bernard glanced at his wrist-watch. "I'm not due there till ten thirty, you know. Just a quick quick one."

He speculated on a patina of grayness that covered Father Lingard and a new habit he seemed to have of rubbing one ruminative fingertip along the corner of his mouth. "Ah, yes," he would say to fill in the gaps, and when Leverson looked at him once too suddenly, too inquisitively, he explained, "I am nature abhorring a vacuum."

"How is your family?" the priest inquired, out of politeness, guessed Bernard, rather than real curiosity, and he thought, I could shock his calm by saying, "My wife's an adulteress and my son has been seduced," but then he re-membered it was almost impossible to shock priests and that all Doug Lingard would say would be a grave "Tell me about it," that was indeed exactly what he did say when, next morning as they lunched together on his return from Stan-thorpe, he finally admitted, "My wife is unfaithful, my son has lost his innocence." (Note that gentler wording, Ber-nard, he said to himself.) But at that time and in that place, he was unable to qualify the new emptiness that exhilarated as it isolated each tree in the forest and singly discovered the birds.

He could merely shrug.

There were, he noticed, some careless stains on Father Lingard's stock.

"I'm a little tired, I think perhaps of this town."

"Aren't you being heretical?"

Lingard smiled wryly. "Well, that would be something. A stir. I think I could bear the Inquisition and a panel of beady-eyed Dominicans pinning me to the wall."

Leverson sipped thoughtfully. "But I didn't think you people ever suffered from boredom. You're so wrapped up in sacrifice, wouldn't even the boredom be part of the pleasure?"

"You sound most Dominican yourself." Lingard managed a small laugh. "It's not a boredom so much. It's hard to ex-plain. A kind of spiritual aridity when all the springs dry up, you know, and there seems to be pointlessness about it all." He inspected his bony wrist. "Look, it must be a problem of my years."

"We all feel it," Leverson said.

"You too?"

"Me too."

"And how does it attack you? The same restlessness, the same discontent? The examination of the heart in the hours when others are asleep? The wish to strip oneself right down to the bone and escape?"

Bernard nodded.

"One must persist, persist, persist. You know what we say—believe in spite of appearances, trust despite all evidence to the contrary, hope against hope. It should be easy, but it's damned hard work. I say damned advisedly." He pushed his beer away and left it unfinished, sad and flat. "I think we'll have to go now. They'll be rushing about in twenty different directions."

Condamine's main street will remain unchanged forever. It was, and still is, a scrubby little town drowned in dust and flies. Around the corner Lingard had angle-parked his car with its nose poked in at a second-hand store. The car was black and clerical, too. It had white sidewall tires that repeated the liturgical motif and it stood, expensive and desperate, ready to rush into life and drive both of them nowhere.

The convent was a double-storied timber building with a brick façade, a chapel on the southern wall beyond which tennis courts lay behind a grape trellis, and a big barn of an assembly hall in the northern shoulder of the grounds. Plaster saints idled in the front garden, peering over the wall at Condamine's Fitzherbert Street—all leaf and old colonial (three verandas, bow windows, hallway)—that sauntered by to join the main highway east. At a variety of points along this road, camphor-laurel trees tangled lushly overhead, obliterating the sky with a turbulent scrawl-screen of leaves whose shadows lay felt-thick across concrete. From the privacy of the grape trellis in the winy summer, various white coifs might be seen moving and observing the cars traveling east or west; observing with envy or pity or indifference or a kind of jealous rage that Sister Matthew endeavored to repress each time she discovered the world she had given up years ago, so close, its pulsing might still be felt in her blood.

Pallid as last winter she slipped quietly now from the practice room block near the stables and glided across to the main buildings to ring the period bell, for she was portress this year, her junior classes being so small she had netted half a dozen further irritating chores that she performed not always lovingly. In high winds she might use hammer and

51

nails to good effect on clashing windows or imprison vine tendrils on a fly-away trellis. Her practicality unclogged hand basins and mended fuses, but was sometimes unable, more often as she grew older, to mend human relationships.

A ginger tuft of hair sprouted grassily beneath her starched coif. Her thin face, clever as an eagle's, was impassive when she reached the waxy hallway where the parlor clock swung its pendulum fifteen seconds off ten. Exactly on the hour she pressed the button, and deep in the convent's conscience a peal, virginal and icy, claimed all eight women in the classrooms and two lay nuns plaiting a net of pastry across a community apple tart. Sister Matthew's acid breath misted the clock's glass as she leaned close to watch the cog-wheels, so like her own unhappy heart, while mechanically she drew her watch from inside a deep apron pocket and adjusted it, took note of her white clever face in the mirror of glass and polished oak, looked hard for a second into her own undeceived eyes, and went gently down the hall towards the parlor.

The bells had rung like twins.

Through the translucent jujubes of stained glass, even before she swung the door open, she could see the dark shadows of both men.

In this asexual world they were exotics.

"Father Lingard," she said, and waited.

"This is Mr. Leverson, Sister. Sister Matthew," he said. "Mr. Leverson is our Board music examiner, I'm sure you will look after him. Not that he's new here—years and years of it. Isn't that so?"

"That is so," Bernard agreed. He wondered where all the children were, what they would be like, recalling Keith, smart as paint, quiz-kid bright, blond, rude, withdrawn.

Father Lingard fiddled his hat around on a white impractical hand.

"If you will wait," Sister Matthew suggested, not quite absorbing them with her strangely illuminated eyes, "I will fetch Sister Beatrice."

"I shan't wait," Father Lingard said. "But you might ask

Reverend Mother to send the Monsignor a list of First Communicants before Saturday week."

"Yes, Father," Sister Matthew said. She had not the near-fawning acquiescence of so many nuns, even her voice conveying not indifference but a self-sufficiency that made Leverson think of Scott or Sturt or Magellan—or any man at all with a desert within that must be explored.

Leverson found himself alone. The small nun had made him uneasy, for she kept her eyelids down and below the ghost of a moustache her mouth was too full and too clever, and for the few moments they had all confronted each other, they had stood like antagonists gripping nothing but space.

Then she was gone, and through the window, he could see Father Lingard thinly striding to his car; and he sat on with his heart suddenly overturned for no reason at all, waiting and fingering the pages of a religious monthly. Priests surrounded by lepers in Sierra Leone and smiling shiny black acolytes in Mombasa seminaries grinned back. His Protestantism was both affronted and moved. " 'St. Joachim, pray for us,' " he read softly. A flock of aspirations beat up in an echelon from the page but he could only repeat the words cynically, standing on his own bland desert, and watch the birds flap away. They were not homing pigeons.

Sister Beatrice rattled in and startled the last one.

A big, warm creature, she was given to enormous gusty spirals of laughter whose vulgarity shocked some of the community that retained a special memory of her, colored according to the personality of the recorder, singing "Macushla" in a throbbing mezzo-soprano at a St. Patrick's night concert. Phrases like "your red lips are saying" came back startlingly to each. There she had stood, lumpy, generous, and lovable in her habit, one hand on the piano lid, the other, forgetful of circumstances, merely that of Miss Moira Stanners underlining the passion of an Irish love song. "That death is a dream and that love is for aye," she had sung richly and ripely. And the audience had gone quite mad and stamped until she had sung once more, her own enjoyment glowing across the hall. Reverend Mother St. Jude had reprimanded her rather acidly later—"A woman in your position, consecrated to spiritual things . . . overtones of the music hall!"—a reprimand which still could not drown the echoes, a year old, of community choruses dominated by the lovely unused voice; nor later that of Father Lake (phony American accent, red hair) who had done Bing Crosby imitations that same evening and was entirely unself-conscious in his clerical black. "To the point of profanity," remembered Sister Philomene, compressing her elderly lips whenever she recalled his "Dearly beloved, as the collection plates go around I will sing for you 'Pennies from Heaven!' " Cheers and cheers! Shocking!

Sister Beatrice laid her warm moist hand briefly on Mr. Leverson's.

"We are ready to begin," she announced. "All the little girls are waiting in the hall, including those from private teachers. While we're walking over to the practice block I shall send for the first one."

He marveled at the discipline of organization.

"If you don't mind," Bernard suggested, "I intend starting with the beginners—to shorten their anguish."

"Of course. Of course. There are only three of them." Sister Beatrice braced herself for gentle bribery and said, "Don't be too hard on the babies, Mr. Leverson. They're a timid little lot this year."

"We shall do our best," Bernard said, not committing himself. "I don't feel particularly fierce. I shall save it for the seniors."

Sister Beatrice opened the front door and they walked out into the garden alongside the convent, through the May damp and across to the old block of music rooms near the stables. She opened the door of the last room and Bernard, gazing in, saw it had been decorated for his benefit with a great bunch of leaves in a concrete pot in one corner against the wall. A terrible print of Saint Cecilia playing a primitive pipe organ hung over the piano. He felt the familiarity in this room and all rooms like it entrap his fingers so that they went automatically through preparatory movements: the laying out of papers on the table, the syllabus lists, the question sheets. The piano lid had been opened; it was an elderly Lipp, black, loyal, but with sad yellow teeth. He hit a few melancholy chords—and discovered its brilliant tone.

"As soon as you're ready, Sister," he said.

One pupil seemed no different from another, but the small anemone hands uncurled over the keys with different mannerisms. By eleven thirty he was only on his fifth, a horribly nervous child with licorice plaits and unhealthy fudge skin. At first she had trembled so much her hands could barely impress tone from this over-willing keyboard, so Bernard had instructed her to stop for a minute and he chatted to her about school until she was almost at ease and able to play, though not well. As he watched the smudged profile he thought of his own son's withdrawn and sulky confidence. He wanted to say to this skinny, plaited mite, "And do you love your parents? Tell me honestly. I won't tell a soul." And he knew if he crossed his empty heart she would believe him. But he could not. She would choke with fright or giggle and some misinterpreter would complain and he would become the bogy man under the house where the rain-water tank sheltered the frogs or the unseen sound glanced at over the shoulder, the padding nothing that one must beware of.

He wrote fifteen out of thirty-five on the mark form.

"All right," he said when she had reached the end of the Köhler study. "That's all. It's all over."

Her mouth felt for and caught a smile. He patted her bony shoulder.

"Off you go. And ask the next one to come."

He ticked the name off on his list and shuffled his papers around. This was a diploma candidate, the first of the morning. His back to the door, he sensed something unusual when this opened—a difference in quality of sound, of footstep which made him turn quickly.

Sister Matthew, poised as a hawk, hovered in the doorway.

"Is something wrong?" he asked.

"No."

"Where is the next candidate, Sister? I'm afraid I'm running a little late."

"I am she." A smile began on the clever mouth, then gained control.

"Oh. Oh, I see. Yes, of course."

"It's not merely the indulgence of a hobby, Mr. Leverson. I'm taking over some of the preparatory pupils for Sister Beatrice. Actually I've been teaching most of my life here—but without qualifications."

"They soothe parents, I believe."

She smiled—but a long way off. And her confidence seemed to crack a little then, for she shook her head briefly.

"All right, Elizabeth," he would have been saying comfily to the child he had expected. "Let's start with the scales, shall we?" And there would have been none of this hesitancy that plucked the poise from him like feathers, leaving him awkwardly squawking.

But she was now sitting at the piano, awaiting his directions. They went through the usual preliminaries. Something had put her out of gear, he was aware, but she answered well enough, and then he said, "The Bach, then," glancing at his lists.

Pianistically she was entirely equipped to investigate the Bach manner, but without the joyousness full interpretation demanded. Leaning back, Bernard admired her facility, the ginger-haired, light-boned fingers that moved transparently across the keyboard. She knew she was good. She tossed the fugue off as if she were only at practice and her indifference merely added to the technical accuracy of her playing. At the end her smile was all awry and he had to compliment her, though she did not look up.

"What about List C?"

"Bartok."

It would be, he thought. She thrust her crucifix like a dagger into a newer and more comfortable position in her girdle and the rosary beads smacked out a decade of amens on the piano stool.

It was, Bernard reflected, hardly worth going through the rest of her work, and only convention made him do so, for she was so sufficient he knew it would be unnecessary to penalize her seriously on any points.

"Very satisfying," he said. "Would you be hurt if I made a small suggestion?"

"Not at all."

"Well, then, on the question of emotion."

"Emotion?"

"Yes."

"You mean my playing lacks it?"

"Not altogether."

She looked amused. "Nuns are not given to grand passion."

"I suppose not." Her frankness startled him. "But in musical interpretation surely even the celibate is allowed a little latitude."

"It has never been declared heresy that I know. But I can only play what the music causes me to feel, Mr. Leverson. Once . . . well, never mind. The Bach is like an algebraic problem. Eventually a must equal b and there is the immense satisfaction of the logic of it."

"There's joy in that. Somehow I didn't feel you discovered it."

"I have probably forgotten how." But if she were not uncomfortable—and he had no means of ascertaining, for she concealed her face behind the curve of her veil—then Bernard writhed and felt she was assessing his preoccupation with the world she had lost.

"Well, then," he said, edging about on his chair and pretending to fuss with his papers, "you'd better get on with the Beethoven."

She nodded, and when she bent over the piano he was struck sharply and terribly by the grace of her arms in the rolled black sleeves now pinned at the wrists, the carved turn of the head under black folds, and the folds themselves; a still music, the flow or the rapture of it stilled. He found he had not listened to her playing even when she lowered her head at the end, awaiting dismissal.

The sky beyond the convent perimeters had the eggshell brittleness of late winter against which shellacked trees might crack above the papery beige grass of the frost-dry country. I am beginning to lose myself, he knew. And now this strange creature is found here, abandoned to perfection in some wasteland where even God withdrew ecstasy. The spiritual carrot of fulfillment dangled eternally out of reach.

"Thank you," he said. "You need have no worries, Sister."

"Need I not?"

"Not as far as the examination is concerned anyway."

"Surely it's rather unprofessional of you to put my mind at rest, Mr. Leverson," Sister Matthew said. She rose from the stool and went to the door, which Bernard opened.

"Kindness in high places, Sister," he suggested. "You must be used to that at least?"

"There, least of all," she said. "I will see that one of the girls brings you morning tea."

But there were no gem scones this time—instead a delicious half-dozen pastry cases with pockets of homemade jam, a vesper-tinted confiture that Father Lingard told him later the good nuns made out of prickly pear, a device they had had to fall back on during the war shortages in order to sate the boarders.

Sharp at twelve thirty, synchronizing her entry with his crumb-brushing, came his last candidate but one, a bold as brass fifteen-year-old who moved through the scales, ear tests, and sight-reading without batting one of her over-long lashes, but allowing her plaits to hang very *jeune fille* in front of her shoulders. She played with a serious and restrained savagery.

Leverson sucked another sweet thoughtfully as he marked her slightly higher than Sister Matthew, wondering at the reaction when the lists should be officially posted back. *Bonnet blanc . . .* murmured Bernard with his mouth full of candy.

She was an unsurprised adolescent whose coloring and I.Q. were both high, with an adult ease of manner that left oldsters fish-gaping at her poise. The most innocent question —("Did you say melodic or harmonic, Mr. Leverson?")— seemed to include an adumbration of no-innocence, of exploratory device intended to wring a response from any male around.

"You were a good girl," Bernard said, amused by her nonsense. "You deserve a sweet for playing so well." And he held the bag out, hoping to put her in her place.

But she would flirt with a shark.

"Oh, Mr. Leverson! You are so kind. And I've always been terrified of examiners before. Don't I deserve two?"

She pouted just enough and looked him full in the eye for one terrible soul-opening second before she rang a curtain of modesty across the stage.

Little harlot, Bernard thought with good-natured amusement, and offered the bag once more as Sister Matthew knocked and entered.

Ridiculously they were caught by the situation in attitudes of irritation and amusement and resentment.

"You have done well, Eva?" inquired Sister Matthew who did not really ask. "I'm afraid that is your last examinee for the day, Mr. Leverson. The child who was supposed to come next has not arrived. Her mother rang to say she is ill and will have to miss the examination this time. Perhaps when you return next session."

Bernard checked his pigtailed lists. "O'Donovan?"

"Yes."

"Very well." He drew a tired thick line through her name. "That packs it up then."

"You may go," Sister Matthew suggested to the girl, touching her arm very gently with a force that was not at all physical, but held the compulsion that brings mountains to Muhammad. "Be a good child, Eva, and run over and close the hall windows."

"Thank you for the sweets, Mr. Leverson," Eva said, ignoring the nun. She dimpled dark as dusk, and only said good-by to Sister Matthew after she had left the room so that the words called back through the door had their own effrontery, coming in from emptiness and empty, too, of goodwill.

Closing the piano lid, Bernard tussled with the impulse to explain the sweets, repressed the confession angrily, and was amazed he should feel obliged to justify the most casual of gestures. My home does not justify its indifference, he thought. I do that for them. And he thought of the lepers and the self-martyring priests justifying themselves and a God he didn't really believe in not caring a tittle whether one justified or not or sweated or suffered or spat defiance into the skies with its blistering eye forcing something profane or sanctified from each member of the race.

He was buckling his briefcase as Sister Beatrice bounced in breathing desperately, red as purging fires and frightened of no one. She was all smiles and high blood pressure, and in her younger days not only had taught two generations of small boys how to bowl but had tucked her skirts a little higher into her girdle and instructed fifteen grubby admirers in the art of tackling. Now, spiritually bringing Mr. Leverson down, she bustled him through to the front parlor for formal good-bys to Reverend Mother, a ritualistic function that he had discovered went on at all convents. Behind him, more silent than prayer, Sister Matthew had faded away without his having time to say good-by, but the carved thinness of her soul and her person remained in his inward eye.

"Would you like Paddy to drive you to your hotel?" Reverend Mother asked, her square jaw defying heaven.

"Paddy?" Leverson asked.

"Our buggy man." Buggy, indeed!

"Oh, of course. No, really, thank you," he protested. "The walk will do me good. Well, walks are supposed to do one good." He felt dreadfully vague. "And it's all in the attitude, probably. I sit too much, you know. Or drive. And driving one never really sees."

They smiled upon him beatifically and this departure seemed harder to achieve than ever, but he went through the polite door and found the rain threat had moved away. "How is your family?" they asked as a final question, briefed no doubt as to his status by some divine grapevine.

He hesitated with one punctuating foot a step below, half turning on its comma of space and time.

"Like Eva," he said. "Growing up, and having difficulty."

And he went away between the carved saints to the roadway and the camphor laurels, and Reverend Mother puzzled over this exit line for some time.

"Now really, Sister Beatrice," she asked rhetorically, "what precisely do you think he meant by that? One loses, after half a lifetime of enclosure, an apprehension of the exact nature of irony in secular matters."

She touched her broken front tooth delicately with her crucifix while she reflected behind her closed door and her authority.

Sister Beatrice knew, but hadn't the heart to tell her.

During the evening examen of conscience, Sister Beatrice admitted actively and sharply to an uncharity that had lain behind her heart for seven months. Within the minute it took for this understanding to reach home her large mind shrank from the fact and her broad face contracted with both the internal and the external annoyance. She shifted roly-poly against the polished oak of her stall and tried not to see the core of discontent. Through the chapel door in deliberate inattention she looked across the downlands.

There was, she knew, no chronological equivalent for that past season of acid frost and snapping winds, the black veils curling in the blue-white weather, the ring fingers with chilblain cushions, the toes swollen and reshaping the black shoes; no equivalent for the purple frost-lines against aqueous sunrise or the desolate settings beyond the range to the south; no equivalent for the time spent on the clauses of the Treaty of Utrecht or the causes of the Counter-Reformation; all those months made unbearably longer as if a bell had begun to chime its statement to her outraged ears by Sister Matthew's voice, attitude, manner of walking, eating and— God forgive the presumptuous human outrage—even of praying. For pray she did in her dry cool tones, assiduously acidulously distorting the Latin that was one of her own teaching subjects with Italianate vowels of maddening length that trailed all over the chapel, syllables behind. Like Sir Roger, but not as lovable.

The pale, closed lids forbade criticism; the ginger hands clenched God between them and made you afraid of your irritation. Even Sister Philomene, whose elderly body inclined dangerously to one side as it moved its gravity-defying path through domitory, refectory, and chapel, was not nearly as maddening. She was old, cranky, and prejudiced, but the other was virtuous, cold, and frightening. She told her beads in no uncertain manner. Sister Beatrice envied that sureness, that confident belief in the infallibility almost—no, surely that was unfair—of her smallest action.

Mother Rectress rose and the community rustled to its feet. Guimpes crackled, beads chattered brief aspirations and, on the way out of the chapel when they must pass, their eyes regarded each other briefly and turned away lest God split the husks off their souls as if they were nuts and reveal each dazzling kernel of love-hate to the other.

Reverend Mother, a square-jawed intellectual (frozen gray eyes, cheesy skin, two higher degrees and fluent Italian) beckoned Sister Beatrice into the downstairs office. Reverend Mother painted a little, abstracts by taste but icons and medal containers worked in blanket-stitched leather through necessity. Fleurs-de-lis and bouquets of Lisieux roses, scrolled rosary cases and imitation-skin missal holders—all would later be sold absurdly cheaply at convent fêtes. A glass-fronted press in the corner of the room held many of these objects, all executed with a kind of standard workmanship and lovelessness but the same mania for perfection that she was also giving to a translation of sections of the *Inferno* suitable to be used with senior pupils. The manuscript sections of this lay beside the neat piles of scapular cases. Reverend Mother took little credit for either.

"Come in, Sister Beatrice," she ordered, "and close the door. I have something to discuss with you."

Even through the closed door the busy silence of the community's movement along the passage came with its swirling voluminous displacement of air, the subdued voices, cool fingers, white skin, fanatic cleaniness, and a vocal detachment from the world.

"How did the examinations go this morning?"

"Satisfactorily enough, I think, Reverend Mother."

"I don't want mere passes, you know, Sister. I want high passes."

"Yes, I know."

"Well?"

Sister Beatrice went quite red. "I can't say. You must make allowances for examination nerves."

"Mmmm." Mother St. Jude regarded her calmly for some moments.

"Would young Eva Kastner suffer in that way?" she asked drily.

"Eva? Oh, I don't imagine so."

"Then you think she would have done—say—superlatively well?"

"It's quite possible."

"That's good then, Sister Beatrice, for I've decided that Eva will have to continue her musical studies elsewhere. She is leaving soon, anyway. And I'm afraid I could not consider her returning here for lessons next year."

Sister Beatrice rose in her instant indignation, but subsided under the surprised eye of the other.

"But why?" she asked. "Why?" She noticed how Reverend Mother's lower jaw fitted in front of the upper and reflected on the hopelessness of argument.

"I am not satisfied with her behavior."

"I see. Has she done anything specifically terrible?"

"Are you making fun, Sister Beatrice?"

"No, Reverend Mother. Not at all. But you can't expect me to be overjoyed at losing a pupil into whom I've put so much work."

"We all have to make sacrifices."

"Yes. But who is being sacrificed? Eva or me?"

Reverend Mother breathed heavily and the fingertips of each hand sought and rested against each other for more than physical support.

"Really, Sister Beatrice," she managed after an almost asthmatic pause, "that strikes me as rather impertinent."

"I'm sorry, Reverend Mother," Sister Beatrice said without in the least meaning it. "But the child still has one more year before matriculation."

"Yes. Well, that will no longer be our problem."

"I think it is our problem. If we have any influence for good, surely it is worth helping her."

Reverend Mother put down her pen (To dear Sister St. Jude from Senior 1948) with which she had been doodling, and said firmly, "What I am afraid of is that her influence may take effect on other pupils before ours does on her. Now, Sister, that is all I have to say on the matter."

Sister Beatrice waded through a neap tide of indignation on her way to the door which she might wish to slam but would not.

"Oh, and one more thing . . ."

They faced each other, but Sister Beatrice retained hold of the doorknob and endured.

"How did Sister Matthew acquit herself, do you know?"

"Quite well, I should imagine."

"Now she would be more nervous than Miss Kastner, I think." When Reverend Mother "thought" it was not to express doubt—it was a pronouncement, entirely dogmatic. "Did she mention any particular difficulties?"

"No, Reverend Mother. None at all."

I shall not ask you why, decided Sister Beatrice. I will not give you the satisfaction of refusing to say. And she thanked God for the little sins that acted as release for her.

In her cell that night sleeplessness and a cold moon in the full drove her to the rear window that opened out on the courtyard and the practice rooms. A diffusion of light appeared to come from the end room where the dumb piano was kept, but she could not be sure, for the rimy glass glittered cruelly and tree movement tumbled papery shadow. She began a litany, sky-gazing as she had not done since childhood, returned to her narrow freezing bed, and fell asleep half-way through, conscious of a few bars of uneasy music as they entwined dream images; but she did not wake until the five o'clock bell that Sister Matthew rang on the guillotine stroke of the hour. Make me more kind, she begged during Mass, and added hopefully, or perhaps less intolerant. Perhaps that will do.

The day was to be waded through as well, tides still in

and beating about Convent Primary School, music apprecia-
tion classes, and an almost biblical battle with the senior
choir after school as they pounded through a four-part version
of "Nymphs and Shepherds" and a Dom Moreno Mass.

"Fake Gregorian. Tumtittitum! I love it," she had said,
to Mother St. Jude's disapproval. (Dufay? Palestrina?)

"Too arty," she defied. "I leave that to the Sacré Coeur!"

"Really, Sister Beatrice!"

So when Father Lingard came to conduct mid-week Benediction she was too tired altogether even to play the harmonium with any enthusiasm.

"May I?" Sister Matthew had whispered in the corridor on
the way in.

With his especial flourish of the cope (a spiritual veronica!)
Father Lingard, in a glitter of white satin and gold, strode
from the sacristy and began the exposition of the Blessed
Sacrament. Incense flowerets whorled, spiraled in the chapel
bowl above the bony glossy stalls and the red plush where
Sister Celestine watched for one dazed wordly second her
beautiful and strange reflected Renaissance twin singing back
to her from the wooden mirror . . . *quoniam confirmata est
super nos misericordia eius* . . . in the long distended rhythm
of the chant. Behind her Sister Beatrice's full contralto
dropped each syllable like a rich gold pebble into this holy
pool and the ripples widened as behind them came some
unusual concentricities of Sister Matthew's dangerous experi-
mentation with chords of a most secular kind. Sister Imelda,
meanwhile, swung the censer in a voluptuous arc whose per-
fume drenched the room. Flowers could scarcely breathe.
Ecstasy, believed little Sister Celestine. Ecstasy.

At the end of the chapel Sister Matthew had turned the
page of her music, which served only as the barest of guides.
Her profile carved itself against the whitened wall and for a
spasm Sister Celestine was distracted by the smile behind
the smile she imagined she detected there. One lifts back the
flesh of mirth and beneath, curved in an entirely different
way, is uncovered the second smile, the real mouth-mirth
and recoil. It glimmered like a white knife against the gray

clouds of love that were being swung, cutting its dangerous crescent into it. Like a stamp, a tiny stamp with a double image. Sister Mary Celestine lowered her Byzantine eyelids and saw the high hard arm-rests, her fully flowing gown, and herself lost inside this medieval robe, still the small girl she had always been at early Mass. She knew nothing else.

When the organ voluntary was over Sister Celestine came down to earth, watched Father Lingard replacing the fiery dandelion of the monstrance, and in the currents of arum lily and incense the voices launched a sturdy ship of Latin that sailed over horizons of stained-glass blue and the green leaf waters, window-reflected by Fitzherbert Street.

Afterward there would be tea and pikelets in the front parlor, some genteel exchanges about the town and parish, and then the reverend gentleman would belt away in the Monsignor's car. The inroads of modernity into medievalism constituted barbaric jokes: telephones, electric intercommunication—they functioned better, it seemed, oiled by prayer. Visiting sisters from the mother house drove their own car daringly over the western highway from the coast to laugh at the unsophisticated buggy that driver Paddy rattled across the downland town.

Sister Celestine went to the refectory. For the good of her soul it was her turn to assist this week with kitchen chores and she had to set the long community table for early supper. As she pushed open the kitchen door her arm was touched feather-lightly, and, turning, she saw Sister Matthew flushed and strange. Her lips still smiled above that secondary smile and both her hands curved up like—like—Sister Celestine thrust aside the obvious word and stepped back just a little.

"Tell me," Sister Matthew was unbelievably pleading, with her lost eyes fixed on the other's face, "how did my playing sound?"

"Sound? When?"

"During Benediction. Just now. Tell me, Sister, honestly. How was it?"

"Oh, very nice, I thought," Sister Celestine replied limply.

"No, no! Not nice! Oh please!" Sister Matthew seemed

66

to have lost her normal poise and was teetering on some kind of collapse that needed others to aid. "Was there any feeling in it?"

"Oh!" Sister Celestine was relieved, but embarrassed, yet had to contribute. "Of course. Of course there was. It affected me—" she nearly said "oddly" but managed "—deeply. Especially during the *Tantum ergo.*"

"Did it really?"

Sister Matthew's hands flashed and clung most thinly, strongly and horribly to Sister Celestine's wrist.

"Yes, indeed. Please, Sister Matthew, you're hurting me."

She did not hear. "I was improvising, you know," she explained with a deaf enthusiasm.

"Were you? Oh please, my wrist."

"Yes. I couldn't help thinking I rather improved on Sister Beatrice's arrangement. Hers is somewhat unemotional, I think." She dropped her hands. "Tell me," she whispered, "do you think our way of life—I mean—do you think in this state, the holy state, one should forgo all emotion?"

Sister Celestine nearly died of shame. There was something unhealthily prolonged in the anxiety and the questioning.

"I really don't know, Sister Matthew," she said "I only . . ."

But the other had turned away, some of the color gone from her face, one plump lip bitten terribly by her strong teeth. Find the truth and you find God, some earlier instructress had stated. But by then you would be dead, she had wanted to reply. Yet never had.

She went away, but her insanity remained, that replacement for an earlier grief which had fragmented her spirit long before she had sought solution within the convent rule, and that evening while the community ate its meal in compulsory silence, listening to one of the sisters reading from the *Little Flowers of Saint Francis*, Sister Matthew dropped her spoon with an enraged clatter and said, "Apple crumble again!"

The lector stopped on the prong of a word and looked for guidance to Mother Superior, who could only frown.

"Continue reading, Sister," she suggested. The skin on her face appeared to have been tightened like drumskins, over-pitched to the point where they might give off unaccustomed sounds that would not merely startle but shock.

Sister Matthew had made her point. Completely satisfied, she laid down her spoon and watched the others eat. Too outraged by the breach of rules, they could not immediately resume their meal, and when they did so the intrinsic virtue in the way each spoon conveyed its load of pudding to the lips was reproachful. Long since she had learned in private circumstances that the outsider must be spiritually self-sufficient—and it was recent failure that so disturbed, that revoked images she had not forgotten but managed to conceal beneath layers of sacrifice; that made her hand tremble on her concealed black lap, her profile hint at some interior crumbling.

The evening drew in one petal of spiritual perfection after another, folded them through the ritual of vespers, office and evening prayers. The toothbrushes worked, teeth were placed in glasses, veils hung neatly on chairs, and last-minute con-secrations before slumber, like a calyx, tightened the safe knot of the flower.

O rose, Blake said, *thou art sick.*

Insomniac Sister Mary Matthew, re-robing in the winter chill of her cell, shook about like fine sand the piled-up hour-glass frettings of the last year into a powder at the bottom of midnight's black glass, and, slippered for safety, glided down the stairs through the re-set, gleam-thick refectory to the bare moon-lapped grounds.

Taut as madness, fine as frenzy, she found her way to the practice rooms behind the hedges and there, in the blazing exposure of the bare light bulb, played angrily, worried the keys and the same theme with her mad uncontrolled dis-sonances, an emotional *rubato* that shocked, shocked.

During this terrible reshaping which awoke both Sister Beatrice and Mother St. Jude, the light bulb failed, and when they came across in the crisp saner air of silence it was to find her pivoting madly, tiptoe on the revolving stool, while she attempted to replace the globe with another she had brought from the next practice room.

Mother St. Jude did the only thing that seemed feasible in the circumstances. She knelt them all down and proceeded to say a decade of the rosary.

4

FATHER LINGARD, ON the back veranda of the presbytery, considered the roll of film he had developed. Coils of it snaked over his alpaca in the unraveling easiness of the basket chair, and those color transparencies he held to the lamp flowed from his hand like a rainbow. Kin Kin, Gungee, Mount Bilpin, the road up through the Mary Valley above the dairy-squared landscape. His eyes moved down the transparencies again and the landscape periphery became the high lush walls that trapped him so that he felt he could hack through the country jungle longingly into some macadamized desert where petrol smells supplanted pasture, and the petrol pumps sprang up like trees, and buildings of steel and glass and concrete blossomed in thickets.

He sighed. Little did the good sisters know when he presented them every so often with scenic movie strips for their projector that they were flashing across the screen for fifteen minutes his silent, anguished protestations.

There were domestic irritations, too. Irascible Monsignor Connelly, squinting over his shoulder in the dark-room he had set up at the end of the laundry: "Now that one, Father. I don't think that's at all suitable, do you?"

"Which one?"

"Ah. There. It's gone now. Run it back, man. There. God

love us, Doug, you've missed it again. With the boys swimming."

"I couldn't see much wrong with that. They all seemed clad."

"No. It's not that. It's the spirit of the thing, now. It had a sort of pagan flavor, you might say. Remember, as their spiritual pastor I ought to know what's good for them and what isn't."

He was very old. He won all arguments.

"I'm sure you do," Lingard would sigh, careful not to excite him.

"Well, there's a good fellow. We'll snip it off before we send it up now."

"Spyros Skouros," said Lingard good-humoredly enough to Father Lake, and they called the Mons that privately, but not even the jokes and the shared smiles could warm the coldness that seeped in from his own Antarctic.

Yet God being on his side should have made the difference that palpably touched his one lung, his thin blood, even his seedy suits. Gardening, getting the air in a gray cardigan and braces, the festival wear of relaxing clerics, his handsome ashy face rose above the collarless neckline of his shirt where the stud still plopped dangerously, a second Adam's apple wagging and glistening in the sun. The thin gray biretta of his thin hair was worn a little uncertainly. His lips compressed over aphides or scale on the lemon or grimaced tenderly at his dog's ripped paw. He was good with all manner of growing things, blessing them perhaps unconsciously and without unction or sentimentality, for he was a man who gave few backward glances at his own kindnesses. During his seminary years he had pasted to the surface of his desk a few lines of Hopkins:

I remember a house where all were good
To me, God knows, deserving no such thing . . .

Someone had scraped it off without reading it a few months after his ordination and parish appointment, but it could not

71

be scraped from him. He was fond of quoting Saint John of the Cross, recalling his "where there is no love, put love, and there you will find love." And sometimes he went so far as to say this to various people he knew who were wrestling with God and each other—but never didactically, for he had believed since his illness that over-active apostleship did more harm than good. (One day in the Sanatorium not long after his lobectomy, a tract-bearing enthusiast had insisted on praying aloud over him for his conversion to a more acceptable faith, and he had joined his voice with the other man's, for reasons of the most exquisite charity.) Yes, he would say it absentmindedly, as if recalling the advice for himself, so that not a soul could have been affronted by aggressive pietism.

Last March at St. Scholastica's concert literal collapse had been near from silent banked-up laughter in his single lung when Father Lake had done his imitations. Not so much was it the skill of his colleague as the stunned faces of two elderly nuns a row away—Sister Philomene was leaning sideways against shock and the gray moustache on Sister Aloysius's face shook with outrage. He thought they might have been saying aspirations but couldn't be sure.

"The top o' the mornin' to you!" bellowed Tom Brophy, sweating into a borrowed stiff front while choruses drowned the crashing supper cups that clinked like the money being counted at the door. Irish reels. St. Patrick tableaux, the mountains o' Mourne. Fake brogues thickened with treacle of nostalgia and sentimental expatriates all Hibernian tipsy in the school hall until eleven o'clock tipped them out, nuns scandalously late to crunch back to their cells above the courtyard. Father Lake had driven him and the Mons home like a lair cabbie, both of his passengers clutching special St. Patrick medals mounted on pads of green and white satin which Mother St. Jude had worked with bredes of shamrocks. Father Lingard gave his to the housekeeper, a keepsake she slipped into her bag to be forgotten with half a dozen blessed articles and a memory of lavender water and Palm Sunday.

He inspected the last negative and rewound. From the

parlor came confusion and distorted television blare that he dreaded but offered himself to in private atonement.

"Tarradiddle!" Monsignor Connolly was saying testily as he pottered across the sitting room and fiddled with the aerial and then an array of adjustment knobs. Four horse-riding thugs blurred, wobbled, faded completely, and returned with phantom doubles.

"I do think if you tried contrast it would help," Father Lake said stubbornly. "You can't expect divine intervention every time." But the Mons twitched at the knobs without bothering to reply.

"The only decent program, too," he moaned. His chins gave the simplest statement a pontifical veneer of authority that caused Father Lingard, sitting back against the book-wall, to smile and smile.

"Why don't you try the national channel?" he asked mildly. "It's the best reception on the Downs."

"Why?" Monsignor Connolly held the aerial two feet over the cabinet. "Why? Because—oh! That's it! Look at that now! I said before it was—oh, God love us! It's gone again!—because I can't stand the heavyweight stuff after a day around the parish. This sort of thing relaxes me. I'm no stuffy intellectual, thank God, and I'm not ashamed to admit there's nothing I like more than a Western. There now—now . . . c'mon now. . . ." He coaxed the aerial across the set and put it down gently as the screen sharpened. "There." He watched entranced as a baby. "Ooh, did you see that now! Ooh! There's a nasty customer for you, Father Vince. I'd give him a good stiff penance."

Father Lingard shifted sadly and tried not to watch. If only he wouldn't talk, he thought. If only he'd stop and let the racket on the hellish machine batter them insensible.

Hideously clear a cigarette ad dominated the eye.

"No wonder all the Children of Mary smoke," commented Monsignor Connolly, glaring at a pretty thing on a ski-lift. "They've made it a snob symbol."

Lingard soothed. "I never understand why you get so

worked up about it. Everyone does it. It doesn't seem a sign of moral turpitude to me."

Connolly scowled under his peat-thick eyebrows. "That's just it. The smoke, then the teeny drink, and then on to—ah, here it comes again. Faint as ever."

"An old film, perhaps," Lake said placatingly.

Monsignor Connolly sagged fatly into his chair. "Never mind," he said. "I'll offer it up. Remember the time I went on that Bay trip and caught the wrong launch with a lot of gospel students from some exclusive sect now. There I was, trapped on a teeny island down the Bay, with nothing but me breviary to read and not a sausage to eat. And there they were with their barbecue steaks going like mad things. But I kept right out of their way. I was in me cassock, y'see, being a church picnic and all, and God knows what happened to the other ferry."

"But surely they called you over and shared lunch," Father Lingard said wonderingly.

"Well, now, it was only a bit of an island, mind you, but there was a hill on it and all, and I was too proud—me dreadful pride—and too cross having got the wrong boat, and I wouldn't give in and go 'round. Not till the launch came back late that afternoon and we all got on together."

Lingard laughed as he went out to heat the cocoa, rattling cups in gigantic signal to bring Lake from the other room. Each evening after she had prepared dinner, the housekeeper went home and the three men shared out cleaning up and getting breakfast. Everything had shabbiness and shoddiness, except for a row of gleaming vulgarity, a marching rank of plastic food containers given by a mother's committee last Christmas. Gold. Frankincense. Myrrh. And now plastic. He hummed a hymn savagely as he put the spoons and sugar out on the tray. Even on Palm Sunday last, the Pascal palm had been piled and tumbled into two enormous green plastic washing baskets over which Monsignor Connolly swung an anachronistic censer.

Through kitchen window and across whiter grass the white

stone church hung over him in the moonlight, came at him across the lawn through the narrow pane, leaned, crushed.

His tongue swelled around conversational nothings as he found the difficulty of being cheerful, of creating illusions of light in his almost ever-present dusk.

"Want a hand?" inquired cheerful Father Lake, who was schoolboy sanguine.

"In more ways than this."

"Oh? Two lumps for the Mons?"

"Cut him down to one, Vince. He's always complaining about the weight he's putting on."

"Shan't we even let him make his own sacrifices?"

"Oh dear, no," Lingard said, smiling smoothly. "Some are born sacrificed, some achieve sacrifice, and others . . . but set him out an extra biscuit then."

God knows, he tried to be sprightly, to keep it up, to live with eyes unblinking and aware in the full blinding light of divine love which, he seemed to feel more and more intensely, appeared to withdraw itself until one day it would become the eye-ball splitting pinhead of light, or to flow just past him or beyond or fall short of that distance requisite for ecstasy. But he was a nothing-man this year, a priest with his vocation askew, no other object in view but a detailless desert whose wells of prayer had all dried up.

It was not, he supposed, that he had lost faith; or perhaps it was that and he didn't know any more. Who had he become but the confessor with the automatic replies? You put a mortal sin into the slot and out gushes the advice with your penance in small change.

"Do you know, Vince"—his confession gushed unexpectedly—"last Sunday, quite suddenly in the middle of Mass, looking down at face after face raised blindly to receive its God at the altar rails, I was filled with terrible boredom. Not horror, mind you. Or rage or anger or anything understandable, really. Just boredom." He poured the cocoa deliberately from saucepan to pot, carefully spilling nothing physical, and added salt to it—or his wound. "If I could care enough, you understand, to weep, to be emotional, to cry out against or to God. But no. I feel like the symbol of a yawn. A great yawn incarnate."

Simple Lake was staggered. But he managed, "It's nothing, Doug. We all get it. It's just a patch to be lived through." He remembered something he never could bear to remember.

"But what do I do?" Lingard asked. "Do I need a holiday? Could it be as easy as that?"

Once, he recalled, he used to be a sponge, an emotional junky, a soak during a *Missa Cantata*, enjoying himself enjoying God, and his superiors had warned him that emotionalism would fail him, that during the barren patches all he could do would be wait until he emerged to find God exactly where He had always been. When you are our age, they said, the false comforters, you will be aware of the symptoms long before the despair sets in.

"Perhaps," Lingard suggested dubiously, "I could confess this to you. Perhaps if I committed some whacking great sin I'd regain the sense of communication, of being taken back."

"It would hardly be worth it," Lake said. "Breaking a leg to get to know your doctor!" And again the little thing he hated to remember hailed him jauntily across the park of his soul.

"Oh, for God's sake," snapped Lingard, "spare me the corny comparisons of the mission pulpit." He hesitated. "Sorry, Vince. I didn't mean to be rude."

"Check!" said Father Lake in fake American to disguise his embarrassment. "It was rather silly. It's too hard to talk about without being sententious. Maybe all you do need is a holiday like me."

He groaned and grinned, the shape, the substance of apology just not here. He was doing all the inner parish rounds on a push-bike, not from asceticism, but because for the second time he had overturned Monsignor Connolly's car on the Killarney Road. Not that the Mons drove any less recklessly. "Never bother about me insurance, man," he'd say, spinning the wheel at a bend. "I just say a Hail Mary and hope for the best. Put your trust in God now, is

what I say, and there's nothing we can do about it after that."
Parishoners being kindly transported to christenings shuddered whitely in the back seat as Monsignor Connolly overtook at seventy, gabbling "prayforusnowandatthehourof"—then, turning at right angles from the steering to say to transfixed passengers, "What a wonderful thing to know there's no death." Yet . . .

"You make it very hard for me to keep me temper, Father Vince," he complained. "Very hard. God knows being a Christian isn't a profitable business at all." For the three weeks the parish car had been at the repair shop the Mons was forced to share the apostolate with his good friend and golfing partner, the Presbyterian minister. "Drop me a little farther along," he'd say, "and I can be calling at the Mumbersons while you drop in on the Duckworths."

"Shall we make it the other way 'round, John," Rod Auld used to suggest, "and let's see who gets a conversion first?"

"Let's get back to the gangsters," Lingard said, balancing their tray.

The parlor whined with bullets while Connolly, sitting a bucking metaphor like an old stager, loped across the mesa toward heaven, easy in the saddle. The sixty seconds of commercial were a special purgatory that made him aware of time and place.

"Where's me cocoa, Father Vince?" he called over his querulous old shoulder.

And it rocked toward him obligingly as he swung back on to the trail.

Lingard, conscious only of his spiritual weightlessness, settled with difficulty into a chair and supported the next unendurable half-hour for the sake of charity and the glittering-eyed sponsor who, somewhere behind packets of useless goodies, would be counting gold nuggets.

"I am a nothing-man," he prayed later that evening after he finished reading his office. "Deliver me."

Sick to his core, he edged his way between the cold still sheets and remembered as he did so that he had forgotten to put the presbytery cat into the laundry at the back where it could coil up near the boiler. So he went out again, shivering in pajamas, and called and mewed till a narrow shadow pelted across the frosty grass and gave his thin legs one bleak rub.

Through late afternoon air, ale-pale, Bernard drove back from Stanthorpe, sucking a jaw-breaker, longing for a cigarette, and promising faithfully across his untuned heart a double Scotch as soon as he reached town. Events followed their deadly sequence. Ten miles out he had to refill his gas tank, and between the space of that and one more piece of hard candy he found the outskirts of Condamine again, crunched the last bits of the candy, and was all in order sluicing cold water over his face, his soul coming up for air. Jupiter Pluvius in shirt-sleeves, he made chopping movements with a comb, straightened a less conservative tie, and went shaggily down to the lounge where he waited for Father Lingard to join him for lunch. He arrived sick, late, calm, pushing through the gluey pre-summer air of the pub like a drowning man.

"Are you ill?" Bernard asked, concerned.

"Not really." Lingard gave what he intended as a smile. "Nothing the medico could put his finger on. There was some worry with a parishioner. Monsignor Connolly asked me along and it all took more time than we expected. I'm sorry. Why, do I look sick?"

"You're very pale."

"Hunger, perhaps. Shall we go in?"

There were two travelers, the dusty men in suits two years out of date, the wide-lapelled boys with the wide line of talk. They had red faces and gluttonous eyes, and expense accounts that worried them even as they diddled their bosses. They were spooning up soup. And at the proprietor's table a proprietorial wife managed a steak and put it in its place.

"Everything finished now?" Lingard asked out of politeness as they separated salad leaves in a search for ham.

How true! Bernard thought, sensing irony. He extracts it

from me, this prelate with the persuasive voice and the unhappy eyes.

"Yes. Everything. After everything is finished there's a feeling of complete relaxation."

"True," the other agreed with his own irony. "True, true. Yet I cannot say relaxed is the exact word . . . more butter? . . . empty, rather. Or nothingness."

"Yes, thank you," Bernard said. He greased another fraction of his bread roll. "That gets very close to my feelings lately. Seven days ago it hit me at last that I was adult and freed of certain relationships that had bound me for years. For a couple of days, you know, I was sustained by a tremendous exhilaration. Saw things for the first time. Read posters and the legalese on the back of bus tickets. It felt exactly like the time I had a stroke and afterward discovered I'd sharpened a semitone."

The gloom lightened.

"A semitone?"

"Yes. After perfect pitch, you know, very odd my dear fellow to hear things like the Bach Passion in C when you're expecting it in B minor. Everything—well, not exactly—had a rebirth. But there was certainly a fillip to everything."

"And your feelings? You were saying something about your feelings?"

Bernard paused. The volta in the sonnet. He saw Keith come up the back stairs in his creased jeans, his sweater wrinkled and grimy, his face sullen, his words insolent. He watched Iris plead with him and he said, "Well, my marriage is—not on the rocks—one hardly knows what to say when that is a positive condition which would be better than it is now. My marriage is not on the rocks, but should be."

"It perseveres then?"

"Yes. It perseveres."

"Against reason? Against comfort?"

"Against all those things."

"Without love, too?"

"Yes. Certainly that."

His doggy eyes became curious. Here was that confessional precision that insisted on the exact nature, and how often and with whom.

"But your boy? You have a son. There's your love."

Bernard waggled his head. "No. There is something wrong. Lately he even hates—I think that may be the word—his mother. I can't say that the love is there for me."

With the penultimate care of the executioner Father Lingard placed the knife and fork together over a piece of beetroot.

"Perhaps he has discovered you hate each other," he said.

"But we don't. Not at all. That's what I'm trying to explain. There's nothing positive like hatred. There's simply—nothing."

Lingard almost smiled. Brother, he said inwardly, come in! And welcome!

"Does this upset you, this conversation?"

"No. You see, not even that. It *would* upset me if I cared. I think maybe I do care about Keith and his mother—but not sufficiently."

"Have his feelings toward you changed?"

"Not appreciably. He's been going through a difficult spot. Goes he won't say where. Arrives home at impossible hours, dresses shockingly."

"That's natural enough, though," Lingard said. "Every third family has teen-age sons behaving that way. But it does seem odd he directs his hostility toward only one of you." He reflected. "You know, Leverson, on second thoughts, maybe that is not so odd. His age. His mother. Curiosity and hostility might be intermingled. Sex does idiotic things with boys."

Bernard, although unwilling to release his son's conscience, managed to admit awkwardly, "He insists he is no longer innocent."

"Oh?"

"Some woman picked him up one night when he walked out."

"The top of the iceberg, as the brain-shrinkers say! Why did he walk out?"

"Who knows?"

"Do you believe him?"

"No. Not really."

"It's an explanation, of course."

"Yes, of course, but it's one of those histrionic remarks Keith is rather given to."

"Well, there's his guilt, and then there's the simple fact that at fourteen—is that his age?—he simply hasn't the maturity to cope with the situation. It could be perfectly true. And he could be suffering the most fearful shock. You didn't punish him, did you?"

"No, of course not!" Bernard protested indignantly. "You surely don't think I'm a complete medievalist."

"Shouldn't I be?" Lingard inquired wryly. "No, I never suggested it. You anticipated me. I was only going to say we carry our own hells within."

They ate somberly, dealing with geometric custards and stewed tea from some eternally brewing urn. Yet after lunch the attraction one unhappiness has for another trapped them together, so that despite a generalized sense of guilt and sloth, Lingard sat defiantly on in the lounge, gloomily matching Leverson beer for beer. The room filled up with crustaceans—varnished hard-jawed mums and small-bit farmers all coated with the same malty staleness that made disgust palpable.

"They'll think I'm a whisky priest," he said. "Occasioning bad example."

Leverson smiled. "Would you care to take your vices farther afield?"

"It might be better," reflected Lingard, looking out of the window at the winter flies and the trail of dead ones cluttering the inner sill. The pale gradations of umber and fawn shivered away behind the war memorial and the Masonic hall. There was a time, he knew, when he had been more aware of the liturgical seasons and the changing color of vestments than he was of actual summers or springs; the sonic modulations of the Latin Gospels troubled him more than

July westerlies blowing from the gold-streaked, cold-blinkered skies, washing with wave and waft of cloud.

Crosses melted into swastikas, symbols of light and dark, ball, crescent, winged like gannets that zoomed around a wartime sky that was as devoid now, he could see, of actual bird, of bird heart (which means spirit) or bright bird eye (that was perception) as he of grace-greeting or welcome at the Lord's table.

But he could not bring himself to confide in the apparent grumble-heavy, comfy-confidence that faced him sympathetically across the table, yet was still a stranger, who then drove him to drunken careering scenic outlooks, a vast number of loquacious grogs and a multitude of moral and technical arguments about marriage and the uninterest of God that brought neither closer to solution when they came in, tipsy with a variety of things, back along the late western road.

Someone hailed them at the five-mile turn-off, and Bernard, kind to hikers, drew up to find a face familiar, though it could have been years away. There were skin-tight matadors and a slick shirt, a knowing eye and a skin prettier than paint and without any, a lot of confused and phony thanks. She was wheeling a sick bicycle with a dreadfully limp tire and wheel-frame. No explanations were really needed, and with it hoisted into the back of the sedan she smirked and said, "Thank you, Mr. Leverson," to his appalled astonishment.

"Do I know you?" he asked. "There's something familiar..."

"You examined me," she said, inching her wordly thigh away from Father Lingard's now pivoted upon the hand-brake with his bony knees knocking the gear-stick.

"Did I? It must have been a long time ago."

"Oh please," she complained pertly, "not that long. I'm Eva Kastner. I was doing Associate."

"Yes, of course," said Bernard, remembering suddenly and acutely. She carried a climate of danger with her. "I hope you are keeping your playing up?"

"Yes and no," the dreadful girl said with unbearable archness.

Yet she was more taken in observing Father Lingard, his mournful profile stamped against the other's ginger abstractedness. He smelt strongly of liquor and, fascinated, she watched while his head lolled and dropped forward on his chest so that he looked sawdust-filled and limp. Just like a rag doll, she thought. Just like. And giggled, recalling the nun dolls (Dress them yourself!) unbelievably for sale in the local toy shop some years ago until Monsignor Connolly's purple-faced protests had the shocking things withdrawn. Suddenly he collapsed against her and closed his eyes as she tried to prop him up.

"Heavens, Mr. Leverson," the little liar said, "is Father Lingard sick?"

Something slowed down within and the car followed suit.

"Yes, he is," he said shortly, drawing in to the grassy edge of the road. "Would you mind climbing in the back with your bicycle, and I'll try to make him comfortable in the corner?"

Lingard made lizard eyes. "Feel ghastly," he said. "But impenitent. Yet still ghastly."

His one slowly expanding and contracting sponge could not keep pace with either the alcohol or the false excitement his behavior had top-whipped and that his guilt insisted upon. Lazy legs in the back swung her limbs across the bicycle frame pert as she, nickel-plated and also built for speed. But her glossy smiles met with no reassurance, her conversational openings were blocked, and the pressure of her personality eased when she was dropped off at a side street near the convent.

"I'm thinking of doing a higher grade one of these days," she said. "Maybe I'll see you next year."

"Perhaps," Bernard said, tolerant now she was going, and added absentmindedly, "Keep up your practice."

"Ooh, I *will*," she said with such appalling innuendo and breathiness that Bernard was flabbergasted and could not bring himself to acknowledge her wave.

Outside the presbytery of St. Scholastica's the sprinklers rained through the brown evening, but not as the quality of mercy, for there was in the air a silent hullabaloo of doom, on which Lingard's eyes opened but could not focus.

"Don't move me," he said. "I'll be ill."

"Will I fetch someone out?"

"Heavens, no! Just let me sit for a minute while I regain balance. Shouldn't drink like that, you know. Not used to the stuff. Can't cope with my bunged-up innards."

He leaned heavily against Leverson, almost falling as he struggled from the car, and like a couple of Mack Sennett comics they wobbled up the path to the veranda, where Monsignor Connolly was watering the staghorns that hung all along the railing between the pots of maidenhair and begonia. He was pretending not to notice while he watered yet watched from a crafty Irish eye. They reached the foot of the steps.

"What's the matter, Father Lingard?" he asked, all formal, his brogue thickening in mysterious ratio with splenetic secretions.

Father Lingard looked hazily at the two monsignors glaring down like Moses from the top of the veranda. "I'm drunk," he said. "Let me past."

"Oh, and that's very obvious now. Good God, you ought to be ashamed to be seen at all, let alone announcing the fact to all and sundry at the top of yer disgraceful voice." His anger swung around on Leverson's distress. "And as for you, now, are y' responsible for this? Taking a man of God off on one of yer drunken orgies for the whole town to see?"

"I suppose in a way I am."

Monsignor Connolly swung his watering can like a weapon. "Git out!" he ordered thickly. "Out with y' or I'll throw you out, God give me strength!"

Lingard flapped his hands like wings. "Now," he said, "not his fault at all. Leverson, dear fellow, forgive him. He knows not what etcetera."

"Blasphemy, too, Father Lingard!" thundered the Mons.

"Profanity, I think," Lingard corrected maddeningly. And swayed.

"Dear God, that I should live to hear it," moaned Monsignor Connolly. "The Bishop will have to discipline you. I wash me hands of it. It's beyond me, it is." He squawked down the hall, "Father Vince!" and flapped excitedly and without direction. "Father Vince! Father Vince! Come here, will you?"

Father Lake hovered his discretion in a bedroom door and tried placatory devices.

"Now, now, Monsignor," he said, "please no fuss. What's a drink too many? Surely half the parish is guilty."

"Half the parish!" screamed the Mons. "What's half the blithering parish when it's us that should be leading them to virtue?"

"That's true," soothed Lake discreetly. "True, true." He came down the steps and levered Lingard up them. "Come on, feller. We'll sleep this off." In his room the priest flopped on his bed amid the failed prayers, like so many dead roses of twenty-five winters, not even the fragrance as reminder, but thorns of failure, the dead twigs of pleas and pleas and pleas. Not until the others moved away could he begin to contemplate the nonsense that Connolly was going on with, the sanctimonious hubbub frozen all over the room like non-fail novenas or miraculous medals. But above a slow-burning Pascal candle the other handsome tragic face of the Christ figure, essentially human and sympathetic, moved in across confetti-leaved lawns of his pastures; Christ, the friend of pimps and prostitutes. He prayed with humble reverence, and sensed the drunken tears move from behind his shuttered eye.

"I'm sorry," he could hear Leverson saying futilely behind the closed door.

"Sorry! It's a bit late for that now indeed. And so y' should be," the Mons added rudely. "We've got the good name of the parish to think of. But that wouldn't mean a thing to you, I suppose, with yer city ways and yer fleshpots and all."

"Look," Leverson began to explain desperately. "We were unhappy. Unhappy, do you understand? You should understand. I told him a little of my own problems and, believe me, I have them. But he said nothing of his. And I think he, too, is a desperately unhappy man. Can't you overlook a silly little thing like this?"

"Don't teach me me job now, Mr. Leverson, please. I think I know what ought and ought not be overlooked."

"Ach, you stuffy provincial Irishman," Leverson hissed, losing his temper. "I don't think you do."

"You—what?"

"I said I don't think you do. You're supposed to be a man of sympathy and understanding and all you offer to someone in need of kindness is a suburban sense of outraged propriety."

"God give me strength!" Monsignor Connolly said. "Father Lake, will y' remove this impertinent man from me consecrated house?"

"He doesn't have to. I'm going. I can say no more than that I'm sorry. I think kindness might be more effective than censure."

The sick white of a dying man spread over Connolly's outraged face. Fence-sitting on a Sunday after ten-o'clock Mass and greeting his flock, he would recapitulate by his presence the affirmation of doctrines, convince of the efficacy of prayer. There was a dogmatic assurance in his no-nonsense Irish brogue that was the speech of medium of poetry and fantasy and every delicious deviation or tricksy reapplication of the truth. But he was flabbergasted now.

"Make me a pot of tea, Father Vince," he commanded, speaking from the seat of the Fisherman, the leather smoking-chair before the television set. "And make it strong for the love of God. I've never been spoken to like that at all before."

Do you good, thought red-head, who had squirmed through countless sulphuric sermons. ("Yes, y'd rush rush quick as a flash now if y' was told y'd won the lottery. But catch y' rushin' to Mass for fear y' might be five minutes late! Oh, not at all. Not on yer life.") Or in the litanied evenings, after Benediction was over, making a late consolatory call to a sick parishioner on a farm, as the car skittered around dirt roads at sixty. ("I just say a Hail Mary now. It's me best insurance.") The Mons, he thought. The Mons. Parish figurehead, death-pale, snow-white, inflexible, stubborn as a mule. His soul, doily-neat, had scalloped edges of predictable pattern, and forty years in the confessional had made no difference to his expectations of the conventional. Monthly he still lashed the Children of Mary on the viciousness of alcohol and cigarettes, and although he had inveighed for a long time against the Jezebels who flaunted their cosmetic-bright faces, sheer weight of behavior had defeated him.

"Tell me now, girls," he pleaded once, "tell me now, why is it a woman shouldn't drink or smoke?"

"Please, Monsignor," some willful suffragette smart alec had said from the side of the room, "it reduces us to the level of men."

He'd kept quiet for a long time after that.

Now he sulked in the front room, scowling and tugging unprayerfully at his rosary beads; but after a while the pull of the brave cowboys was too much and he was off with the cussing, drinking men, the Galahads of the saddle, with the volume turned up extra loud—for, while he was a good old man, he had a venial sinner's simple belief in the virtue of punishment.

"Libera nos domine," Father Lake prayed, and went out to the kitchen solitude with his thriller.

Leverson went back to the Focus and the compressed cooking smells superimposed like transfers of the day before the day before—steak, cabbage-rolls, pie, mince, roast. Sitting on the edge of his bed, he took out the photo he always carried with him and inspected with some curiosity these stranger faces—a woman called Iris and a boy called Keith.

Quite beside himself with his hollow-sounding soul, Bernard could not refrain during the week from writing some sort of letter to Doug Lingard, a letter that contrived to be friend-ship without unction.

    . . . this final balm [he wrote—rather too artily, he felt, but could not avoid] that you talk to me about, this solace one can expect at the end—I simply cannot believe in it. In any case it's hardly for myself I'm concerned but you whom I seem so terribly to have embarrassed. Did you manage to smooth things over? Are you friends again (forgive my humor!)—if not with God, at least with the Mons?

I think my Protestant wilderness may be less frightening than yours. No saints turned raveners lurk in the coverts. No fleshed images have reverted to plaster. The incense hasn't failed and there never were any candles to go out. There's just this rolling dullness in human relationships and only myself in it, though I must confess that a few days ago some remnants of feeling did seem to return to me. I wanted badly to strike Keith, who has been pestering like a genius. Surely this is a sign of returning life! Could I suggest it to you as a pick-me-up or are personal relationships quite closed?

There should be a new page for mundanity, you understand. But I'll be back in Condamine for two days at the end of the fortnight. We can mundate then.

Yours,
LEVERSON

Three or four days later he opened Lingard's reply with an excitement he could not decipher, it so hung streamers above his bare walls, colored windmills out of place, out of time.

I admit myself flummoxed. Endure is the watchword [Lingard had written]. Perhaps when you're here we'll have a chance to discuss this further—unaided by spirits! —but I write now because you deserve some warning of a rather unpleasant series of happenings. Forgive me, my dear Leverson, for thus rushing it at you, but I must.

A week or so ago Connolly received a quite scandalous letter, unsigned of course, alleging that your conduct with the examinees was more interested than might be proper in the circumstances. Euphemism on euphemism, you understand. The Monsignor's first reaction, of course, was to rush to the convent where the nuns very properly were outraged and skeptical. Following upon this, he next decided to send a furious denunciation to the Board demanding an investigation, but we managed to calm him and reduce him to sense after the Sisters had assured him that no parent had ever made the slightest complaint. Finally he agreed that when you return next week you should be shown this appalling letter and be allowed to take whatever action you think fit. Unbelievable victory!

I can't say how upset I am to have to write like this. Forgive me. I don't have to assure you, do I, that I know it is nonsense.

Yours in Jesus Christ,
DOUGLAS LINGARD

The seasonless country was barely changed by frost when Leverson returned at the end of the week.

In the deadly brown smoking room of the Focus, Leverson watched Father Lingard cautiously. The room harbored the stale breaths and jokes and hopelessness of commercial travelers in wine and underwear, of spielers in farm machinery and irrigation, of overnight politicians who had to cadge special votes and out-of-town tract-bearers, of belchings and one-too-many and the terrible dreariness of forced good cheer.

Father Lingard might have been unrolling one of the Dead Sea Scrolls, so carefully did he pry back the paper from its envenomed folds until the center of its deadliness was exposed.

"It's ridiculous," Bernard said, having read it. "And rather pathetic. One can only ignore it."

"Yes, I thought it sounded like the petulant outburst of some failed candidate. Hardly the parents of one, do you think? Have you any enemies?"

"Oh, my dear Lingard! What a question! Of course. But who knows them? My wife. My son. My wife's lover."

Lingard winced, but not from outrage. "Please," he said, "you cannot be so cynical."

Then Leverson did laugh, for he was angry enough with this letter. His soul felt as if it might heat and vanish through the lattice of his bones. "How about you?" he asked too loudly. "How about you? You have the most wonderful enemy of all—God. Oh, I envy you that. Remember what Wilde said, 'A man cannot be too careful in the choice of his enemies.' And you have the most wonderful antagonist of all."

He puffed and was red with the climax of irritation and popped two jaw-breakers at once into his mouth for control. Lingard, however, understanding right to the marrow of the moment, held the grayness of his lips in tight check before he could spit out the protests and cries. "I wish I could see that."

"See what? What I say?"

"Yes. That mine is the most—well, most wonderful."

"Ah well," Bernard said, calming down and sucking away, but not intending the patronage. "Be happy in my envy. My genuine envy."

The convent door looked twice as thick and swung back like a chunk of stone when Sister Matthew opened it to him, letting both the man and the sunlight in.

"How are you?" he asked, observing some feverish shimmer of youth behind the skin. She was so small he might have blown her aside with one breath of annoyance. But she avoided his eye, which she remembered as being directly and disconcertingly blue. A forlornness enveloped the bird look of her. Had she read the letter or heard of its contents? He hoped not, quite urgently, for some inexplicable reason.

Sister Beatrice bustled him away to the music block, where he examined the few pupils who had failed to report for the examination the previous month. He was surprised when the same frightened child that he had failed before reappeared and sat desperate before the piano. She was even less capable of playing this time and her plaits hung more sadly than life, dangling on the keys. Bernard was about to pat her shoulder when he remembered the letter. He would, he imagined, be pricked by this over and over again in like situations. He withdrew his paternal hand.

"We could try again next year, couldn't we?" he suggested. And some muffled voice agreed vaguely. Was Christine—it was Christine, wasn't it?—he consulted his lists—a pupil at the convent? No. She was Miss Trumper's. And did she like Miss Trumper? Only a bit? Well, never mind, he would be going to see Miss Trumper and he would see what could be seen.

Just as he was finishing packing his books away, Sister Matthew entered without knocking. Having closed the door and heard it click, she leaned back, clutching her music and regarding him steadily.

"Well, now," Bernard said, baffled, "what can I do to help?" And he experienced once more the unorthodox persistence of emotion.

"May I try again?" she asked. "May I try that Bach again for you?"

He was staggered by her seriousness. "But you passed most creditably," he argued. "You couldn't have wanted to do much better, could you?"

Her fingers seemed stripped to the bone; the flesh, her only protection, was gone. "I have been working on it." She faltered. "I think—I think the interpretation has improved."

Neither looking at him directly nor waiting for his answer, she jerked across to the piano and began to play with terrible emotionalism what she had once performed with such mathematical accuracy. He waited until she had finished, impatiently, but resigned.

"Would you like me to show you?" he asked gently, attempting to align himself with her, but she did not stir.

"Here," he said, "sit in my chair, and I'll show you my version."

Years ago one of his pupils had told him his fingers smelt of tobacco and biscuits and, watching now the reddish hairs on the back of his fingers, he wondered if they still affected pupils that way. Slyly he glanced at the little nun but could see nothing except the curve of black shaping her neat and, he suspected, crazy head. Preposterously, all the same, when he finished and lifted his hands from the keys, swiveling on the stool so that he could look directly at her, she was crying silently with her eyes shut tight, her mouth open as a child's, rebelliously unsure, and as a child making no effort to hide her face.

"I'm sorry," he apologized. The grating timbre of his voice was grotesque. "I didn't mean to upset you."

He ground his teeth over his mundanity, its idiocy; but she unexpectedly replied with her eyelids still gripping each other as if she might let the world in should they open, "I'm fit for nothing. Neither in this life nor any other."

The room whirled with embarrassment. Should he be involved like this in personal confidences? He thought not. The reversal of what he had assumed secure hit him blow upon blow. Three of a kind, he told himself. And the numerical situation gave him comfort.

"That's a drastic statement," he said weakly. (One could hardly pat the hand of a religious.) "Do you mean life in general? The religious life?"

"Perhaps."

"How long have you been professed?" he asked.

"Nine years." She opened her eyes. "Since my eighteenth birthday."

"You don't know much about any other sort of life, then, do you? Do you think it's so much better?"

"Are you lonely?" she inquired, changing the subject with an abruptness that was outrageous.

"I suppose so." Bernard smiled at her but she stared whitely into his face, cold as wax, and he added to placate her, "Everybody is. All knotted up inside."

"But you have a family, haven't you?"

"Yes. I have a boy. But we are very much apart these days. He's growing up. He doesn't seem to need me any more. I wish he did, you know."

Impossibly the memory of the eight-year-old recurred. "Dad, Tommy told Chris he was a dirty rotten bloody bastard." Eyes radiant. "True. He did. He says dirty rotten bloody bastard. I'd never say dirty rotten bloody bastard." Coming at sin obliquely for a week after that until the novelty wore off. "Dad, is it really wrong to say dirty rotten bloody bastard?" And he had ruined it all for Keith by saying, "No, son. Not really."

Sister Matthew stood up convulsively as if she had been twitched from an occasion of sin.

"I'm sorry, Mr. Leverson." She was so formal and dry, her tears might have been his own fabrication to ease an intolerable situation. Just as unexpectedly she put one of her small-boned hands on his and with a limpid smile, which cut past that secondary one and curved her face into that of a child, she said, "My playing certainly didn't deserve a sweet."

The bell rang! That was it. Ten years ago he might have laughed at her distress and five years before that again he would not even have noticed; but charity, like cancer, grows slowly until it involves the whole being and he could only regard her through the increased understanding of his own unhappiness.

"I haven't got any with me, you know. I usually do. I'm giving up smoking. It's bad for my heart and I simply have to have something to distract me. Gum. Candy."

"Perhaps next time," she insisted. She was pinning him down.

"Certainly next time. I owe you one, anyway, for your examination work."

It all was incredibly silly, though he could not have been more gently amused. Having opened the door for her, he walked across the grounds to the front of the building, the circular grass plot where unacclimatized bauhinias wrestled with the weather. The saints were on guard, calculating with their hollowed eyes, and he was conscious as he walked down the short drive of agitation behind and flapping of veil and habit where Sister Beatrice and Reverend Mother endeavored to catch him before he left. The lopsided conversation was never completed.

As he moved back toward Mother St. Jude to deal with polite reassurances, he was surprised and not surprised to notice Sister Matthew's gliding departure in the direction they had come and to see Reverend Mother's jutting jaw pursue the last fold of the vanishing habit.

5

CHOOKIE MUMBERSON UNDER the leaves, under the probing twigs of Miss Trumper's garden. Mold heaps, fertility rites with bone-dust from his biblically broadcasting hand in a snail-trail so that we can follow him into the shrubbery near the rubbish dump where he is having a furtive afternoon smoke. Behind the polka-dot freckles bumpy moldings of his short-nosed face with its light-blue eyes can be observed without much pleasure. Only a mother could—and she never did. He is and always has been too much of a burlesque of the tough little boy. Now at seventeen he is just not tall enough, kid-freckled still and with his largest fingernails not quite half-an-inch deep, over whose pink segments wet, nibbled, flesh bulges cushions. He would squat on a laundry bucket by the bottle heap or relieve himself, still the small boy, making a wet pattern on the paling fence. C-H-O-O-K-I-E he would write, awkwardly button up, roll a cigarette clumsily and puff tiny smoke signals he hoped Miss Trumper might not read in her weekly time. But . . .

"Tea," she would trill from the house. "Tea, Chookie!" Standing on the back step, upright as glory, her myopic eyes blinking against daylight. To convince her he would make a few digging sounds with his hoe while she cried, "Chookie," in a frantic hopeless way into the long lost acre, her voice finding him out down the overgrown paths, across parterres, with its trickle of doubt and anxiety: "Chookie . . . Chookie. . . ." Once he had cackled like a hen in reply all the mad freckled way to the back veranda where she had gaped her humility and leaned her shock against the fly-screen door.

"But I never thought you minded," she protested, her limp mouth kneaded by her own guilt. "I didn't know. Really I didn't."

"'Course I don't," said Chookie, glad she was upset. "I was only kiddin'. Everyone calls me Chookie, ever since I can remember like."

She mumbled something.

"Silly ole woman," Chookie had thought, following her into the kitchen, all germ-free chrome and laminated plastics reeking of disinfectant. "Ain't got no sensa humor."

He ground his cigarette out carefully and scraped a little dirt over it with his boot. Germs. Smoking was dirty. She was always tellin' him. Silly ole nut. But he didn't want to lose a sweet cop like this. One day a week, but she paid as much as if it was two. Almost as much as he got at the convent for three. Nope! This was for him. And in a few months maybe he'd push off to Brissy and look the girls over there. That's what he told himself, anyway. Not that Chookie had ever had a girl, but he'd thought about it sadly and desperately since he had his first set of long strides. All his mates used to rib him and he couldn't stick that.

He trailed after her voice.

Where the concrete path began between an apple tree and a hedge her anxious face could be observed at the back window. Grinning, he dragged a hand across his mouth.

She had the tea made this time when he got in. "Scrape them please, Chookie," she had said, and he had lumbered back to the steel dormat and ground off a little mound of twigs and clay. But she had two goes at rinsing his cup and it took her quite a while to make up her mind to pour his tea into it.

"I hope it's not dirty," she pleaded, not looking at him. And he played it along with her, poor biddy.

"That's okay, Miss Trumper," he said. "That's how I like it."

"Biscuit?" she inquired. "No. Not the top one. I'll take that. There you are." Relieved, she nibbled safely.

"Good-oh," Chookie said. He ate two fast, and poured himself a second cup.

"How's your mother?" Miss Trumper always inquired. And he always said she was okay.

"And your father?" Chookie used to marvel at the routine and suspect she never listened to his answers. Or cared.

"Shot froo," he said for a change, putting two heaped ones into his cup.

"But only last week you said he was all right."

"Did I?" Chookie grinned, showing a row of teeth that badly needed bracing. "Well, he wasn't really." He shoved the last corner of a biscuit into his mouth. "He's been gone for a month now, only Mum didn't want me to tell no one. But last week she heard he'd been smashed up in his truck near Longreach and she says she don't care who knows now. Serves him right."

"Was he badly hurt?"

"Only enough for it to be a warnin', Mum says."

Miss Trumper's mind reeled. Backing from the sugar, she pushed her chair out a little. Chookie dropped his eyes and reached for another biscuit.

"Shot froo," he repeated, surveying the fabric of this tale with artistic satisfaction. "Yeah. We think there was some dame at the back of it. Mum says he's a regular rooster an' he shot froo."

Miss Trumper took the envelope (floral motif in corner) containing his thirty shillings from where she always slipped it beneath the clock. Something made her re-check the contents, but then, as she pressed her long gray fingers on its crispness before giving it to him, the doorbell cut through the ceremony and she had to thrust it at him suddenly and then vanish down the hall while Chookie stuffed the envelope into one pocket and three of the biscuits into another.

Background noises—female cluckings—and he slipped out of the kitchen door, re-coiled the hose, and put the gardening tools in the garage where no car but an old harmonium propped its age against the wall upborne by the harmonics of nonconformist hymns. Chookie dragged up a fruit case, squeezed the bellows with his knees and very softly picked out with one audacious finger a wheezing version of "When the Saints Come Marching In." It was so vulgar it made him laugh out loud, like the time he had crept into St. Scholastica's and played "Roll Out of the Barrel" before Sister Beatrice pulled him by his ear from the stool. Wish the ole girl'd gimme this crate, he thought vamping softly with his left hand. But he closed the lid down before she got mad, and sloped around the front where she and Miss Paradise were practically nibbling the shoots off an umbrella tree. Miss Paradise inclined the hideous painted flower of her face over the shiny leaves so she would not have to speak, but Miss Trumper, who hated all good-bys, kept waving until he allowed his eyes to see hers.

"Next Tuesday, Chookie?" she asked unnecessarily.

And he answered with mock solemnity, "God willing and weather permitting!" She was delighted, the old superstitious dear, the thrower of salt, the avoider of ladders, the reader of astrological forecasts.

"Good-by then," she caroled. But he did not answer, following his shadow absorbedly along Fitzherbert Street. Before the plate glass should begin he paused to run a clogged comb through his carrot-crop and clean his fingernails on the teeth of it.

Thoughtful in a shade patch. Side lanes ran north and south through a lantana scrub at the backs of houses. He waited in the sun-pocket and felt a perspiration film like jelly over his freckled mug. Chookie in aspic! He giggled at the thought, fingered his pay, and watched a town lovely swing past. He gave her a wolf whistle, but she just tipped her profile upward. "Snoot!" he hissed softly. "Snoot." All the desperation of his adolescence rushed through him so horribly he could have cried. "What's up with me?" he asked himself them. And as he went down the shortcut he burned with some terrible force that sharpened when he saw the skinny kid he'd seen once or twice before come down the lane after him, bouncing a ball which entirely occupied her as she whacked it along the cow track. Smackety-smack. Miss, grab, smack, smack; until his fairy-tale giant loomed over her as the ball rolled right to his clumsy feet.

He kicked it gently backward.

They stood very still in the sun.

The ball rolled red, green, blue, across the rut. There was no one coming or going, only their two-ness and the rubber ball beneath a bramble. Her innocence inflated like a monstrous blister on his eyes.

"Come here," Chookie ordered, frantic, and unable to stop himself.

The child backed away. "I want my ball."

"Get yer ball." Chookie grinned, hideously nervous. "Then come here."

The child felt her throat grow solid and God move away into the sky like a star going out. Edging past him she bent and picked up her ball while Chookie measured her thin frame, terrified by a guilt that grabbed him in its hand and squeezed and urged him. It made him angry.

"Come on," he said very softly and dreadfully. "I'll show you something. I got a pound. Come here an' I'll show you."

She sprang around and started to run as Chookie pounced across the track. In her constricted throat a soundless scream formed, higher than fear, the high-pitched nothing of hysteria that broke into rain-patter of breathing when he grabbed her fleeing cardigan tail and dragged her around. But she wrestled viciously and silently on the path under the lantana cliffs, and between the bites and kicks and guilt and rage Chookie wanted terribly to let her go but could hear only his blind self saying over and over, "I wanter show you somethink. I wanter. Lemme show you. Lemme show. Lemme." Her heel caught his anguished shin so that he wanted to hurt her now, she made him so mad; shake her and shake her till she rattled her silly little bloody head off and it banged away down the path like the ball. Then on the thought, the rhythm began and he shook, shook, shook, the blackness dazzling him, shaking her stupid light-boned body all over the path, scattered like lantana flowers to break in a gust away from him down the laneway, right down between the cubby-holed scrub, away from him collapsed suddenly to his haunches on the track, watching with his blind eyes and dropping his head between his knees to vomit sparsely the bitter bile of his spasm and catching the last trickle down the side of his mouth on a checked sleeve.

The second day he'd lost his school money, a whole two shillings, and when he first discovered it had slipped from the knot Mum had made in the corner of his hanky, his flat little stomach had contracted and given him a belly-ache. "Tell Sister," the ginger-headed girl in the jazz garters had said. "Tell Sister." And he told, but no one found it or if they did they weren't saying, and that night Mum had nearly given him a hiding except he was so upset and hadn't eaten anything. Sister made him share his orange, too, at play-time and one of the other boys had shoved him over on the slope behind the church so that he cut his knee and it bled. "I don't like school much," he told them between his grimy sobs. "No one would play with me." And the next day when he saw the girl in the beautiful jazz garters—all pink and blue stuff like little dobs of flowers round the crinkly tops of her gleaming white socks—she had looked away and pretended that . . . and then he got in the way of the big boys playing footie. Weeks of it, he remembered. Weeks of it. Later on he settled down and a big slob of a kid who had jug ears and couldn't multiply a thing used to catch it every lesson while Chook shone with sixty per cent brightness and watched the new victim gratefully. But there were some bad spots. Like the time Sister Gabriel pinned his inky copy page to his back and he had to wear it all afternoon, half dead with shame. All the girls laughed at him. "Chookie!" they trilled across the playground. "Inky!" Not that the boys were so bad. And the next day the lime-light shifted from him because Gabe announced that there was a lot of cheating going on in the class and even if they thought she didn't see, their guardian angel did and anyway she'd prepared a big pasteboard sign with CHEAT printed large across it and the first one she caught would wear it all day. It was ole Barbie Jazz Garters. She had hysterics later and her parents came up to the convent and Reverend Mother saw them in the parlor and even Father Keefer came over from the presbytery. All the kids had sneaked around by the coleus hedge near the music-room windows that looked across to the front parlor, but they couldn't see or hear a thing and he had to go and spoil it all by laughing out loud. Later on Gabe gave him the strap—one on each hand—with a leather-bound discipline beater from whose impersonal guts he could still see the sawdust oozing. *Wish!* Don't cry, Chook! *Wish!* Geez. Geez. It hurts! And he'd cut out sharp into the grins waiting to rip him, with his blue eyes watering and his mouth twisting a way he didn't mean it to go. But ole Jazz Garters left the next day and went over to the state school and none of the convent kids ever spoke of her afterward except in soft secret voices because of the scandal. For a couple of Sundays, too, Father Keefer had been strong on sending the children to government schools. "God-less institutions!" he'd thundered from the pulpit. "Godless. Given to the world and mammon." "What's mammon, Mum?" he'd whispered urgently in church. "Wait till you're older," she'd said, and folded her neatly mended tan gloves over the worn color-lost edges of her old handbag. He only put two out of three pennies she'd given him on to the plate, but he never really enjoyed the candy he bought afterward.

I wish I hadn't done it, he said then. And he said now, in the hot dusty lane, I wish I hadn't. He looked up at the exposing yellow afternoon light and saw himself trapped in that place, discovered, and he began to run back to the street and left past the bungalows, past the convent and the courts down toward the riverbank and the fellow-feeling willows.

Miss Trumper. Miss Paradise. Chookie Mumberson. Miss Trumper. Miss Paradise.

Before a cheval mirror whose surface needed loving-kindness, the once lovely Trumper made nifty waists still with a glacé kid belt not suited to her age but daringly retained from a last late spring flurry during the war.

Still lush in her mid-thirties, but desperately discreet about the exact position of time's finger ("I was never good at telling the time!"), she had sported an American Colonel of Distinction with iron-gray temples for three mad weeks of invasion summer. Verna Paradise had gone crazy, dyed her hair orange, plastered her eyebrows, built out her bust. They'd been in business college together and knew every pale-skinned curve of each other's face. Foursome cozy they razzed down to Brisbane in a staff car, grogged at pubs, waved streamers, blew hooters, swooned, necked, made love and parted. Now Trumper could hardly believe it of herself. She had never been the racy kind.

But the Yanks were different. Soft as honey. They melted with good manners. Subtle, Verna asserted, and brave spenders.

"Got me bitta fur!" she used to mock, long after her hope had died, would never come tight-pantedly drawling. And the desperation would glare ferociously from under the blue-silver lids of her eyes. Spin that molting rabbit, sister! Twist it this or that way. Peer out, across oceans now, and not see the lost Yanks from Minnesota or Baton Rouge or Tucson. The Brisbane streets filled up with slouch hats once more after the forage caps had gone, so that the girls who had lost their hearts or their good sense at bus stops and good-bying railway platforms were jolted back to terrible sanities.

Miss Trumper tightened her belt in the flattering half-lit room and remembered the return trip to Condamine and a certain anguish and guilt she side-stepped but could never forget, and she waggled her poor sad head at her reflection.

How can I absorb this day? she wondered. And the next? And the next? I am eternal, she accused herself. And groaned at her face making lipstick mouths in the glass. Eternal.

Sometimes she read, martyred in wicker slices on the front veranda's shady afternoon where now, still kidded along by her belt, she took her fifty plus years and sat them behind the silver spotted leaves of begonias whose fleshiness soothed. From corner posts erupted staghorns in wire baskets that netted a view of the convent wall and lawn and the weather-beaten saints impervious to her guilty bloodshot suppliant eyes.

"It's really," she said aloud, for these days she said aloud more and more frequently, "it's really that I want to be a saint."

"Verna," she asked as they took tea in this leafed corner, "is it silly to want to be a saint?"

Miss Paradise paused, stunned, in the act of adding sugar, but she did not allow this to sweeten her words. "Yes," she said. "Pass the bikkies, Kitty."

"But truly," persisted Miss Trumper handing them across with a few jerky retractions. "I can't see that it is. I mean, think of all the marvelous people. St. Francis and Joan and Lawrence. The one who was roasted, I mean."

"Why do you want to be a saint?" asked Miss Paradise, settling her rainbow-striped dress in a sickly candy flounce about the edge of her bony knees.

Miss Trumper sipped her tea and had two goes at putting her cup back on the saucer. "To atone," she said.

"Oh Heavens!" Miss Paradise sighed. "You are feeling bad today, aren't you? You're one of millions. No one knows. No one cares. It's all years away and you do yourself no good by being miserable."

I must be wretched, Miss Trumper decided, when I am not inanely gay, making licorice eyes at tradesmen who go away and gag over my gush. Yes. I know. Gag gag gag gag gag. Oh why, she asked herself, why did I do it. And all across her forehead barbed-wire worries writhed as she saw once more the struck-off quack's rooms and felt every bleeding inch of the walk afterward along the Terrace to the cab-rank. Fifteen years. And she had carried that half-hour and that walk for every day ever since until the minutes pressed their spikes into her and she told herself this is it, this is the end, and began saving her sleeping tablets like a miser awaiting the final luxury. But at the end something always intervened. She would tell herself it was nobler to go on living if you could stand it. Isn't it, Verna? Isn't it? Seeking reassurance like a child. And, yes dear, Verna would say, of course it is. Of course it's nobler. And they would hover, dry as sticks, over their pot of tea and pretend they weren't quite so old and things weren't so terrible and giggle a bit, gay-girlishly with the lipstick hooking onto the wrinkled corners of their mouths, the sad runnels, but exposing the dry lips. Or the dry souls.

"Are you still having Chookie for one day only?" Miss Paradise inquired.

"Oh yes," said Miss Trumper. "Sometimes he drops in if he has left something he needs in the tool shed. He's not a bad lad."

"Just primitive," Miss Paradise suggested, gashing Chookie wide open.

"Well, perhaps. You know, he does do some awful things. This morning down by the back fence . . . I was going down to fetch him in for tea when. . . ." She subsided into shocked gossip that still managed to distract, for if she placed another's transgression alongside her own, the harsh light of conscience ceased beating upon her with quite as much acidity. Oh, she was avid for crime sheets and scandals and went through the paper for meaty bones which she would bury in the crumbling earth of her eroded mind and unearth much later, slightly altered in shape, for soothing comparisons. She had a shocking familiarity with famous rapers, mutilators, necrophiles, and poisoners, altogether unbelievable in this gentle tottering soul who could not now harm a fly without some pang of heart.

"Disgusting," decided Miss Paradise. "I'd tell his mother."

"Oh, I couldn't! How could I? Could you tell anyone a thing like that? I mean, how would you say it?"

"You certainly can. Exposing himself that way. Say if someone else had seen. . . ."

"But it was hardly exposing. I mean, he might have wanted to go and couldn't. . . . Wouldn't you say it was more vulgar than vicious?" She always sought timidly for excuses after the revelation.

"Vulgar or vicious, it shouldn't be." Miss Paradise was rather angrily envious. No scandal had touched her for years. "My dear," she whispered then, "there's someone coming. I think you have a visitor." And her voice trailed into italics as she slit-eyed a portly figure hesitating at the wicket gate.

Bernard had met Miss Trumper before. Six times? Seven? He was not sure, but she could have given him a total of minutes devastatingly accurate, a summation of trade, an analysis (false) of looks exchanged or emphasis (misread). Her frantic hands automatically began to twitch curls into provocative positions and one forefinger, desperate digit, rubbed the corner of her mouth to erase the trapped carmine grease she knew from experience would be there. Then one hand stroked pleats, and then pushed at puffs of hair at her nape. Her hair style had not changed since she wowed them during the war. And she went, naked as birth, across the concrete veranda to the man who had never yet really seen her.

"Hullo," said hearty Bernard, all pipe and chuckles. "What splendid weather for lotus-eating! And how are you?"

Miss Trumper always found that an exceedingly difficult question to answer, some ethical principle rearing itself at one, so that she shied away like a nervous horse.

"How are *you*?" she emphasized. "It must be ages."

"I'm sorry for coming unannounced," Bernard said. "I'm going back this evening and I wanted to see you before I went."

"Oh!" See me, she thought, pulsating with miracles. See me? Oh, *do* see me. "It's a delightful surprise. Stay and have some tea, and meet my dear friend, Miss Paradise."

Miss Paradise's paint had hardened like lacquer. A smile might have caused terrible damage. So she did not smile, but inclined her head coldly, going all *grande dame*. From the narrow rainbow sleeve an over-ringed hand, unlucky with opals, trembled into his and withdrew after withered contact of a minimal kind.

"How are you," she stated and could not have cared less for an answer, aloof behind her public image. She had always played hard to get, the cunning thing, from sixteen on, and had been noticeably more successful with men than her dear friend Kitty, so that now she carried the nonsense on into middle age by habit. Underneath the speculation bubbled, though her eye missed no detail as she stripped him mentally —but only to the underwear. She had always been a bit of a prude.

"Tea?" Miss Trumper asked, kitty-cat cute and blessedly relieved from guilt for a few brilliant moments.

"Thank you," he said and tried not to watch her having trouble with the hot water that she added. During the few moments she was gone to get another cup he rumbled about in his briefcase for papers, watched by the brilliant phoenix opposite who sipped her tea and nibbled biscuits with the utmost icy composure.

"It's about the little Garnett girl," he said when the tea-table settled itself. "I've had to fail her again. In fact, I didn't really examine her. She was so nervous she couldn't play a note, poor little thing. Wept like a sponge. I told her I'd come and have a talk with you."

Miss Trumper knocked the sugar bowl, dodging sideways in an effort to avoid contaminating it before she passed it through her agony to Bernard, who recalled her foibles acutely.

"Not that one," she suggested as he reached for a biscuit. "Try that top one. It doesn't look so—so battered." She laughed foolishly, afraid to say "germy."

"Thank you." Bernard took it as swiftly as possible to cut short her indecision and nibbled into its icing. "If you like," he said, breathing vanilla, "I'll see if a different examiner could come up next May. She might feel happier with a woman, say. I often wonder if I'm getting too old and crusty."

"Oh dear!" Temporarily Miss Trumper was seized by a spasm of panic. Not come? Oh please not not come! She looked forward to these little meetings they had had for the last few years when over tea and scones they would conduct post-mortems of the trials of music-teaching and the changes in the syllabus. He was so kindly and gentle, so good, so genuinely good and worthwhile, she felt. No. She could not bear it if he ceased to come. Bold as brass, she put a racy hand on his sleeve.

"We'd all miss you," she said. "You're part of the system now. Christine is a silly little girl. I'll speak to her."

"No. Don't do that. She was very upset."

"I do know her mother's rather odd," Miss Trumper said, twitching just the merest bit. "I don't think she bothers about her. 'Neglects' is too strong a word, I suppose. But I don't think she ever makes her practice, and then she gets so upset when Christine's results are terrible. But what can I do?"

"It's very hard," Bernard soothed. "Very hard. Having children is buying oneself trouble."

Miss Trumper went dreadfully white. "Do you think that?"

"Well, it's only a saying, isn't it? But I suppose one's worries only really begin with parenthood."

"More tea?" Miss Paradise interposed, attempting to save her drowning friend.

Miss Trumper wrestled silently, inwardly, and terribly with her guilt, which cast a slime over the entire day, her face strained and absent.

The man, aware that something dreadful was happening within her, would have made amends, but all he was capable of doing was turning to her companion and asking fatuously, "Have you live in Condamine long, Miss Paramour, or are you merely visiting?"

It was shocking when Kitty Trumper screeched with wild laughter then, as if a thick plug had been wrenched out. Miss Paradise was straight as a stick, but propelled her reply with much effort so that the very sound of the words and their sense were stiff as glue. "Paradise, Mr. Loverson," she said coldly. "And I reside in a house across town."

Behind his smile he hunted around for table talk, but was inhibited by her eyes drilling across an ellipse of tea.

"My father was born here," he said weakly, "across the river on the flats."

"Was he, indeed?"

"Yes. We used to come up from Brisbane when I was a boy so that he could look around the old place and say how much it had changed. You know."

"Do we not?" Miss Paradise would never unbend now.

"Did you really?" Miss Trumper appeared to be recovering. "Oh, that makes us school friends almost! I was at school here. This is the old family home." She rejoiced excessively and longed at once for the innocence and the untroubled eye, the animal spirit that had once been able to lose itself in simplicities—the high tea after tennis in winter dusk and the long horse-rides out toward Toowoomba with the exaltation of movement and the daringly jodhpured leg become one freedom; a certain aspect of landscape at a turn on the Gap road when a valley revealed its sunny ripeness to the eye focusing between trees and hills. "School," she said softly. "I wish I could be there again."

"You're crazy!" snapped Miss Paradise rudely. "It was cruel and terrible, inky-stockinged, verbal, nagged and primitive."

"That's the second time you've used that word, Verna."

"Is it? Well, I like it." She could feel a quarrel beginning to boil. "*Primitif. Très, très primitif.* We had to kowtow and and behave abnormally and fawn and debase our individualism."

"Oh dear," Miss Trumper said. "Oh dear, Verna. But we were safe."

"Safe!" scoffed the other. "Safe! . . . I'll have to be starting back," she said abruptly. The older, the huffier. There was some ratio. She fluffed about quite a bit before she actually edged the heavy garden chair back, Bernard assisting somberly. "Who wants to be safe?"

Miss Trumper's eyes popped. "We all do. Oh, I know I do. Don't you think everyone does, Mr. Leverson?"

"We're never safe," Bernard said rather sententiously. "There's unexplained nastiness squinting across any unexpected lull, eyeing us off and waiting to pounce." But he smiled.

"Lovely!" approved Miss Paradise, quite viciously, a rainbow monster. "I like that. I like the feeling of something about to happen even if it never does. And it never does. You and your stuffy little school womb! All tight with authority and chalk and hours for prep and prayer! Oh, those gay times with the short-sheeted beds!"

Miss Trumper retreated and fiddled with her teacup and then removed her hands suddenly as if . . .

"You've never lost it," Kitty Trumper suggested, "or you'd never say."

"Neither have you, you silly thing," Miss Paradise said rudely, "only you just won't realize it or believe it. You love to crucify yourself. You're a born martyr. You know what they used to call her at school, Mr. Leverson? Alma Martyr!" She laughed and laughed.

"Please," Miss Trumper pleaded, anguished before the visitor. "Please." Her voice almost flapped away.

Bernard attempted to appear engrossed with the potted plants. He strolled a few feet away into a late square of afternoon sun, but in the silence at his back could be felt the protestations of the one and the amusement of the other.

"Good-by then, Kitty," he heard Miss Paradise say. "I'll see you later on when you feel more cheerful. Good afternoon, Mr. Leverson." She looked him up and down and held his eye for ten pulsing beats. "I like big men," she said, "with pockmarks."

"Sorry I can't oblige," Bernard said, taken aback. His tongue seemed stuck to the roof of his mouth. "Good-by."

Maypole straight and mad she went down the path between the ornamental cabbages and the gerberas.

"Don't take any notice please," Miss Trumper said, battling with something she was not prepared to reveal. "She's a bit—well—crazy, you know, and doesn't mean a thing by it."

"Thank God I'm not pockmarked," Bernard said drily.

"Now, just before we get side-tracked, let's settle about young Garnett."

Before he left, Miss Trumper, putting all her coin on the red, asked if he would care to try her piano; after all, she pointed out coyly, he had visited her several times and never yet . . . (never yet what, sad Trumper?) . . . and it was a rather pleasant little Carl Mand and she wondered what he . . . she would like his opinion . . . her father had imported it direct from Germany, Coblenz to be exact.

"Show me," Bernard said, practicing charity.

Horrible as a museum, the sitting room was a photographic Tussaud's with only one subject. Impressions of a striped wallpaper barred like a cage gave way before the fixed tinted plight of the paper prisoners. Here was Kitty Trumper at three in a ballerina's tutu with one chubby leg extended in an awkward arabesque (her hands clutched two wires eliminated by photographic processes), and the little subject glanced shyly backward at the camera lens which had caught her candid eyes gleaming from beneath a completely geometrical fringe line. And here she was at seven in Cossack costume, one leg heel-toeing it, hands on hips; and again at ten (plaits this time and a brace), tutu stiff as pudding performing a *bourrée* on *pointes*, her round, smiling face upturned. And surely not much older, there she was at a baby grand, her unplaying fingers resting on the eisteddfoded keys, her face a map of musical rapture. ("Imagine you are far away, my dear. Do you hear the lovely music?") All her poor shrunken little soul was looking out of those large eyes. And again at fourteen and eighteen and twenty-two (a straight photograph, this, in a lacy pink sweater with a lot of cleavage and two blond curls glued into false positions below the ripple marks left by the curling grips). When she had begun to give lessons: "I'm nice the first time, but not so nice the second!" And it was only two and six a time, nice or not, with abridged versions of the "Moonlight Sonata" and the Rachmaninoff Prelude and Mendelssohn's "Spring Song."

They were everywhere, at every age and with every face—full, profile, three-quarter—starry-eyed glancing up, gazing into misty distances; looking down shyly, peeping coyly, and one (a mistake obviously) almost leering out of a leprechaun's costume. They were framed and hanging. Mounted on stands. Turned into glossy plaques. They were in high gloss, sepia and tinted.

Bernard blinked, re-focused, blinked again. It was as if he had raped a diary. Later on the padded blue furniture came into being and at an occasional table, set also with twin plaques of Miss Trumper as a shepherd and shepherdess, the ultimate insanity of the ego.

"What do you think of it?" she asked proudly.

He coughed desperately until he remembered she meant the piano. But where? he asked himself. Where? And there it was, a gay walnut upright, a little beauty, bearing the weight of a massive plaster stag that reclined casually along its lid and looked down at the performer.

"Amazing!" Bernard said. "Truly amazing!"

"Yes. Yes, it is." Dear Miss Trumper was pink with pride. "There were candlesticks, but I had them taken off and polished." She jerked away and set a framed photo rocking metronomically on the veneer.

"Do try it," she urged. "I have it tuned every six months. Tell me if you think it's worth the trouble."

"Ooooh," Bernard said. Like most music teachers he hated performing and at this stage in his life remembered fragments from scores of things but hardly anything in its entirety. "You'll mark me out of ten and not give me a pass."

"No, no! No, no." Masses of exclamations and protestations, and Bernard, pelted by these gasped rebuttals, seated himself heavily at the brow-beaten piano and rushed through one of the earlier Bach preludes. Oppressively close, Miss Trumper lowered her face to watch him and all the other Misses Trumper pranced or peered and the stag impassively observed him make a couple of sloppy mistakes.

Now, decided some insane gambler in Miss Trumper. Oh

now. And she laid one gabbling hand on his sleeve as he played the last chord and shook her head from side to side as if words had collapsed or abandoned her.

Some mumbled thanks were managed, some garbled inquiry achieved.

"A lovely instrument," Bernard soothed, rather astonished at the piano's full tone.

But it was like being buried in pot-pourri, and burrowing through rose leaves he attempted to rise, flapped tweed wings, not a ministering but an escaping angel.

Miss Trumper burst into tears.

Before he could slide from the polished seat, she had dropped to her knees beside him and his horrified eyes riveted on her head which she had rested on his lap.

"Please? Oh please please please?" she asked, several times.

Instantly he understood what she wanted, but he could do nothing except put her back gently and not ask what was the matter.

I shall die, Kitty Trumper told herself deliberately. I must. I shall take pills or drop from moving cars or walk into space. I shall court locomotives and precipices and open windows. I shall cut off this knot that pretends to be me.

"Once," she dribbled into the tweed thigh that sought to escape. "Once. . . ."

But Bernard merely said "Now" awkwardly or "Don't" or "There. You're over-tired."

Her humiliation could not prolong itself like some litany of self-abnegation, yet she did not know how to end the situation that struggled weakly in the wild flare of the lighted moment. Bernard managed to get to his feet and he bent down to help her also, unwillingly to have her suffer by seeing him out. Putting one hand under the desperately fragile arm protected only by silk, he helped her into a chair. Her mouth kept breaking words to pieces as if she were feeding them to the youngest and tenderest of animals and he felt very near to weeping himself as he saw her, an old velvet-framed ballet dancer, collapsed on cushions. Somehow he conveyed his own grief through the touch he gave her shoulder before he escaped into the garden.

Chookie was still trembling with rage when he returned through the side gate and went around to the back of the garage where the rakes and hoes were stacked. He didn't quite know why he had come back. Maybe it was to look at the harmonium again or maybe it was to conceal himself from home and repercussions. Inside there was some fierce acid burning steadily that seemed to be in control of his veins through which no blood could flow, only the heavy pulsatings of anger and frustrated needs.

He sat steadily on an upturned box and had a quiet cigarette to steady himself, but nothing was any good any more and he found the cigarette drooping from his hand, spilling ash telltale on the concrete floor while he watched the sleepy afternoon house through the door. There wasn't any sign of the old girl any place, not even a sound from the house. He hoped she'd gone out. He hoped this and he hoped this and he pulled a bit of paspalum up near the door and chewed it for a bit and watched the wet end dribble across his knee and said, "Crikey, O Gawd," and threw both grass and cigarette away and lit another cigarette. I never meant to touch her, he said, he told himself. I never hurt her none. Just give her a bit of a shaking. Strewth. What the hell will I do? I only shook her up a bit and off she went. Am I glad she went or aren't I? Glad, I suppose. O Gawd. He sat on the box and leaned his head against the door, and the trembling, for another reason, took him and he bent over his stomach and moaned and spat tobacco shreds and coughed a bit too loudly, for somewhere back in the house he heard a movement and then the old girl calling out something.

He stared steadily at a clump of bright leaves and waited for her to call again. I'll just get what she owes me for that extra day I did last month, he thought, and push off. Now he shivered under his sweater.

Someone was fumbling at the side window, making ineffectual pushes at the stuck casement. Watching, he almost grinned. She looked so funny struggling with the catch and peering blindly through to see who it was in the garden. He slouched over to the doorway and stood against it until she focused into recognition and he could tell by the shape of her mouth that she was calling him, for her hand appeared to be beckoning, too, in a spidery fashion behind the lace; so he ambled across the lawn and path and went around to the back.

"Coming," he called, but not really loud enough for her to hear, and he leaped spindle-leg over a hydrangea clump and put on his sandy grin to the bland back door.

"Come through, Chookie," he could hear her cry, faint as cobwebs, as distant as death, from somewhere away in, and it made him hesitate, the house was so dim. No light anywhere. The afternoon of watered silk cut off as he pushed the door close behind him and stepped down the too-glossy linoleum. Even the kitchen clock had stopped. He was aware of his own heart. Or, hers, pounding in another room. Bumping against the dining-room table, he narrowed his eyes into cat vision, and heard her movement in the music room beyond.

"Yeah?" he asked, pushing past bead curtains into the haunted arcades of Trumperie.

There she was, curled up funny on the settee. Something was wrong. He took another look. Her face was mucked up as if she'd been crying and the funny thing was she turned away when he came in and he could see she had bare feet and was sitting there in nothing but an old sateen slip. White and sad, her shoulders looked as if they'd been crying, too, and the small shiny mounds of her breasts, tokens, preserved a lonely little sorrow. Sadly her thin knees pressed against each other for comfort.

Some awful curiosity and excitement lunged back through Chookie as he looked at her coiled up on her pathetic sacrificial table and he swallowed a couple of times and kept very still by the end of the sofa, waiting for her to say something.

But Kitty Trumper said everything in her tearless silence, in her pleading dress, in the dejected rejection of her slopped-down figure. She wept inwardly and the tears ran inwardly and threatened to drown. She wanted and was not really sure what she wanted.

Me? wondered Chookie. Kind. Frightened. Lustful. Appalled. Me? Me?

114

He prickled all over and was so silent she, who did not raise her eyes lest he observe too closely, imagined for a moment that he had slipped backward through irresolution and escaped. Hoped so.

But he had not and remained, gauche, unable to murmur the most clumsily hewn of consolatory words, too young to do anything except the one terrible final thing which she both wanted and rejected. Slowly he advanced his feet over the deserts of carpet, draggingly, touching before resting weight as if he were on some crumbling margin—as indeed he was—and came at last to pause before her lowered eyes and soul. He heard her breath gasp like an old tire. One hand jerked convusively on her black sateen lap and one raised itself to him to be hauled up this mountain.

Chookie put an opened awkward palm, patting, comforting upon the thin hair and he marveled, as touch nearly brought him to his senses, at the fragility of the skull under his fingers. His tongue was looping itself about words that refused to untie themselves into proper sounds. Gawd, he prayed. Gawd. And then they were both blinded.

And afterward, when they had fled to opposite poles like mad creatures, he ducking out in the early darkness stamped all over with watching photographs and she rushing from pretended rapine toward the angelus gates of the convent, that patting horny hand remained raised like an eternal blessing, recalling, at least to her, endless pictures of tear-stained benedictions.

But Miss Trumper had to sob and moan through the guilt of her satisfaction, rushing crazy as goats across the half-clad road across the lawns past the startled saints and finding her wildly flapping arms in some terrible collision with a small mad nun who was running also across the garden after her lost God.

In the hurtling dark, bleeding with remorse and the batterings of escape, Bernard drove east, aware of guilt. I could have been kinder, he acknowledged, could have flirted or pretended or touched just momentarily, laid one Christian healing palm on her dried-up loneliness. It wouldn't have meant anything at all except the sacrifice of seconds. You selfish bastard, he said. No wonder Iris . . . and swerved in the dim light to avoid what might have been the materialization of his sin, the waving, thumbing figure on the edge of the road.

"Givus a lift, mister," it asked out of the shadow as he drew up, but Bernard waited until the figure moved closer to the light before he spoke. "Give us a lift?" There was the merest trace of whine. And then he saw it wasn't a man, but a boy not much older than . . . and with an absurdly spotted face.

"Where to?" Bernard asked.

"As far as you're goin'."

"Oh?" He looked down at the empty hands. "No luggage?"

"Nope. On a walkin' trip." Chookie grinned nervously. "I been comin' from Dalby and me bundle got pinched when I was in the station washroom back there."

"Back in Dalby?"

"No. Condamine."

Liar, said Bernard to himself, and, "Hop in," he said aloud. "I'm going through to Brisbane."

"Good-oh," Chookie agreed, slamming the door. He leaned back in the corner. "That's where I'm goin', too."

6

Sharp as tacks Leo Varga slid his sports car into the city crushed with trams and cars, himself crushed rather delightfully by two students whom he had picked up in glancing as it were on the way out of the last lesson. Mr. Varga was wearing a thigh-gripping shortie coat with a real (but real, kids) astrakhan collar, even in July a wee bit hot and unsuitable for Brisbane. His cravat was spotted foulard and somewhere above or below this barrier there was plenty of after-shave lotion that he dabbled also generously between his thonged toes. Wow wowee! Generously and keenly interested in young minds, he had been taking Tom Seabrook and Keith Leverson on an adult outing, an after-six invitation to a preview of paintings at an *avant-garde* gallery in a South Brisbane basement. He had two or three rather limp crayon nudes hung, and it was always good to take disciples who might make suitable and overheard remarks.

Tommy Seabrook was a double of his dad—a town innocent, when it was all boiled down. Yet he and Keith, after the initial horror had worn off, discussed their parents with unpleasant detachment and kept their real feelings, their bruised soft souls for private exposure at those times when each reverted to the little boy who cried for lost fairylands. Avuncular Varga latched on quickly to the fact that the relationship knit the two of them matily. Disgusting little beggars, he mused, when they showed off and were hard-boiled and super blasé before him, stripping their pathetic erring parents naked, coupling them and laughing them into pieces. What he simply did not know was that each witty dissection was agony, though the boys suspected this of each other, and sometimes after a particularly amusing comment by Keith one would catch the other's eye with an apology lurking there afraid to reveal itself fully.

"What do you think of Leo really?" Tommy Seabrook ventured, unable to imagine the suitable reply he wanted.

"Oh, he's okay." Keith was cautious. "The only adult I know who's human."

"Human?"

"Yes. Intelligent. Interesting. Interested in us."

"I suppose he is. You don't think he's too interested, do you?"

"What do you mean?"

"Oh . . . well, just that. I don't know. Skip it!"

But they knew all right.

Leo could be charming when he wanted. And he wanted now. As if they were contemporaries, he gossiped with the lads, introduced them to other adults who were holding opinions and tiny glasses, bought them coffee, listened to what they said—and then drove them home.

"Pretty neat, Leo!" Keith said. That meant "thank you."

"Yes. Keen!" Tommy said. "Me, too."

"Don't forget, laddies"—that was just his fun!—"we're off to the big surf when the weather lets up."

They nodded gravely while Leo leaned out of his car like a fun-in-the-sun ad to drop them off at their street corner.

"Wonder if Father's home?" Tommy said, kicking it along but hoping wildly that he was.

"Wonder if Mother is!"

They all laughed, extra cynically, and Mr. Varga supplied the slow wink.

Later that evening, during an especially interesting television documentary on Poland, Keith began saying, "Duffle coat, duffle coat," over and over. The words were not loud, but distinct.

"Shut up!" Bernard ordered with lukewarm reaction as he missed something he was straining to catch. Somber as lye, Keith smiled and watched the glassy images distort and coalesce, holding fifteen minutes' silence out like a floral tribute to dad, but when the interviewer was questioning a particularly pretty student in a turtleneck who was eager to be voluble, Keith began intoning firmly the same pair of words.

"Ah, get to bed!" Bernard ordered, raising the volume and contemptuously not looking. The phone clucked as if it were about to lay an egg.

"Dear God!" Bernard said, reaching across.

"Duffle coat," Keith repeated, smiling gently.

Bernard handed the receiver out to knitting Iris, who fulfilled every function of the women's magazines from snappy sweaters even to her adultery.

"It's Kathleen Seabrook," he said. "Tell her to hurry up and get off."

Keith went white suddenly. He watched his mother, his eyes glinting like a prophet's about to uncover a truth, and Bernard, noticing this, could only sigh.

"Cut along, son," he said, remembering the closed tight fists of babyhood and the pinkness, the sweet-smelling firmness, the gentle fuzz of hair. Love fell, just for a few seconds, a wild and unexpected rain, with memories of bath-times, animal-shaped cakes of soap, red-faced tantrums and small fierce fingers curling about his own.

"If you're old enough to listen, Bernard," the bright lad said, "I'm sure I am."

Refusing to move, he lounged along the carpet over a copy of *Swot*, the threepenny weekly he and Tommy Seabrook had begun at the high school. He was busy compiling the pre-vacation issue editorial and was sweating over a variety of headings. "Oh the thickening thilence!" he had just written and was moodily chewing the end of a ballpoint over it. "Gone, the patter of enormous feet," he had scribbled underneath, "as our favorite sadists sneak from room to room, canings, the detentions, the pieces of flying chalk hurled diligent in their search for victims. Gone, the happy carefree with expertise by masters of modern languages."

I like that last bit, he thought, and said, "Hey Bernard, what do you think of this?" He began to read through his mother's endless voice, trying to drown the lies and the insincerity, the fake friendship. "What do you think of this for a profile on old Slugs? 'It has been rumored among the dim brains from Junior School that *liaisons dangereuses'*—how d'you spell *'dangereuses'* Bernard?—'are imperiling the morals of susceptible teen-agers. One of our slower-moving staff members, Slugs being the frivolous nomenclature given him by discerning students, has become involved'—is 'involved' the word, Dad?—'with a set of vital statistics from the economics faculty. What the school wants to know is—what do all these figures add up to?' How's that, huh?"

There seemed no end to it, Bernard thought, like one of those dream roads, hazardless and empty, that never touch the horizon, or round the hill or even reach the boat-yearning sea. The television flickered; Iris talked inanities and Keith, smiling somewhat madly (wherever have I seen that smile before? Leverson asked himself) visually negotiated the room as if he were setting an enormous trap and were awaiting the exact moment to spring it. Sheltered by telly buzz, what seemed a foreign language and radiant commercials, Iris began confidential side comments into the mouth-piece, looking as if she would never tear herself away from its two-way comfort, so that finally Bernard switched off the set and hid in his small study where the four walls with their brown stains and shabbiness accepted and did not criticize. Piles of undone work rammed home their obligation, forcing him to close the door very gently on his still listening, spying son. Softly, too, he turned the key and, shoving aside the pile of unmarked theory papers, he put on a record and mentally dug in.

Throughout his instant porridge, Keith said "duffle coat" approximately fifteen times. Bernard had almost ceased to hear it by now, but Iris poured acid into the breakfast compounds, witchily hexed them both, nerves on edge, and watched her own edges curl over and crisp. When I pray, she decided, the saints cease to be flesh and become plaster. They turn bland plaster saintly smiles toward me, calm as the Inquisitors and as unmoved by others' endurance. Let someone, anyone, love me, she prayed, burning the toast. . . . But half a mile away Gerald curled up behind his newspaper and wondered anxiously how he could extricate himself. Keith watched her with amused hatred and Bernard for once failed to notice anything.

"*Tum tee tum, tum tee tum, tum tee ti ti,*" he sang absently marmalading his blackened bread. "*Now your days of philandering are over!*"

And Keith left without apology and gathered up his school bag.

But he did not go there. Normally he picked up with Tommy Seabrook at the Edward Street ferry and together they loafed over to school through the Gardens and down again. But this time he went straight toward the Bridge and came up into the city through the Valley, prowling around Anzac Square and mesmerizing the goldfish in the fonts. " 'The gold fin in the porphyry font,' " he quoted dreamily to the rhythm of trams and out loud, startling the old ladies or the early shoppers, not caring either, and wondering if he could have written it better. In the state in which his emotions daily rested he was half drugged—intermediate between nothing and fantasy, with ideal parents who drove long cars and flirted and were gay but intelligent, who kept him in his place and said No often and firmly.

Oh, how they said No and how often and how firmly.

But the big tower rang and, prompt on the final hurly-burly of the bells, he slipped, a knowing minnow, into the open doors of the store. Everywhere the black-clad girls primped goods and clicked cash registers and patted their hair-dos—but there weren't nearly enough customers, so he went back to the square again and, taking off his school blazer, folded it neatly, tightly, and packed it into his bag. Then he bought himself a slow peppermint-flavored julep to be sucked through a lingering straw, minute after minute. He was boxed a bit by the morning's crossword, but filled in half the blanks untidily though accurately before he went back to the store and up the escalator to men's wear.

There were plenty of shoppers now. Keith slid unnoticed into the mob, sidled along a rack of jackets, and selected the one he fancied long before obsequiousness tottered up, all iron-gray and florid.

"Yes, sir?" it said—because it was certainly desexed and dehumanized by the sanctions of its employment. "Can I help you?"

Keith put on his open, blond, urchin smile that worked so well in tight spots.

"Could I try on a couple of these coats?" he asked. He was at his most engaging.

"Any particular color?"

"Well, I can't quite make up my mind."

"What size would you be? Youth's?"

"Oh, about thirty-six I think. My mother told me to get thirty-six," he added dazzlingly.

"Then this rack over here. Anything along here would do. Just select a couple and I'll be with you in a minute. There. That's a nice bit of camel hair. Pricey but good. And that worsted is imported."

"May I use a dressing room?" Keith asked.

"Through over there."

"Right."

Keith did not hurry. Casualness was the thing. He selected four coats from the rack and managed to hold them as if he had three; then, sauntering easy as could be, he went into the dressing-room block, the confessional, and it didn't take him more than half a minute to swap coat for blazer and be found casually and elegantly admiring his back view when the salesman poked his head around the curtain.

"How's that, sir?" he inquired. Pretending he cares, Keith thought savagely. I'll fix him.

"I think it's a little too big across the shoulders." He pivoted slowly.

It was balletic. As he divested himself of one, the older man stood poised with the next garment outstretched for him to slip into. They proceeded with the farce. Somewhere an orchestra should have been playing *pizzicato*. Excuses came so easily from the boy it might have been assumed the salesman wanted them too, for when Keith finally sorted his blazed from under the discards, both were glad.

"Sorry to bother you," he said. "I've always been hard to fit."

"That's all right, sir." The salesman had barely looked at him or seen the straw bright hair, the blue eyes, the rose tan of skin. He hated his job and he hated the customers who were faceless shapes with voices persistent or nagging. Some chaps blew smoke and some shifted false teeth but most never wanted to buy at all, just kid themselves along a little, and he was prepared to oblige so long as not much effort was expected, the minimum that kept the departmental head's eye off him and left him alone to brood among the hand-woven tweeds and the shoddy.

Sauntering for the heck of it, stopping to take in a few suits on the way out, you'd swear this kid was an old hand at the game. Far too late for school, he headed for a phone booth at the post office, dialed the principal, and pulled off another purler of deception that made his toes curl with pleasure.

"Leverson speaking." He could do a take off of the old boy like a dream.

"Oh yes, Mr. Leverson." The fawning wasn't what some of the wealthier lads got, but there was enough. The teachers are frightened of the head, the head of the inspector, the inspector of the local member, the local member of the parents, the parents of the kids, and the kids of nobody.

"The boy's a bit off color today. I thought we'd keep him home."

"Indeed. I'm sorry to hear that." Distance emasculated the keep-a-straight-bat voice of the pompous old bugger who preened it around on speech days with his pass-degree silk dangling showily over his humped shoulders.

"I think he'll be in tomorrow. Sorry, Hendrix." That omission of the "mister" was especially pleasing.

They clicked each other into silence, and Keith wandered into a newsreel and then a support film in the after-lunch period, so that he arrived home in nice coincidence with the local ferry, his round face innocent as goosegogs, round as johnny-cake. This guileless mask he bent over a late-evening forgery that said, dear sir Keith has been absent because of an intestinal upset, please excuse him yours sincerely Iris Leverson. It was pleasant to have both parents display such concern and he could just imagine Slugs writing it up on his blue record card: "Parents over-interested in their son's health. Appears coddled." It took him quite a time achieving a passable likeness in handwriting, and by eleven his mother was fretting at his door for him to get to bed, while he, active as a cartoon character, rammed the note under a blotter. Maybe he'd keep this for another time.

For two weeks now he had avoided communication. She questioned, but he did not answer. Whore, he accused her as he walked over to the door and unturned the key.

"Why did you lock yourself in, silly?"

He shrugged.

"Do get your light out." Iris's eyes begged and begged of him to relent. He thought of the duffle coat and smiled—but not at her, so that she winced, a wince that like some small pool's throb spread ripples to the farthest margin. Her adultery had not been a success. Half the fun would have been in having Bernard care and the other half in having Gerald "tortured by desire"—that was the phrase she knew from her usual reading. But one did not not care and the other was not tortured. The indifference of one she could have endured after the inadequacy of marriage for twenty years—stamina parties, they used to call them—but the reluctant lover turned the whole thing into a farce. Gerald must feel like Byron, she reflected, raped oftener than anyone since the Trojan Wars. And without much amusement, for she was a humorless woman. I am not as shallow as I seem, Iris would have prayed or exhorted anyone to believe. The nightmare is the daytime stay-awake one. I move into normality through sleep and wake to unending dissatisfaction.

Keith shut his door again. The house was like a set of interlocking boxes, absorbed Bernard being closeted in his study, battered by Parsifal. Please God, prayed Iris to some faceless power, and did the only thing she could think of, which was to run a long hot bath.

Keith wore his duffle coat at school the next day, sweltering it out for vanity until one of the other boys made a pertinent remark about a certain sloppiness of fit and an extra length that appeared undesirable. So, having dumped the garment in his locker, Keith did some practical brooding over failure and achievement, and at the end of the week returned with it to the shop to attain the real climax. Seeking out a different assistant, Keith managed to exchange the coat for one of sharper cut.

"Keen!" Keith admitted, admiring himself in a three-way mirror. "Sharply elegant!—I'm sorry, but I seem to have lost the docket."

But this big store had said for years it aimed to please.

"That's quite all right, sir. That's one of our special lines."

Keith felt as elated as a first-time drunk, even nodding pleasantly to his former salesman when he passed him on the way out between suits and *après*-swim wear at the top of the escalator. But his blank eyes did not remember a thing, Keith knew, and he literally pranced to the lifts in his trim new skin, rode to the basement, and absorbed his guilt and victory through a long vanilla milk-shake. Five minutes later, pursuing victory past the tape, he gave a jovial smack to a cringing cigarette machine as he passed and was rewarded by its spewing out a pack of twenty and taped-on change.

Just for a handful of silver he left them,
Just for a riband to stick in his duffle coat,

parodied cultured Keith and went out at a half-skip from the arcade to take in the morning.

Gardens. River tawniness. On the other side of the water a raised swimming pool with portholes for voyeurs, across which flashed the ochre limbs of swimmers. The park was pimpled with mums and ice-creamed children and newspapered old men who slept in the near-summer sun with the headlines pulled down over their eyes to keep out the brighter glare. Behind the groves of *Chamaerops excelsa*, braces and flatties and flapping dirndl skirts—the town was always six fashions behind.

Chookie Mumberson, anybody's meat, good ole Chookie, sneakered and flapped down the tar path from the kiosk where he'd been looking over the field for residual deposits. The Technical College boys floated in a recess and grubbed up pies and cokes and left propelling pencils and cheap pens behind, and sometimes fought over or dropped the change that was scuffed accidently beneath the tables and chairs, filthy with tea dribbles and fizzy drinks.

Chookie ambled along by the artificial waterfalls and sent some twigs downstream with messages to all relatives: Am having a wonderful time, love, Chookie. Sorry, Miss Trumper. Wish you was here, yours respectfully (Jesus! respect!), Chookie. Cheerio pop you drunken old sot, Chook. He watched the little girls for a while, weighed himself at the gates, then came back again along by the river on the path above the water. Just to his left a ferry beetled backward and forward, backward and forward, and the typists and the business types piled out and a bundle of kids in uniform, all lugging cases, the mugs, before they headed up town. Two hundred yards away in the direction of the gardens was another of them, heading wrong way round the point to the domain. He was a tubby blond in school grays, gripping in one hand a plump and glossy leather briefcase that even at that distance glinted expensively, and in the other a thumbed-open book.

"Fool!" Chookie said bitterly, while moving up casual as Friday nights to get a closer look. This bait settled on a sunny bench beyond the greenhouses, removed his coat, and folded it carefully over the back of the seat while from his case he extracted a lunch packet and a blazer that he re-rolled tightly before ramming it back among the books. Sybaritic in sun, he began to chew and to read.

From a grove of exotics, Chookie observed for a while, rolled himself a snappy fag, and counted his small change, twice because he had always been superstitious and then once more because he discovered unexpectedly a shilling in the back pocket of his jeans. It had some sort of relationship with two theater hand-outs and a few packaged food coupons he couldn't bring himself to throw away. They had all the magic of folding money.

As the sun became more garrulous the midday voices receded, the families trailing off for tea and scones that they could share with the flies of the unwashed kiosk, and Chookie, patient as a crab and just as oblique, moved in.

Perhaps it was his shadow that first touched Keith or came between the sunlight and flesh to make him start.

"Good book?" Chookie inquired, trying a friendly grin. You bleeding fool, he told himself. Something twisted.

Keith hated chummy strangers, but when he looked up and saw a spotty red-head he was too bored even to feel annoyance. This would be no trouble to handle. That accent! It was the persistent drunk or the too smooth fifty-year-old he found hardest to push off.

"Not bad," he replied, letting his eyes drop back to the page he ravished but could no longer read. Chookie leaned against the back of the seat and kicked gently.

"What's it about?" Not that he cared.

But this fat chump didn't answer, like Dad on a drunk when his mum had asked and asked and asked about the housekeeping and it was as if suddenly the old man had gone deaf as a post with determination not to tell.

"I said what's it about?" Chookie's voice took on a few more decibels.

With the deliberate finger of one bored to extinction Keith marked his place and stared stiffly behind.

"You wouldn't be the least interested, and I want to read, if you don't mind." He put on his snootiest tone.

Dirty rotten nance, thought Chookie, but he grinned and scuffed the dirt at his feet and said, "How d'*you* know? Y' might be surprised." Like Brother Bernard the day he caught him reading that story by the Italian bloke, Mor—somethin' or other, that the kids had been passing around.

"Why, Chookie? A culture bug? How surprising! Show me now. I always like to share my pupils' pleasures," I'll bet, wretched Chookie agreed silently handing it across. "Oh, I see. What's this? 'Conjugal . . .' really, Mumberson, have you time to spare from your studies for this sort of thing? Later, surely. Now cut along to my room and we'll see if we can find something a little more suitable, shall we?" It had taken him three days to copy out the great slab of the *Imitation* that was given him for punishment and he never found out what happened to the book.

Long silence.

"I said y' might be surprised. Looks like a diary."

"It is a diary."

"Them things are okay to read if they're someone's y' know. I keep a diary."

O God, Keith prayed, make him go away.

"Got some pretty funny things in it, too. Things I bet you wouldn't've heard before."

This was all planned and practical, a gambit that took him closer, breathing nasally, with his freckled paws resting a grab away from the coat, the piggy bank he longed for, the cover-up he had forgotten to take in his flight from the town. If he wasn't careful this other chap might get up and—bingo!—there it would go, this winged security, roosting on another bench, and he'd be back where he started.

Ferociously ostentatious, Keith turned an unread page as cold-blooded Chookie smiled nervously at his back.

"Bittuva snob," Chookie suggested, keeping it casual.

Very gently, like kindness to animals week, Chookie lifted

the duffle coat and stepped lightly back on the lawn, standing still again on its muffling green to reassure.

Then his speed, the lightning dash, surprised even Arch Mumberson—"Run with it, Mumberson, run, you silly drongo! Oh pass, you idiot, idiot." "Sorry Brother Bernard!" —and he was back in the palm groves before you could say rape and running up the hill toward the kiosk and the college buildings.

Keith had read the same sentence twice before he sensed he was alone, and the first thing his eye apprehended was the bland emptiness of the long park bench and the burst bubble of his sin.

Premonitions had always played an enormous part in Iris Leverson's salt-over-the-shoulder, touching-wood life. She gorged herself on astrological forecasts, read "Personal and Missing Friends" in the hope that—, had a lucky color which never seemed to bring her anything but disaster, and an aversion to opal jewelry. "Darling," Bernard used to remonstrate in earlier days when the term meant something, "you are so mad you would cross the street only when the lights turned red!" And, of course, it became a legend about her. But although she laughed lightly, chromatically, disclaiming all this nonsense, she had secret belief in faith healers who would create circles of patients clutching colored strings to test the oscillations of disaster, would tie cords of a certain red around tops (the vibrations or right!), and indulge in all sorts of eccentricities that were private, harmless, and gave her day a lift.

Now she had premonitions.

Gerald. Yes. On the way out. The second week Bernard had gone to Condamine she had been casually munching her marmalade toast when eye and heart had both leapt as they read in the agony column:

Take notice Iris, and be warned. Even though you may be observed by no earthly beholder, God is watching you.

He alone may decide to completely alter this.—Laddie.

"My God!" said Iris, putting her toast down. "Oh my God!"

Quietly during the day she managed to show the clipping to Gerald.

"He's split his infinitive," he said.

"Not you, is it?" she asked suspiciously.

"Not I, my dear. Not I."

"Then who could it be? Could it be Bernard being funny?"

"Oh, come! There must be several thousand Irises in Brisbane. It's simply coincidence. And when you look into it, mad mad mad."

"Have you kept my letters?" Iris demanded.

"Well, maybe one or two," he lied, knowing a negative would distress her.

"Then don't."

"What about you?"

"No. Not that I know of. Could some have been intercepted?"

"Well, that's a point. But I think you're wasting your time worrying about it."

Keith remained bland. Gerald remained aloof. Tremulous Iris scanned columns daily. Other notices appeared—fulsome, pompous, idiotic.

Iris [cried the printed text one memorable Tuesday a week later], if you are discussing this in any way with daddy, he is acting in direct opposition to my instructions. You are not wanted or welcome in my life and will not be tolerated.—Laddie

She did not care to show Bernard.

"Get a lawyer," advised wary Gerald. "By the by, they've been appearing in the evening paper, too. Not nearly as pontifical, though. Short and succinct, like 'Lassie come home.' Only they're addressed to me. 'Gerald, this must cease.' Signed, 'Sonny.'"

"Daddy. Sonny," reflected Iris. "The boys. Do you think

it's the boys?" Nor did she care to admit Keith's on target dinnertime insult.

"Could be," Gerald said. "But I seriously doubt whether any of it is intended for us. Bookies use this sort of thing as code, you know."

But when the letter came Iris felt the pincers squeeze.

Dear Mrs. Leverson,

I suspect you have been engaged in a sustained and complicated relationship with someone who has duties that must call him elsewhere. Though there is no concrete evidence to support this feeling, it persists, and I do not wish to see you caused hurt and worry by a connection that can only end disastrously. This must not be allowed, and the subsequent difficulties in which you involve all connected with you, only serve to exacerbate the situation and drive one to the limits of endurance.

Do you want to be hated?

Laddie

"Exacebrate! Exacebrate!" Gerald exclaimed. "He can't spell either."

"It's moral victimization," Iris said indignantly. "That's what. No, don't touch me, Gerald." (He wasn't going to.) "It's too risky altogether. From now on we must try to—well —" Gerald knew. He didn't have to be told. If Iris saw the relief in his eye she pretended not to.

Their frequent post-four-o'clock meetings of tea-drinking innocence had frequently been interrupted by Keith, close-buddied with other blond pals, sullen and hilarious in turn, secretive, transistorized, unbearable and adorable despite all that.

They hated games. They would hang maddeningly about the living room, sidling and listening in.

"Are strictly for boneheads," they would explain, when Gerald suggested a hearty round of football or cricket in the yard. "Crude, man, crude."

Sometimes Keith would stalk in as if Gerald and Iris were

not there, saying casually to a pal, "Yes, my mother thinks this . . ." or "my mother thinks that," loudly, as if she were not even in the room. Then they would pour themselves great tumblers of milk, scoop ice cream into them, and shake them up in a metal beaker like cocktail slickers, all the time looking past the sinful pair on the sofa, yet standing before them, then wandering away to Keith's veranda to sprawl with their great boots all over the coverlet and chairs.

"When," he inquired insolently one afternoon, " is lover-man going to be *in absentia*? A boy is getting so he doesn't know his own dad!"

"Please," Iris whispered, making silent mouths at him from the hall, and "Please," his bitter baby face shaped mimicking back at her, merciless and carried away by brazenness he neither wanted to nor could control. And when she begged, "Stop it," with her eyes welling, he mocked tragedy, too, yet his own eyes remained dry despite the fact that his heart was swimming for its life. If just once she had seized his head and turned him back into the small boy, rubbing his hair and holding him close with nonsense and endearment, he might have succumbed.

Or he might have thrust her rudely away.

But he longed for her to take the gamble, yearning for the kiss-it-better-days of childhood that he had wanted, could not bear to leave, and had been forced to resign. Sometimes the preciosity of his pose was almost more than he could maintain: an exhausted Rimbaud duffling in and out the espresso bars at the Valley or the Gabba and absorbing on moonlit nights the shifting leaves shadow-mapped on stone as he strode, hand pocketed, along River Road up toward Kangaroo Point past Leo's flat with its sham emotionalism, lights out and *Clair de Lune* stringing out over the river. He would watch the ferry palpitating like his pulse, hear the clump of water, of cable, of trolly bus bound for the bright lights.

And he was so lonely he could hardly bear it, lounging around the Valley ("For God's sake, Keith, where do you get to on Saturday afternoons?" "Pitchers, Bernard! Pitchers!") and watching them drift out of Leo's coaching-college rooms before he went on up the stairs from the wasted noon.

"You don't really need me," Leo said to him. "You're simply wasting your father's money. I'll be candid, laddie. I know less about calculus than you."

"Someone's got to flog me through matric, Leo. I'd rather it was you. The bird at school tramples all the refinements underfoot and horses around with the stuff like a pro rider. I just can't follow. Anyway, you've done wonders for my Galic accent! 'Voulez-vous danser, monsieur?'"

Mr. Varga's coaching college was a fly-by-night affair. It had started off in a rented room in the center of town where Leo compensated for the slowness of incoming fees by dossing down on the floor, eating salamis and cheese, and washing his socks in the tea-urn. When arrears became intolerable he would move on. He was shifty as sandhills yet always giving the appearance of affluence. He ran a bigger car than he could afford, dressed exquisitely on several credit accounts, oiled his beard and made himself socially acceptable by remembering to bring little gifts that not quite compensated for the money he had borrowed a month before. His beach shack, which he had built himself from concrete blocks and bamboo, was smarter than paint. "Twenty tricksy ways with hessian," he used to say. "When one is poor . . ."

Yet it worked.

Ultimately he made his college pay. It was all puffed-up bluff and the hard work of teachers who wanted to make a little extra in the evenings. Leo would admit lovably, "I'm a cunning old swine!" And they'd all laugh at honest Leo.

"Keith, dear boy," he would instruct, "you must learn the gentle art of lying by telling the truth which, when it is outrageous, will never be believed. Never. Never."

Iris was not sure of him. And with reason.

"How's Gerald?" he would always ask her. And of Seabrook, "How's Iris?"

He inquired continually of each about all.

"Sweet solitious Leo," Bernard snarled one evening at a

party. "I'm beginning to hate that bloody malicious pseudo-Christian tenderness."

Gerald was dancing with Iris in a corner by the gramophone. Professor Geoghegan was smoking and observing with a scientist's interest from another corner of the room. Abruptly, and killing the crooner's phrase, Gerald announced, "This has got to be it, Iris. I'm sorry, old dear."

In his not too closely gripping arms he felt her sag heavily, weighed down by disaster, and during the clarity of this moment she observed, as Bernard three weeks before had observed, single extraordinarily beautiful gerbera spikes of decorator colors, dusty, off-beat, and behind their reflected selves an open glossy magazine displaying a model wearing an Emba mink clutching a man with an eye patch. She's beautiful, Iris thought with the insane distraction that comes at tragic moments. And what a dish of a coat!

"Oh my God!" she said. "Why tell me now?"

"Kathleen."

"Knows?"

"Yes. Do keep dancing, there's a dear. Tum tee tee *tee* tee. That's it! People will suspect I'm maltreating you. Yes. She knows."

"Aren't you?"

"Aren't I what?"

"Maltreating me."

"Oh, for Heaven's sake! Be your age!" *That* was unforgivable. "Even the placid Bernard must have some idea."

"How did she find out?"

"I'm not sure for certain, but something absolutely crazy happened. Did you see yesterday's personal? Evening edition?" He laughed suddenly.

"No. I don't get it. The ink comes off on my clothes," she explained crazily.

"Well, there was another. To me again. 'Gerald,' it said, 'you are disgusting and ridiculous. I shall play kettle to your pot!—Sonny!'"

"You see," he explained, "it's a threat. I'm sorry, Iris, but we never did intend our marriages to collapse."

The storm clouds obscured delight. Iris might have continued to argue or plead her case, but the self-important lawyer of her pride cautioned her against action that she might later not redeem, so she was gay and gallant through the ordeal of finger sandwiches and Yankee lemon pie, not eating a great deal but pretending and cracking gay cross-chat with bamboozled Bernard, who, still in his own ecstatic state of self-discovery, was examining with new interest open pores or dewlaps or unpleasantly rough fingers with chewed nails.

Within the marital cot that evening from the depths of lost pride she tried to coax; but he no longer cared and turned his yawning face to the wall while she lay awake in the headaching darkness, taking like powders the recollections of romanticized but stinking little adulteries committed with difficulty in the backs of cars, cheap motels, and on riverbanks.

In his own home, Gerald slept soundly for the first time for weeks.

7

Leo's beach shack seemed packed with boys, but there were only two of them horsing about near the radio-gramophone against a window full of acid-blue sea.

Varga smiled angelically and did a crazy Charleston, swinging yards and yards of imaginary beads while Tommy Seabrook giggled insanely, sprawled against a backdrop of cushions.

"Marvelous! Do it again!"

"I've broken me beads," Leo said. "Can't do a Charleston without me beads and me bobble fringe."

He was so genial above his bristling torpedo—the sort of spy who'd be spotted at once!—it was hard to believe he could ever, ever . . . ever what? Keith asked himself. Ever dish dirt? Ever hand out the hard facts? But he had. Sliced right across his family like one of those keen vegetable peelers that tore carrots to neat red ribbons. Seabrook's, too. I feel old all of a sudden, Keith hated. Or young. Or what is it? His bafflement hauled him to a pause with an adolescently rushing pillow in one raised hand.

"Can this!" he ordered.

"Can what!"

"This bunk."

"Okay. So so. Don't get your hair off, man!"

Mr. Varga ceased his merry pranks (Call me Till, bud!)

and suggested juicily that they get their boards from the garage and tread a few, before tempers, tempers . . . waggling that admonitory jocular forefinger.

Without a word Keith strode out to the bamboo-slatted *lanai* Varga had built across the dune side of the shack and found his gun board slouched against a lattice railing. Carelessly he stripped off his shirt and began oiling his shoulders, smacking a greasy palm against the bottletop as he upended it, and then slapping it even harder against his skin.

"Can I do that?" Leo questioned from the shelter of his sunglasses.

"No thanks."

"What's up? Anything amiss?"

"No."

"Oh? You sound a teensy bit put out, laddie. Here. Let me do it for you."

Mr. Varga reached confidently for the lotion bottle, his hand rapacious for more than oil, but Keith snatched it back.

"Oh, come on, you silly young bugger! Give it me. You've splashed my shirt."

They wrestled silently for a half a minute.

"My, my!" Mr. Varga said, getting possession at last and watching the boy warily. "We are in a temper, aren't we? Something's surely bitten you. More trouble with the folks?"

"Leave it!" Keith said slowly. "Just leave it."

"Leave what?"

"That stuff about my family."

"Dear boy, you have my sympathy. I'm on your side. I'll stand *in loco parentis*, if you'll pardon the cliché."

"I'll—never mind. Just don't keep reviving it, will you?"

"Ah," queried kind Leo, "does it hurt? I'm sorry, Keithy. Truly. Take it like Seabrook. He stands the pace. His attitude —I hope you won't mind my saying this, Keith—is more mature than yours. He laughs the whole thing off. Treats it as the nonsense it is. Really, it is time you started to grow up."

Wordlessly Keith picked up his board and started off up the sliding dune toward the waiting sky and the watching sea.

"Wait for us. We'll be with you."

Get lost, get lost, Keith pronounced to his foraging toes.

From the top of the sandhill he looked down the coast to Burleigh and the spot where, half a mile away, lollipop umbrellas had their color sucked from them by the sun, spinning their windmills over a score of bathers who fried in noon heat. Voices scrambled breathlessly upward from the rear, so he stumbled into the dip on the seaward side and sprinted his confusion across the hard strip into the first gnawing line of surf. Dropping to his knees, he began to paddle his fiber-glass prayer mat out beyond the breaking water where purple currents moved along the sleeping coast, weeping purple, violet, cobalt rivers of salt salt tears. On the bosomy swell he knelt easily, holding the surf under him like a beating heart that moved him here and then there, that bucked a little when he shifted his weight, but, like blood, took his impulse for lost horizons farther and farther away from the beach and its puny people. Now and again he flickered his hands under water and steered in toward shore which already had the vague quality of something lost in anger. But this was something. This was a lull, a calm, the space between border fence lines he'd explored as a small boy in a fisherman's rag hat. ("Look, Dad! I'm not in Queensland. I'm not in New South. I'm nowhere, dad!") Nowhere, he assured himself, lazily riding the world's blood.

Two specks that were Leo and Tommy had tottered down to the sand flats and were waving their towels, orange and white, against the green tree-line. They were very small. Leo's towel had a dirty big bronze Roman gladiator that he'd screen-painted himself, but from here it was all welded into a mucky orange.

He didn't bother to wave back, but paddled slowly along the shark-line south toward the umbrellas. Funny, this. He thought of something funny and laughed out loud, but it sounded queer over the hum of the moving sea. Those big sea-riders down at Kirra used to go out so far on their boards they could yell out to each other, "Well, which beach will it be, Turk? Greenmount or Kirra?" Funny, that. Funny if they'd said Tugun. "Get lost, Leo!" he said loudly, and then he shouted, "Get lost, bum!" and paddled his board suddenly a little closer to the rising waves and crouched, waiting for a boomer. When he caught the third he came in, his feet pressing forward, back, with tiny dancing steps, changing the pressure and the pull to keep ahead on this big feller that was trying to get away from under his feet. His arms swung out and he felt pudgy and awkward like a drunk gull, but managed to keep upright until the top broke and he was flung forward into the sandy watery turmoil of the sucking fringe.

Tommy began running along the beach toward him, but slicker than seaweed Keith was out again, paddling furiously across the current and moving farther down the beach.

"Let him go," he imagined Leo saying. "Let the little fool go. He's having a tiz about something. He'll calm down by teatime. That's certain."

But Leo was wrong.

The boy crossed the dunes an hour later, a mile away from their bathing spot, and walked back along the road with his board balanced on his head.

The shack was empty. There was shock in this, but he grabbed his shirt from the *lanai* rail, took the key out of the meter box, and went into the bathroom where his trousers were hanging on a peg. A clock gobbled seconds while he dressed, while he stuffed his few clothes into his overnight bag.

Poets, spies, criminals, saints, have just this ecstasy. Cramming the clothes down, zippering his furtiveness and not troubling to leave a note, he swung the door closed with a crash, smiling as he remembered he had left the key on the table inside.

Or like stout Cortez, he told himself. Stout—bloody stout—Cortez.

The township was a-glitter with clip joints and espresso bars and fake continental dining spots where for twice the price of the local brand you could have the same frozen dinners accompanied by the dreadful whining waltzes that were known as French. Or, for even a little less, Spanish American hot chili foods would be de-thawed and served to the hot plunking of electric guitars they called Spanish. It was all a matter of taste. Sharp like razor edges, bright, falsely clean, falsely smart in front of their tiny sordid kitchens, ten minutes ahead of now, all down the main highway. Boutiques. Girls in boutique wear. Old girls in better boutique wear. Boys with boards, hamburgers, chips, wide straw sombreros, Okinui shorts and girls. Their souls like spit spazzled and dried on the hot bitumen and what was left promenaded and searched and never found.

Keith had a coffee and sandwich, and sat to watch the weekend millionaires puddle by toward the ritzy bars and the beach, hardly coping with the heat. He decided—and it was the whip-flash in the blackness—that he would not go home that night. No one would care. Those scenes, those catechistic agonies with Iris and Bernard meant the snap of two fingers to both, he was sure. No one cared. He'd fought them out of love, not hatred, and they were too thick-skulled to see. Not even Keith saw.

Munching a biscuit that was included free with the coffee, he dangled the tiny paper bag of sugar over his cup and emptied it slowly in, pondering over Leo's invitation for the Saturday and Sunday. This gave him all Sunday to flick Mister Varga with. Just for kicks, Leo could stew, simmer as delicately with worry as one of those delicious ragouts he was so fond of carrying on about. He wouldn't go back and they could frighten themselves sick along the beach fronts looking for him under the weed-heaps, or behind dunes or lost lingering walls of blue water.

Jeans went by. Skirts. More skirts. Palm Beach shirts exposing great bellies. A duffle coat. More jeans. Duffle coat? Bright blue? Keith did a re-check—duffle coat, duffle coat. And the hair. Something about the hair. Grabbing his bag and thrusting his chair back, he flung out past the till with his four shillings at the ready. It was like baton passing, and then he yelled down the window fronts at the vanishing coat, "Hey, you! Come back! Hey! Hey, you!" Growing longer, his sprinting legs stretched like rubber between the receding shops. "Hey!"

Chookie dodged into an arcade and behind an eruption of plastic banana palms and rubber plants slipped into a telephone booth and began flipping the directory over. He thought himself smaller, crouched down stupidly under the shelf with the ear-piece stretched agonizedly out on its cord. Gawd, he breathed. Gawd! And heard the door pant open behind him.

"Okay," said Keith, "I thought I knew your face. Give me that coat."

It was the longest shot in the world that they should meet like this in sea-dazzle forty miles from town, so witty, so ghastly, Chookie grinned oafishly, then began to laugh. He had, after all, other problems. "Always in trouble, Chookie," Sister Philomene had said before she whacked him. "Can't you ever learn?"—and apparently he could not. "Bless me, Father," he confessed unsorrowfully in the cubicle, "it was me filled Monsignor's biretta with ink."

"Do you know what profanity is, my child?" came the voice from the other side.

"No, Father."

"It's treating in a light or joking way anything relating to God."

"Yes, Father."

"Now Monsignor is God's representative on earth and what you did was poke fun at him. There you did wrong."

"Yes, Father."

"And I think, if you have real contrition, you will go and tell him you're sorry—as well as telling God."

"I can't, Father."

"Why can't you?"

"Well, I'm not really sorry. I mean I thought it was funny."

There was a sound he could not interpret from the other side of the grille.

"Then why are you confessing?"

"I dunno. I jus' thought I better."

"Do you wish you were sorry?"

"Yes. I guess I do, Father."

And that was how he always felt—wishing he were sorry.

Chookie stepped out of the booth and against the lush plastic background began to peel the coat off, stroking its bright blue lovingly for a minute before he handed it across.

"Thanks," Keith said, looking hard at freckle-face. All he had on underneath was a dirty check sports shirt and a pair of soiled jeans.

They inspected each other carefully, Keith touching penumbra of some tragedy somewhere some lost time on the other boy's shadowed cheek.

"Why did you take it?" he asked. "What gives?"

"Dunno," said Chookie.

"Haven't you got a coat?"

Chookie began to move away.

"Well, haven't you?"

"Not here."

He's too dumb to get one my way, Keith thought. Dimdumb. I could lift me another while he's thinking about it. A foreign emotion took Keith by surprise: looking at that dirty shirt and those grubby jeans he was sorry, sorry because he, too . . .

"Here," he said ungraciously, "I'm lumbered up enough." He joggled his bag. "You might as well keep it now."

Ginger paws dangled the coat stupidly, wanting to say no and shove the thing back but not knowing how, so that all he could do was turn away down the arcade, still trailing it, and dreading what it held—the power to shove him quaking and curdling before a broad oak desk and a mean face over a blue uniform. Theft? Rape? He shuddered away from the word. Five years. For youth. He wasn't *that* lovable. Ten if he got a day looking as he did, back from the glass fronts like a cheap bum in his ground-down jobless heels with half a note in his pocket. Yeronner, I thought she wanted it I thought I thought I thought she was fed up and miserable and then Yeronner I dunno I thought she seemed sittin' there in her under-stuff. . . .

O Gawd, prayed Chookie, sloping out at the far end of the arcade by the garage and trailing snail-wise across the oil streaks and the gravel.

He'd mooched around a bit for a job, but no luck except a three-day break as grease boy at a car park that set him up for a little cash but still had him sleeping in the dry leaves of the park or along the dunes, huddled under the duffle coat. He ate Chinese because you seemed to get more; but afterward, with the gas in his belly and the empty watery feeling of the shredded half-cooked vegetables and the sauce, he ached for a great plate of solid steak. His plan was to hitch a ride, farther down the coast into New South for preference, but he wasn't fussy. The north was pretty big and the old hunger for the hot dry parts gripped him now and again like the incense of prayer. Odd-job Mumberson, he thought. That's me. That's the ole Arch.

"Hey!" Keith called, coming up through unexplainable shame and wishes to atone. "Just a minute."

Chookie shoved truculent hands into his pockets. In one, his fingers took hold for comfort of his harmonica and the tips of his fingers slid along the reed lips, touching the tenderness of this pal.

"What now?" He was holding the coat out. He never had known anyone who hadn't changed his mind after a gift. "Here y'are!" Pop had said to his mum. "Got yer somepin'." He'd tossed the packet on the table and Mum had looked up from the ironing, incredulous because fairy tales had finished twenty years before and pulled the string off without saying a word. It was a new handbag, all shiny black with a gold button for a clip and it looked as if it cost the world. "Like it?" sober-for-once Pop had asked. And Mum had started to cry a bit, not much, but Chook had seen her mouth go funny like she was trying to hold it still. Holding the bag and stroking it. But something seemed to have stopped her talking. "Thought you would," the old man said. He seemed pretty pleased with himself that day and Mum took it to church on Sunday instead of the beat-up brown thing she'd been carrying for years and hauling hankies out of for their noses and pennies for the collection plate. "*Domine non sum dignus,*" intoned the priest, and he had seen Mum rub at a dull spot on the glossy black skin. She loved that bag, but during the next drunk his old man had hit around on it and just to watch her squirm had shot it out through the window clean into the water trap. Mum had cried half a day and then shut up with her mouth tight and never said a thing for days and the old man was sorry and tried to clean it up. But it was never the same.

"Here," he said to the other boy. "I don't want it."

"No, it's not that," Keith said uncomfortably. "I thought you might want a coffee or something."

"I don't want nothin', thanks."

"Don't be mad. You look as if you could do with one."

"What's the gag?"

"No gag. Just that. Would you like a coffee? Would you?"

"Not gunner dub me in, are y'?"

"What for?"

"The coat?"

"Oh, that." Keith went red. "Forget it. I'll tell you about that sometime. It wasn't really mine."

Chookie looked suspicious, but the hot white sun wiped faces clean of secondary intent and the dazzled eyes that blinked regularly against glare could cope with nothing more than light. Any sin might be concealed. They fell into step.

"Don't like this place much. Nothin' doin'. And too much, if you know what I mean. Too much to take notice of a nobody and not enough to give us a chance."

"Been here long?"

"About a week. Just lookin' around like. Think I'll push on."

"Don't you have a home?" Keith demanded enviously.

"Not now. I've give that away."

A possibility here for himself, the pussy-footed possibility that had sneaked in and out of the mind-maze for weeks, the sly shadow under the shrubbery, the quick form caught between moonlit trees.

"Don't they care?" he asked curiously, imagining Iris's tentacles stretching all over the state until they burned themselves on the flaming tropical tip of the Cape.

"Maybe." Digging his reluctance into the ground, Chookie hoisted a flag that said no questions yet.

They walked out across the bridge toward the surfing beach where Keith bought two parcels of hot chips topped with glistening salt crystals, and, holding the greasy paper in cat-on-hot-brick hands, they mumbled the potato in, their faces trapped in the heat of the chips and the blustering sea-winds across the water.

"I've never been to the beach before," Chookie confided.

"You mean you've never seen the sea?"

"Not till this week."

Keith was silenced, then he began to laugh.

"Sorry," he said, after a bit. "Sorry. It just seems strange, that's all. I've never met anyone before who . . . I mean . . . I can't imagine. How did it strike you?"

"You ever bin inland?" Chookie demanded angrily. "Right in, I mean."

"Well, no."

"Same thing," Chookie said. "Guess it is funny never havin' seen the sea. But I dunno why everybody thinks you gotta see it. You haven't never seen inside and I don't think that's funny. I have. Same thing, really. Just the same thing—only dry. Rollin' oceans of earth, see? Waves-a hills and no end to it. Just like this. Only brown instead of blue. And still. Terrible still except for the heat shimmer. And just as dangerous."

Shut up, Leverson! the boy told himself. Shut up before this freckle mug knows all the answers.

"Chip?" he asked, thrusting over his yellow paper.

"Still got some. Could do with a drink, but."

They looked around by the dressing sheds for a bubbler and found one whose chrome spout dribbled endlessly into the porcelain basin jammed with leaves and sand. While Chookie sucked away busily, he was aware, as one is aware of shadow or light across closed eyes, that the younger boy had moved behind him in some supplicating fashion.

"I'm leaving, too," Keith said.

"Okay then!" Chookie said, cruel out of embarrassment. "What's stoppin' y'?"

"No. I mean home. I've had it."

"They'll have the cops out after y'," Chookie warned. "Y' too young. Don't be a mug."

"What about you?"

"Me? I'm older. Bin workin' for years. They'll be glad to see the last of me. Well, Mum maybe won't. But the ole man'll give three cheers."

"I thought we could hitch north together," Keith suggested. "Or south. Though that's where they'll think we've gone automatically. Maybe that would be a tactical error."

"What d'y' mean, tactical error?"

Keith sucked his cheeks in. "Strategy. Plan. Get it?" Dim brain, he thought. "I've got a bit of money on me. Not much. A couple of pounds. Enough to buy us meals."

Sated Mr. Mumberson, having been put in his place, picked some fried potato from his front teeth. Cops. That was it. After this kid they'd land him, too, both of them wriggling in the same trap. No, sir! Coppers! When he replied he felt his voice break suddenly.

"Jesus, no!" he said. "Y' can't tag in with me. I'm in real trouble."

A certain pride then gazed down at his dirty nails, inspecting them without repulsion, nicking them together.

"Why? What have you done?"

"You'd split."

"Why should I?"

"Well . . ." Chookie hesitated, torn between confession which would unburden and the need for concealment. Watching the lonely blue water he shuddered with the same convulsive wavesweep. "It was this ole girl I worked for. I done her over."

"You mean killed?" Keith asked, appalled and excited.

"Gawd, no. Done. You know. Stuffed. Well, how old are you?"

"Raped, you mean."

"That's what they call it."

"Did she make a fuss?"

"Oh Geez! That's it! She squawked, the mad old geezer, and shot out of the house and all the time I thought that was what she was after, callin' me in and everything and sittin' aroun' with half her clothes on." Unexpectedly he blubbered because he couldn't do a thing right. "Somethin' got into me. I just couldn't stop m'self once I'd started. And I felt sorry for her, too. I liked her. Can *you* believe that?"

Mournfully he ate his last couple of chips, pushing them one after the other between puffy lips now split and chapped by salt air while he cried without attempting to conceal his face and the tears ran unchecked down his cheeks and onto the jacket at which he swiped with the clumsy palm of his hand.

They were ugly hands, Keith observed, and strangely pitiful with their cracked joints and scaly early-morning-milking surface.

"See that coat," Keith said, not breaking even, not trying oneupmanship, not doing anything at all except attempt grace. "I stole that."

"Did y'?" The other brightened. "Still"—relapsing—"that's only petty theft. Y' notice how well I got me terms. I mean, y' can't compare that with—with what I done. They'll say you done it for kicks and let y' off if y' dad pays."

"So what?"

"So everything. Don't tell, will y'?" pleaded Chookie, grabbing Keith's arm. "Don't tell no one."

"Oh, cut it out!" Keith shook him impatiently. "Repeating things is for bastards. Don't tell me. I hate the gossipmonger!"

"If you do," Chookie threatened, not following the other anyway, "I'll dub you in proper."

They walked back, two of a kind, along the front toward the river into the late afternoon.

Bogus is as bogus does. Gay as all-get-out, Leo tried on before his shaving mirror a false bronze moustache, busy as a squirrel's tail and simply crazy man crazy with the black torpedo. Nevertheless it added a homely something to his too plump lower lip and made nonsense of a scar that ran from the corner of his nose to his mouth.

He fixed it firmly in position with gum arabic, plumped out his green foulard cravat and eased off into the living room.

"Oh my God!" Tommy Seabrook cried involuntarily. "What's happened?"

"Change of face, change of heart!" Leo cried. But underneath, his heart, unalterable as diorite, knocked regularly against his ribs.

"Where's Keithy, lad?" he asked.

"Not back yet. His board's on the porch, though."

"Is it? Little bitch, shutting us out like that. I don't suppose he thought we'd bust in. Well, well!" Leo twiddled his false whiskers reflectively and went back to the dressing room to do something about the window catch he had forced, a matter of not many moments, after which he gave himself into the wardrobe and nosed around.

"Clothes are gone," he called, muffled by artificial fiber, "and his bag." Piqued, but fighting it, he returned to the other room determined not to lose even this false face. "I suppose he's gone home, silly little bastard. What a temper! Well, we'll simply have to struggle through without him, Tommy lad, and I suggest we glue up the pieces of our hearts by stepping townward. Razamatazzy taz!"

He did a soft-shoe routine.

Mad about the boy, he hummed, winking gaily at Tommy, then took it *da capo. There's something sad about the boy.* Exaggeratedly pouting, yet not, not. . . .

But Mr. Varga couldn't quite get the kicks out of it, and around ten he decided to put a trunk call through to the Leversons to see if the laddie were back. Indeed he would be—and he hummed lightly as he waited for the little number ("Bet she's got a bouffant!" he had hissed in aside to Tommy) at the exchange to connect his call. And hello there, Bernard, and yes indeedie, it was Leo Varga speaking. Had the prodigal returned. What? He couldn't quite catch that. Not? Oh, then . . . yes, he realized he was responsible, but there was absolutely nothing at all to be alarmed at after all the lad was fifteen. Yes. He could see all that. No. They'd simply been for a swim—separately—and on returning. . . . In his annoyance at the silly business Leo pulled his moustache too hard and it hung askew until he managed to gum it back insecurely with absent-minded spittle. Pips sounded. Yes, extension please, said Barnard to bouffant, a faint and furious forty miles distant. Police? What was that, the police? Oh Leverson, dear fellow, surely not necessary at this stage, do you think? Give the lad time. Probably on a spree somewhere. Remember how it—you don't? Well, never—till eleven then? All right. If not by eleven . . . after all for God's sake he wouldn't have rung, would he, if he hadn't been anxious? Yes, yes. He'd see to it and he'd ring first thing in the morning if there was no sign.

Dear sweet angels, Leo said softly as he hung up and tottered back to the drooping Seabrook fatigued on a post-office bench. Pal-wise, he squeezed the boy's arm, friend and comforter, and, promenading him back to the car, explained the set-up with the accent in his favor.

"What about my place?" Tommy suggested, not very cleverly.

"Oh, I hardly think so. Remember the situation there, boy. Really!"

Tommy was snuffed out as if some hollow cone had been lowered over his last little spark. Did the sod have to keep reminding him? Did he? In the neon-sparked dark he hated Varga with his phony voice and false moustache and stinking little *objets d'art*. Hated his abilities and techniques, his jokes, his superb cooking, his skill on a board, his coaching college where, weekly, one of the minions pumped him full of matriculation maths. Loathed loathed loathed.

Funnily his oblique eye imagined as they cruised back along the tourist-dabbled main street that it glimpsed Keith emerging from a hamburger bar. He wasn't alone—some sort of ginger lout tailed behind.

"I say!" he started to cry excitedly, but his resentment jerked the reins. Let Leo suffer.

"Mmmm?" Leo asked abstractly, negotiating a welded set of lovers in a car.

"Nothing," Tommy said. "Nothing. Just thought of something."

Leo had every light blazing in the shack like a sailor's

welcome; he set it electrically on fire, drank brandy cokes and spun endless Previn discs. Writhe, clunk! Tommy muttered sleepless on foam-rubber bunk in the sleeping annex. Worry your pansy guts out. And he smiled through his insomnia until eleven when he heard Leo bang out of the shack and restart the car, a signal for him to nose under the bar and pour himself a muscular drink which he took back to bed.

"I'm having my Ovaltine, Mumsie," he murmured to the shadowy wall. "It brings out the best in me."

8

"THIS—BLOODY—PLACE," Sister Beatrice murmured, "will drive me up the wall." She swung her face, stuffed redly with unsaid words, and stared across the placatory landscape. It gave back its unblinking calm.

Sister Celestine nibbled at arguments like the most timid of mice.

"No one can perform miracles," she suggested. "If you can't get it done before September, you can't get it done—and that's all there is to it."

"My dear," Sister Beatrice said, "living, living like this is the great miracle. Oh, don't be shocked. It's true. Reverend Mother doesn't expect miracles"—twisting the ring on her left hand savagely—"she gives cold commands. 'Then all smiles stop together.' Oh, that woman should have been an Inquisitor! Can't you just see her roasting the heretics? Basting, perhaps!"

"Sister! Sister!" Shocked Sister Celestine turned away from the big woman, who laughed out loud.

"Oh, come. It's simply that an old pupil of mine was visiting last month to show me her first baby—a gorgeous little boy. And do you know what she told me? Just as she drifted off under the ether she said, 'Please, Reverend Mother, may I have permission to have this baby without curtseying?' The doctor told her later. Isn't that a scream?"

Sister Celestine went scarlet and could not reply. She turned her beautiful grave face away to the protection of the grape-green trellis.

"No wonder they won't have women in the hierarchy!" Sister Beatrice continued. "Imagine it! Lady Popes!"

"Lady what?" asked a voice from the other side of the leaf curtain.

The vine ceased its writhing and Sister Philomene, angled crazily, came blinking out of the sun with her unshockable eyes and triangular smile. "I'm no Beauvais, no Stogumber. Go on. Finish what you were saying, Sister."

She swung her beads threateningly while Sister Beatrice, knowing that every community must have its spy, pulled a large white handkerchief from her pocket and dabbled at her damp forehead. "Nothing," she said. "It's nothing. The anguish of the servant, that's all. Time-tables. Time-tables. Bells, bells, bells."

"It's nearly end of term," Sister Celestine, the heavenly optimist, consoled. "Then we will all be able to have a change of scene."

"Is it jelly for tea, Sister?" Sister Beatrice demanded blandly and suddenly. "Hadn't you better make it now? It will never set in this heat, despite the refrigerator. You should add a pattern of shamrocks in angelica in case Monsignor might call."

Sister Celestine was shocked, yet although humility and youth both prevented her speaking, she was scorched by the other woman's laughter shivering through the grape trellis and clusters of round plump fruit.

Sister Philomene smiled her crooked, bitter smile and inwardly planned to report this heresy.

"To be Hibernophile is not an article of faith, my dear, though criticism uttered audibly in some places seems to constitute heresy. This country has built the Church on the superstitions and courage of the Irish. It's natural they are a little arrogant among their own."

Elderly Sister Philomene turned away, pointing her feet slowly in their well-polished crinkled black. Examining the toe-cap of each shoe, she was hypnotized by the sun-spot on each, the tiny turbulence of light, the only morsel of warmth she seemed to carry with her, despite the angry red capillaries that latticed her cheeks. Beneath her guimpe she folded her arms and moved crabwise to the rear of the convent building, apexed toward vengeance.

" 'Where there is no love, put love, and there'—so one supposes—'you will find love,' " Sister Beatrice quoted, her eyes absorbing more sky color than they could possibly hold. "Heaven knows, I try. I try to love her, but she affects me the way Sister Matthew used to. But no longer. Once I could not raise a hand, let alone a heart. No one seems to help or touch her. She is so lonely, so alone."

"But we are told you are never alone when you have God," Sister Celestine said, a shade too sanctimoniously, but tearing a grape from a stalk as she passed and putting it to her beautiful mouth.

"My dear, you are so very young." Sister Beatrice patted her arm kindly. "That is the greatest and most terrible loneliness of all."

The younger woman was not sure if she should listen or even if she understood; yet observing Paddy glumly hoeing beyond the basketball court, his face set expressionlessly over routine, she was perplexed. Could it be, she wondered, that there was too much joy in her relationship with her Creator, that sanctity was more arid than she had supposed and all this abandonment of self was a sensual—dreadful word!—pleasure, a subjective one that should not be tolerated? Crossing the lawn in front of the stony saints, she had a further glimpse of him sauntering around the corner of the building trailing his unwilling hoe and whistling mournfully. Too shy to speak she watched him amble past, accepted his grunted good morning and grin with a smile that crept out like a mouse, then saw him bowl up to Sister Beatrice and start chattering away, an old friend.

When does the joy cease? Sister Celestine inquired of the faceless sky. Will I settle into the despairs of these older people? Following Sister Philomene she re-entered the safety of the convent walls, pausing by the chapel door which, opened, gave out its own peculiar atmosphere of silence, prayer, and security. She went in to pray for all of them, but Sister Philomene continued her angular course down the passageway to Mother St. Jude's office where, having entered with her bitter virtue, she proceeded to expose this or that folly, to insist, to complain, to demand.

Like Monsignor Connolly, she was very old and won all arguments.

Father Lingard felt oddly in the presence of all the concern. Negotiations at this level had something of the quality of prayers.

I suppose, he thought blasphemously but honestly, Christ sensed this looking down from the Cross. There they are and there am I and still I remain apart. Listening to the music. Or is it that playing in the orchestra I cannot hear a sound, perceive even the curve of this stupendous aggregate of notes?

Sister Beatrice, still flushed, but without the usual up-lilting mouth, and now mere participatory audience, leaned forward over a concealed anxiety and waited for Mother St. Jude's next words that should, by all calculation of previous results, make the final decision.

"This is not common, thank God," she stated. The set of her jaw defied the frequency of its thrust. "Nor is it an everyday matter. I think here, Father, what we are confronted with is the good of the community posed against that of the individual. What we must ask ourselves is which is the more important."

She waited. The dustless parlor cupped itself hungry for the reply fragmented by the doubts of others while the watching crucified figure silently pleaded. On whose behalf?

"One tends to be overwhelmed by numbers." Father Lingard said after some dubious seconds. "I cannot believe this is always right."

"But such a disrupting influence could cause damage throughout our little community."

"Ah, Mother, forgive me, but should not, on the other hand, your very numbers be a strength against such a happening? Somehow I can't help believing . . ." He stopped altogether and Sister Beatrice's heart thudded shockingly under her starched guimpe.

"Please go on, Father," Reverend Mother said, or ordered.

"That—well—that the care of the individual soul is the first concern of Christianity. Not a sparrow, you know. Not one sparrow. After all, the masses can look after themselves, all welded cozily together, saved by their conventionalism."

"But the scandal? Think of the scandal!"

"One should be able to survive that with the truth on one's side."

"Yes, yes." Reverend Mother's jaw tightened. "But have we the right to expose others to that? Have we?"

"You obviously want Sister Matthew to leave," Father Lingard said. "After all, I am only your spiritual adviser, thank God, and have no ultimate say in the application of your community's Rule."

They were locked in indecision.

After that terrible evening with the unfortunate little music teacher, Sister Matthew had become quite intolerable. They had hardly been able to pry the pair of them apart, clinging to each other for some dreadful succor in the twilight garden of the convent to the distress and scandal of silent observing neighbors. And when eventually a sedated Miss Trumper had been removed by doctor's car to a rest and observation wing of the private hospital, Sister Matthew had plumped herself square in the grass plot and wept loudly and terribly until they had bodily carried her inside where her sobbing had gone on and on until another doctor administered an injection and she fell away from her problems into sleep. But the next day she had vanished before matins and was found in the practice rooms worrying a Bach subject until it cried aloud for release. A false calm cleansed her face. She sat chilly and reserved at table listening to the words of Teresa of Avila until her compressed lips were opened by her heart and she shouted, "Stop it! Stop it!" rushing from the refectory to the chapel where prostrate between the stalls she screamed silently to her deaf God. Somehow, during that night, again she had sought the angry core of her disturbance and scrawled on the white chapel walls the words, "Plaster Saints."

The purple chalk, Lenten in its implications, was still on her fingers.

"Why, Sister? Why?" they had asked. And she could not say—or was unwilling.

"Have you lost your faith?" Reverend Mother had asked fatuously.

"No," she had replied, with a smile behind the smile. "My virtue."

Of course, that was nonsense, everyone agreed at the hysterical consultations in presbytery and convent parlors, but even the utterance of such a thing hinted at an instability of temperament and wavering standards.

"What do you imagine the cause of this breakdown to be?" Father Lingard tried again.

"It's not a sudden illness, you understand, like measles. It's something that has been developing for a long time. In fact, I would venture to say since her noviceship. She was always the strangest of postulants—tense, appearing to conceal yet withholding nothing. Nothing that seemed of importance, anyway."

"Then what triggered it off?"

"Sister Beatrice thinks there is some association with her music. She talks constantly about her interpretation. It really was quite embarrassing after the last examination she took."

"She failed then?"

"No, no. She passed most creditably. It was something the examiner said to her, we feel. Some comment he made, though we are unable to find out what."

"Oh?"

"Oh, nothing—im—improper, Father. Purely relevant." Reverend Mother's face would have lit a line of martyrs to any Coliseum.

"Of course, of course," soothed Lingard, who regarded all

this as ah so much nonsense. "The real thing is, what does Sister Matthew want, poor soul? Does she want to leave? Does she wish for a dispensation?"

"She doesn't know. She is so confused we feel we must make up her mind for her."

"What she really wants," Sister Beatrice interposed, and she couldn't help her smile, "is to play the nineteenth Bach Prelude and Fugue really well."

" 'Bach every time,' " said literate Lingard.

"What's that?" Reverend Mother asked querulously.

"I was just quoting. Could I see her perhaps, alone, and have a little talk about all this?"

"Certainly, if you feel it necessary or helpful." Mother St. Jude, suspicious of mockery or opposition, gazed at her shoes, which she polished with missionary fanaticism. They had the gloss of a soul that could do no wrong. She nodded at Sister Beatrice, who retired to the corridor still astonished at finding her dislike transmuted to love or, if not actually love, sympathy and anxiety.

Sister Matthew was whiter than despair.

With her hands trapped in each other in the concealment of her unpinned sleeves, she entered the parlor. Objects moved away from her, for now she seemed to have no softness to give, no tenderness to explode. She sat straight on the hard chair and looked down at her lap while behind her rustling authority closed the door.

Father Lingard watched the young nun for a half a minute and finally he said gently, "Well, you seem determined to worry us all to death." (The big safe chunky family doctor my dear nothing can go wrong you may have carcinoma but I'm not telling you that just a bit of a lump here is it? or here? We'll have you fixed up in no time at all. The deeper the voice the higher the fee.) He hated himself.

"Can't you cry?" he asked curiously. "I shan't tell."

And abruptly the smlie went out behind the smile like a candle after Mass and without knowing she was weeping, softly and despairingly, she put her face into her cradled hands upon the table.

Father Lingard waited.

"Are you unhappy here?" he asked at last.

"Yes," she spoke between the thin barriers of her prison fingers.

"Have you been for long?"

"I think so. I don't really know."

"Do you think this life is unsuitable, perhaps? Or is it just that there is someone, perhaps, you don't like as well as you might?"

"I don't know."

"Don't be ashamed of not liking it here," he said. "There's nothing to be ashamed of in having mistaken one's vocation."

"You talk in clichés," she said.

"I know," he agreed humbly. "It's the fault of this sort of life, of this sort of training. We must believe in clichés."

She looked up at that. "Perhaps I am unsuitable, then."

"Is there anything special worrying you? That you'd care to tell me—I mean not as a confessor, you know, but just as another human?"

Sister Matthew went sick inside and clutched the slippery edge of the table.

"We aren't human, though, are we? We've lost the habit."

"Oh, but that's just it," he insisted, still gently. "We're very human, and if anything our human qualities are magnified within, even though without they are concealed."

She wondered about this.

"Tell me," Father Lingard persisted. "You must tell me."

"That letter," she confessed at last. "About—Mr. Leverson. I sent it."

Breaths were expelled and the crucified Christ leaned closer.

"Do you hate him?" Father Lingard asked after a small moment.

"No, no. Of course not."

"Perhaps you admire him a little too much? Could that be it?"

She began to cry again.

"Please, Sister," Lingard pleaded, confronted with the open wound, "please don't cry. I do understand. Not fond, that way, I know. I know exactly how it is. He is kind, gifted, fatherly? That is all there is."

"Yes."

"And you were—let us say—hurt in some way?"

"Yes."

"Would you care to tell me why?"

"No, please, Father. Not why."

Lingard sighed, a release that seemed to come more and more frequently in these days of forgotten sun. Would the green ever again surge? "It's no matter. The serious thing is you might have ruined him. Did you send the letter to anyone else?"

"No."

"Well, thank God for that. Now the best thing you can do is make amends, I think, by writing a little note to him saying you're sorry."

She cried suddenly, "It's not so simple. I don't believe any more in sorrow and forgiveness. So what use would there be?"

"The plaster saints?" He looked straight at her bright surfaced eye. "I know. I feel it, too, at times. Not only at times. There seem to be no replies as you shout aloud in a deaf world."

"Then what do you do?"

"You do nothing," he said. "You endure and sit on the tip of each day, a Simeon Stylites, watching the hours tick over the west and come up in the east and eventually the drought breaks. That is what they tell me, anyway."

Sister Matthew, propitiating her inner restless demon, was forced up with her slender face averted so that all the other could see was the pathetic curve of her black-veiled head, her narrow shoulders oppressed with what her self had revealed to her.

"May I go, please?" She remembered a confession once . . . Father, I feel sick, may I go? He had talked and talked, too long as she reeled and wobbled behind the dusty curtains with the air percolated by the drone from the grille. What could he say? But nothing was decided. Nothing seemed even moving toward any natural climax. His intention had been to open the door, even this natural one, for her, but she was through before he could reach it, and running, gauchely flying and flinging down the corridor, past a holy-water stoup toward the side garden grape-green in the half-light of the pepper trees.

Sister Celestine was pacing the sidewalk that served as a cloister, clutching at fragments of medievalism in the hot downlands and saying the Rosary sibilantly when the distressed woman bird-flapped beside her and plucked at her arm.

"What will I do? What will I do, Sister Celestine?" she begged.

"Pray," answered Sister Celestine, who had not yet found it to fail and did not intend to be unkind.

"That's no good! Oh, that's no good!" Sister Matthew cried impatiently. "Oh, no good, no good."

She ran past her across the yard in the twilight, breaking the solid air apart, it had become so heavy, so turgid with unrisen prayers that clung stickily to her face as she wiped and wiped. "Please," she kept praying to the holy-picture faces of childhood that she knew lined the sky in rows, holding their crosses, lilies, roses, racks. "Please."

No one, it seemed, was at home.

Fearful of the question, dreading the answer, Sister Matthew, moving for years as she had in an atmosphere denuded of emotional relationships except for that great familial union with God, began saying nevertheless, "What is afflicting me? What is my restlessnes?" And, as she became braver, or more honest, "Am I in love?"

She reeled back.

But this carnivore came in again across the filthy dust of the arena. "Am I in love?" Literally she leaped to one side of her narrow cell and prayed quickly quickly Jesus Mary and Joseph I give you my heart and my soul. She said this many times but eventually the word "heart" broke into the steady flow of supplication. This word had fleshly connotation.

"Assist me now and in my last agony."

But this was the agony—this intrusion of the world, this desire to be noticed, applauded, approved, smiled upon. Ah, there. There it was. Smiled on. She did not finish the aspiration. She was the small girl again in the expensive coat—Mother always dressed her better than the neighbor's children —so much better she could never play. "Don't spoil your lovely jacket, dear. Mind those new shoes. Elizabeth, Elizabeth there's a spot on your new skirt. What is that spot? Ice cream? Ice cream? But where could you have got ice cream? Then they had no right at all to offer, tempt, seduce and make that dreadful spot on your virtue."

"May I breathe forth my soul in peace with you amen."

She sat down to write her apologies to Mr. Leverson and her pen, as if controlled by evil, said, "Dear Mr. Leverson, I am unhappy and sad. Not because of the letter I wrote to Monsignor Connolly, not because it was lies and wicked, but because I cannot please you. Why does this make me unhappy? I want—" she poised her investigating pen over the abyss and then plunged down, down "—to see you smile on me with kindness and approval." She was so shocked by this, by what she had written, that then she tore the paper across many ways until it was tiny and meaningless as confetti; but all the scraps of white and blue she tossed sadly over her unmarried shoulders, took her birthday pound that small sister had sent last month but which, somehow, had escaped Mother St. Jude's surveillance of the mail. "Little Rosemary," she had said as she handed the letter across. "What a good child to write so often."

God bless again and again that sprawling unformed script.

Outside the hay-scented mouth of the day opened, the sweet white teeth of houses nibbling away at the plummy sky. Quieter than prayer, Sister Matthew went down the stairs past the porridged refectory, through the courtyard where the boarders lined up for their eleven o'clock ration of thick bread and butter, and around the side by the empty school hall. The rest of the community was in chapel, but sedatives and doctor's orders had insisted she remain in bed. While the Office chanted steadily she went, silent and black, through the front gate and courageously unpartnered past the disapproving saints into the shelter of the puritanic trees of Fitzherbert Street that never before had observed nuns ambulant and solitary. Yet the external world neither crashed nor thundered; the sky remained mute and blue, and the only chaos went on within, in the headache that for weeks had accompanied her anxiety and frightened her now into lowering her eyes to watch the renegade feet that carried her almost involuntarily toward the town. The teeth of the street might eat her up.

This was different from those occasions when, lawfully partnered, she had walked briskly, head lowered, to the church or primary school. A problem of concealment confronted her for the hour before the train came in. The station was four credos distant. How often, accompanied by Sister Philomene, had she walked to St. Scholastica's on Saturday afternoon to decorate the altars with flowers, polish the brass candelabra, and lay stiffened white altar cloths across the holy table. Not a minute had been wasted then in secular communion. They did not speak as they sped along the footpaths; rather they prayed, but softly so as not to cause comment, their gloved hands unobtrusively slipping along the wooden beads.

Sister Matthew lingered nervously, unsurely, in the ladies' waiting room, appalled by its grime and mercifully not comprehending its walls. At the last moment she bought her ticket, still in the trance that could not calculate change or what might have to be done on reaching the city or even how she might survive, so conditioned was she by unworldliness.

"Return or single?" asked the curious attendant. But she had only enough money for a single and he watched her oddly as he slicked a stamp across it.

Sister Matthew judged it best not to reply.

Within the slow terror, the outrage of her behavior welled. Not even an umbrella for comfort, she was aware. They are devices made for religious, for the prodding of ferrules into dusty waiting-places, for shelter from the savagery and intolerance of public eyes, for holding, for remembering, for placing the hands in repose. Heretically she pondered the substitution of umbrella for cross, but there was, she knew, in that handle to be gripped, much comfort, whereas the outflung arms supported anguish. The Cross had come not to bring peace but the sword; looked like, but was never held as, the religious dagger it really was.

The umbrella was the symbol of peace.

Her train reeled in. The boxcars hiccuped to a stop. Primly she entered the nearest second-class carriage and took a seat against a far window where silently she addressed the patron saint of delays. Her prayer was answered, for down the line the engine screamed its protest at the enforced journey and they rumbled out again across the downlands she had not crossed for five years—Sister Matthew, two wheat-farmers, and a mother with a small baby.

She was terrified. There was nothing behind which she could hide.

Sister Beatrice found Reverend Mother in close relationship with a confidential phone that whispered urgently in her coif.

"Father Lingard," she explained at last, replacing the receiver, "says he made inquiries at the station and she has bought a ticket to Brisbane. Heaven knows where she obtained the money!"

Sister Beatrice did not know what to say.

"She will have to be brought back at once," stated Reverend Mother, setting her jaw forward and raising her upper lip to reveal the broken tooth. "I can hardly allow her to wander around the countryside creating a scandal."

Sister Beatrice ate her reply.

"If you think I should have taken her off the train before Brisbane, I think not," Reverend Mother continued, uttering strategy aloud. "There could be a most shocking scene. It would do more harm than good." The last phrase comforted her in some way and she repeated it. "We must pray for her,

Sister." She closed her eyes and one knew she had already begun.

"Prayer is hardly enough," Sister Beatrice dared to say. Her heart ached for the delinquent.

Mother St. Jude chose to ignore this. She believed in forgiving much in times of stress.

"It's true! It's true!" Sister Beatrice cried, her red face swollen with pity and unshed tears. "What will she do when she reaches there? She is completely unable to look after herself."

Reverend Mother opened her eyes. "I've wired St. Benedict's. Someone will be there to meet her. She will have to go straight into hospital, where she should undoubtedly have been some weeks ago. She needs prayer, Sister Beatrice, and care."

"But what do we know about her own feelings? Has anyone ever tried to discover?"

"Feelings are not what is important, Sister. One's soul in the sight of God is what matters."

I am by nature a blasphemer and heretic, Sister Beatrice admitted angrily. "You are hard, Reverend Mother," she said. "Forgive me, but you are hard. I cannot even pretend to be fond of that poor little soul, but I feel not only that I want to help, but that I must."

"Hard?" Mother St. Jude rose from her chair abruptly, turned her back on the other woman, and stood for a long time at the window gazing across the garden at the unspeaking saints.

"I suppose I am," she said at last. "I suppose I am. One has to be in this position. I think . . . I'm not sure. Perhaps not." She appeared to plead. "I wasn't once, you know." But she did not turn around, did not face her accuser.

"I'm sorry," Sister Beatrice began to cry. "Oh please—I'm sorry. It's the upset. We all say things."

"No." The icy white handsome face crumbled only slightly as it turned. "No. You are right. I have become hard, without meaning or wanting. But I shall tell you this. I want to tell you. Years ago—not here but in another House—when I was younger, you understand, and I still had my sensitivities and feelings of loss, I sat in a room much like this and held my sister's boy upon my knee. After she had gone I sat on and wept, wept because I could not have a child. I wept until it seemed everything dried up and I grew hard, as you call it, I put up a shell between myself and what I had given up. Oh, I could tell you all sorts of stories against myself."

"Ah, don't." Sister Beatrice's big warm face bent anxiously toward her. "Don't," she begged.

"Yes, I must. I must tell you this. One of my past pupils came back and told me herself. She didn't mean it as a criticism. It was funny and pitiful and I'll never forget. A pretty girl. Always polite. Adrienne was her name. At school she charmed everybody, opened doors, helped with books, never failed to curtsey when she met one of the sisters, won the *prix d'honneur*. A model girl. Sometimes I hoped. . . . However, she married and had her child, which later she brought to show me, all pink and gold and like herself. But that is not the point. Do listen, Sister. Hold this against your soul as a warning. In the labor ward, she told me, under the effects of ether and so on, she had cried out—it was the joke of the hospital—'Please, Reverend Mother, may I have permission to have this baby without curtseying?'"

Shame consumed Sister Beatrice for her day-old treachery.

Mother St. Jude paused, but her hands made some agitated comments on the windowsill.

What could be said?

The slow roses wasted timelessly in their bowl. The Little Flower watched safely behind glass. Mother St. Jude could not turn her tear-distorted face to her subordinate, who, uncertain what to do, acted finally like a woman and went across the room to stand closely beside her superior, her plump hands resting gently, warmly on the stiff authoritative arm.

"There," she said. "There."

Mother St. Jude stopped crying after a moment or two, but the small release had softened and blunted her perception so that, after all, Sister Matthew was not met by colleagues when she arrived at Roma Street. During a halt for refreshments at

Ipswich she had cleverly left the train and traveled down on another running an hour later. She was inured to fasts and long retreats. Those awaiting her in Brisbane were flummoxed, and Sister Matthew, hunting through a telephone directory for Mr. Leverson's home address, felt she might have foxed a court of the Inquisition.

Even this simple action held unknowns. In the gelatinous case of the telephone booth she was an anachronism of such deliciousness several people stopped to look in their Brisbane florals and braces, but she, preserved by the side-wings of her habit, did not see. Outside the afternoon split open like a lemon. Building pips. Tropic clear sun, bitter sour. Directly in front of her a cab-rank held the loitering cabbies, the orange louts who didn't give a damn about fare or foul.

"Where to, Sister?" he asked when she slipped in behind. She counted her change and said, "I only have five shillings. Will that take me to Kangaroo Point?"

"Okay," he said. "It's robbing the poor, but we'll see what we can do." The robbers, it seemed, were everywhere.

In the morning sun truth, the no-news blank, smacked Varga hard. Tommy Seabrook went home on the three-o'clock bus just an hour too late to catch Dad, who, drawn by habit rather than affection, had investigated the suburban distance between himself and Iris, wanting not her company but her reassurance that Varga was all right, was not what he had for some hours been beginning to suspect. Bernard, despite family urgencies, was trapped by impersonal demands of the examinations committee and had gone back to the city to escape Iris's tragic face and insane preoccupation with possibilities, all gloomy, desperate, final. With an indifferent calm that maddened Iris, who had obviously undergone some cathartic soul-searching, Gerald took coffee and conversation. Bewilderment gave her a certain feminine charm and for an hour or so, unaware, she contrived to look younger so that Seabrook Senior was lulled back into misplaced sentiment and was reaching for her hand in order to press it when the doorbell rang.

"Oh God!" Iris cried, snatching her manicured fingers back, and running to the door. "Keith!"

Against the translucent panel a shape was pressed, a shape whose outline presented no familiar document, but seemed like some large and heavy bird curved injured against the entrance. Hesitant, Iris lifted the latch and turned the handle, at whose first movement the shape receded. Yet upon the door's opening there was revealed a pale and fine-featured nun, young, with the desperation of saint or madwoman in her eye.

Each tongue was tied.

"Is Mr. Leverson at home?" at last one managed.

Iris supported her belt with an impatient thumb and shook her head.

"I'm so sorry," apologized the little nun. "I have to see him."

She did not move to go away. The street streamed emptily east and west. Iris, her eyes searching behind for her son, did not know what to do. Religious were in a different category altogether. "I am a Wasp," she used to describe herself whimsically in courting days to a charmed Bernard. "White Australian Single and Protestant."

"Was he expecting you?"

"Oh no."

"But you know him then—I mean, you have met?"

"Yes." The nun smiled gently.

"Oh."

"As a music examiner."

Iris permitted a strained social smile. He must hate you, thought Sister Matthew. But she was wrong.

"Would you care to come in and wait? Only, you see, I don't know when he'll be back, and besides—"

"May I?" the nun asked eagerly. "I've come from Condamine. The train seemed so slow, you know, like another lifetime altogether."

Something was wrong, Iris sensed, some propriety was being outraged. Her thoughts trailed ridiculously. . . . Would she be staying at a hotel, convent, motel? Had she simply come or been sent? Unequal to this, she limply invited her.

"Come in," she said, and wondered frantically if she should show her to the bathroom. "Would you care to wash, perhaps?"

"No, thank you," Sister Matthew said, with her smile a trifle lopsided, and they went back to the sitting room for awkward introduction and interpretation with coffee-drinking Gerald.

"Would you care for some, Sister?" Iris asked in her social manner, indicating the percolator and the cream.

"No." Sister Matthew could not be bothered explaining that it was forbidden to eat publicly and, not being bothered, was overcome by the temptation to outrage the unseen Mother Superior. "Yes, perhaps I will then."

She drank neatly as Chaucer's prioress, not a drop falling upon her white starched coif that creaked so oddly as she leaned forward to reach the sugar.

"It's Lent," she said—and took two lumps.

"But it's not!" Iris exclaimed.

"Figuratively," Sister Matthew said. She glanced carefully under her black veil rim at the man who had absentmindedly said, "Thank you, darling," to one not his wife. She stirred this piece of knowledge reflectively in with the sugar, not really listening while Mr. Seabrook flexed conversation muscles and shouldered the weight of a Socratic-type conversation that finally left him exhausted. Incongruities seemed the natural outcome of his dalliance—agony column cris de coeur, agitated nuns. He was tempted to laugh. When Iris had first told him of Keith's disappearance he had added this to the sum of all the insanities of living that propelled him through the nine to five grind, and became only the comic bric-a-brac that, coated thinly with seriousness, could not at bottom be taken too profoundly.

"I must be off," he said to Iris. "Don't worry. Everything will be right. As soon as Tommy gets in I'll ring and let you know if anything's developed. They'll probably be together."

He paused before the nun, who still kept her eyes down.

"Good-by, Sister," he said. "It's been most interesting meeting—"

"Please don't lie, Mr. Seabrook," she said.

The sandy old fake went scarlet. "Oh, but I assure—"

"Good-by," Sister Matthew interrupted. "Good-by. I feel the calm of frankness. Perhaps it is the coffee. There is something soothing about deliberately disregarding a rule."

Disturbed, lover and lover confronting each other at the door, fumbled and mauled not person but an exposed astonishment cheap as paper flowers, those emotions that had gathered dust and needed flicking with some lightly purple feathered rod making tokens of fastidiousness.

Shiny, long, false, adulterous, his car kept its lamps averted, but he climbed into the familiar stink and handled the crumbling road map, the oil-rag in the glove compartment. It was all safe, known.

"Careful what you say back there," he was compelled to warn.

"Do you think she's mad?"

"Crazy as all-get-out. Maybe she's a salesman in disguise. Maybe she'll nab the cutlery while you're gone."

"Oh, shut up!" Iris snapped, suddenly petulant.

That's why we're through, Gerald thought. You're not only a silly bitch. You're a dominating suburban bitch and it's through for ever and ever.

"I think she was rather a pet," he said, and turned the ignition on fartingly to drown her irritated words. "Poor little thing. You tried to be too *grande dame*."

He skidded off, wanting his son. Parental love, he told himself sourly, the only damn love affair that goes on and on. After all, loving only has to be active to exhilarate and you accept that fact and they love you back sparingly because there is a natural wish to escape. I must have a drink with Bernard, he promised himself, to celebrate my freedom.

Left alone with conscience and visitor, Iris flapped about a little, straightening blinds, cushions, lamps. Thank God for adornment, she might have prayed as she set that part of her house in order, that part which now she knew she must value most or appear to under the lenses of this watcher's eyes. Uncomfortably, refugee to the kitchen, she made more coffee and listened for the phone, a car, a footstep, while the nun, as if somehow she had reached the limits of a necessary journey, accepted silence in the stuffy living room, folded her hands within her sleeves, and waited.

It had been one of those days for Bernard when the natural hues wash back as in some cheap print exposed to rain and only the outlines of events appear, the black upon the white, the conversational bones, the remembered actions branch sharp. He had gone past old Bathgate's studio on the way to the canteen and from outside the door heard a Ravel sonatina played so maturely he thought, Good old Fred, he's not bad when he bothers. But then the choleric features of Bathgate popped at him around the door Punch-like.

"Come in," he hissed, "and listen to this."

A blasé nine-year-old was playing, her cranium barely in line with that of the grand. In a corner of the room, *matrona bellicosa*, crouched Mum.

"Watch your feet," she ordered smartly as Leverson tiptoed in. "Not you. Her." She wasn't really apologetic, and hunched in the chair, her eyes slitted at daughter, at prodigy, at celebrity. Under storm-cloud, the little girl sped smartly to an end and began a no-nonsense blowing of her unformed nose the moment she had lifted her miraculously swift hands from the keyboard.

"Not bad, is she?" Bathgate demanded with pride.

"Excellent," agreed Bernard. The little girl looked him over coldly. "I wish they were all like that."

"Play your Mozart for them," Mum said.

Bored, she flexed her downy narrow arms.

"Which is that?" she whined.

"Oh, you silly!" Mum snapped. "It's the one with the blue cover."

Prodigies, thought Bernard. Prodigies. *De prodigiis domine libera nos.* And he whispered something of the sort to the teacher, who guffawed and disgraced himself.

That was one outline.

And then a public phone, jammed with pennies, stuffed with lovers' fee, had prevented his reaching Iris. And after that a missed bus stamped its green backside on his memory for ever and ever. Then the ferry stalled mid-river on its cable, wallowing in apologetically ten minutes late; and oh God when he walked in. . . . Iris, who was no dispassionate observer, believed they confronted each other like a guilty pair, recognizing some oblique aspect of her own betrayal with such force that even she, who normally lacked finesse, was forced to leave them alone in his study.

"I have to speak with you," Sister Matthew said, making the preposition sound strange. "I've come all this way."

"I'm so tired," Leverson said, but without meaning to be rude, "and my son—" He stopped. "Yes, of course."

Like a child, she sat opposite and again he was struck by the sad curve of her shoulders and the lamenting arch of veil over head and neck. She was watching the piano with an almost obsessive rapacity, but he closed its lid and leaned against it, observing her white face curiously.

"Is something wrong?"

"I have to tell you."

"Tel me what?"

The confession had be executioner-swift.

"I sent it. That letter to Monsignor."

"You!" Bernard flushed annoyedly. "Why, for God's sake?"

"Certainly not for His," Sister Matthew said.

"Oh, don't be witty, please!" Bernard snapped, not detecting her humility, and then watched, horror-struck, the tears sparkle out.

"I was not."

"I'm sorry. I see that. I'm upset, you see. You'll have to excuse me. Why, then?"

She remained silent.

"Don't you realize what a letter like that could have done? God knows I have troubles enough."

"Yes, yes. I know."

"Do you hate me?"

This was one of those traps of sixty seconds where every wild beast of time flared its eyes.

"No. Not at all. No, Mr. Leverson. I wish—I wish to please you."

"That was hardly the way, do you think, to expose me to scurrilous charges, risk my employment, my reputation?"

"I'm sorry. I came because of that, because I'm sorry. To say I'm sorry."

"Never mind then. So long as that is the last of it." Collision of ideas in his mind held his speech in confusion for a moment. Then he joked with her, suggesting that perhaps she *had* come all the way to play the Bach, and opened instantly the old wound and watched it gush in horror. She did not seem able to find her handkerchief or was too embarrassed to search before him.

At last she spoke. "I've finished with all that," she said.

"All what?"

"Music. I intend never to play again. Not ever."

Bernard wondered what should be said now, if protest would soothe or false flattery aid. She seemed, so he imagined, beyond the help of mere words and he knew now that unwittingly he had inflicted hurt he could never mend. Absentmindedly and tactlessly he helped himself to one of the hard candies kept on his desk while Sister Matthew watched through streaming eyes.

"Here," he said ineptly, "would you—" He stopped, horrified. "I want you to have one," he went on, "not for your playing, you know, but for owning up. You were very brave."

Blindly she reached into the jar and took one, holding it without recognition; then with extreme care she put it in the depths of her apron pocket, and rummaged uselessly for a handkerchief.

"Take this," he said hopelessly. He really did not know what to do with her. "I sympathize, Sister. I'm not quite sure what your troubles are. Perhaps if I tell you that those of my own—only—well, only serve to blind me to yours. I don't want to seem unkind. But my boy is missing."

She was nuzzling the linen square wetly. "He is missing and has been since last night."

Selfishly she gave no sign of having heard but continued to dribble sadness into the damp rag she held before her giveaway face.

"You could pray for me," he suggested. "I don't seem able to somehow."

Soon she would go. Had she come with anyone? he inquired, and she shook her small head. Without telling anyone or without permission? To follow her letter up with this was intolerable.

"May I ring your mother house?" he asked. "It is—difficult —to be involved this way. I honestly don't know what to do with you."

The rejection of words was unintended, but struck her Stephen-like martyred body with stone upon ringing stone as she accepted his suggestion that he telephone for a cab.

"You must go back, you know. There is nothing else."

"I don't want to. I don't know what I want really, except that I am so unhappy."

"But isn't it too late? What is there for you to do if you leave such a sheltered life? Where would you be swept? It's worse on the outside, believe me. In there, you're safe. God's on your side. There are people, meals, and salvation."

In that order, they each thought, communing unaware.

Outside a taxi howled like a tiger. Here was one Christian being flung on to the hungry circus floor.

"My wife will go with you," he said, to help. "She will see you safely to the convent." Impulsively he put his arm about the narrow shoulders and held her gently for a minute, then he opened the door.

Beneath his kindness she shuddered, for the world should only shock, and she turned her strange lonely face up to his and said simply, "Thank you for this."

In the hall he found Iris opening the door to the cabby, and then he became the beggar, the one who had to force himself to plead, a thing he hadn't done for years, to squeeze her arm despite his own discovery of her inward shudder. She nodded. Merely that. Nor did Sister Matthew say another word after he saw them to the front gate where his good night fluttered like a moth in the car's headlights and was not answered, though he could see the strangely sculptured profile turned deliberately toward the river and the wet shadows of the city.

This is death, Sister Matthew thought, to have confessed and been absolved and feel no relief.

9

"You're the same as me," Chookie said.

He was looped up in a hollow of the dune. They had walked on down the coast all afternoon and just on six a timber truck had picked them up and run them on past Fingal toward Cudgen Headlands.

"Jesus, it's cold!" Chookie said. "Bloody cold." Foetus-curled, he hunched his skinny knees up under the duffle coat and shivered, looking from the crook of his arm to where Keith sat with his arms coiled around his knees. A caesura in the dactyls of the dunes showed the licking, fawning sea, full of fear and fish and tides that dragged the shore endlessly across the world and back again. Carbon-paper sky stuck all over with stars. Mosquitoes droned up in the damp.

"How do you mean?" Keith asked. "What've we got in common?"

"We're boys," Chookie said, and giggled dirtily. "But I don't mean that, maybe. I mean the inside us like. You know. Not the bits you see, the pricks stuck on, the face-stuff an' all. I mean inside, see. How we feel."

"No," Keith said sulkily in the gripping cold. " I don't see."

"That's 'cause you're such a puking puss," Chookie said amiably. " 'Cause you stink with fancy notions. But don't make no mistake. We're just the same. Two of a kind."

175

Keith stared into the lonely starlit sky and out across the luminous sandhills.

"Maybe," he agreed. "We're both thieves."

He thought of those other two all that time back hanging beside with all their blood dropping south, dropping toward the antipodes, hour after hour.

"What church do you go to?" Keith asked.

"Don't go to none. Give that stuff up years ago."

"No. But what were you brought up as?"

"You're a bit nosey, aren't y'?"

"No. Just wondered."

"Tyke. Catholic. Altar boy, too, if you know what that is. I could spout the ole Latin then orl right. Couldn't have put a finger between you and me, hay? *Credo in unum deum omnipotentem factorem coeli et terrae,*" he began to chant glibly, and crumblingly crushed the words together, back again in his red slippers and cassock, with the white surplice Mum starched so carefully especially along the loving lace, a bit common in its enormous edging, sewn by Mum and torn by Lil (six, and savage, man!). Back with the missals and holy-water containers, the blessed palms and the polished brass, back horsing in the sacristy and parking gum under choir-seat edges, taping notes to girls under Father Lingard's car when he went up to the convent to hear the girls' confessions.

"Well, what is it Chookie?"

"Look over your car, Father?"

"Oh, I don't think so, Chookie. Does it need it?"

"I'll give it me papal blessing, Father. Give her a look-see underneath. Dust y' gaskets!"

"All right, Chookie."

And ungum the replies, Father darling. Oh, the joy of it till they jacked her up at Sid Hancock's and found the blooming caboodle. Yes. Holier-than-thou Mumberson winking across the red carpet at his mates but pulling the Communion cloth with his mouth sucked in and his eyes cast down. Funny, all that stuff. Looking back he couldn't see how he'd got into it. "I was a rough dimand," he said, having grinned through the darkness an explanation that illuminated all the impossibility of his once having held the water and the wine in his hands, having carried the heavily bound gold-hasped missal from epistle to gospel side, having struck the the altar bell and lit candles and snuffed them with a taper and having afterward, to see if he would get struck down by fire, said "bugger" in the sacristy when he had changed back from cassocked sample acolyte to uniformed schoolboy. And, not being scorched on the spot, saying it again to his dazzled mates. "Buggaremus, you mean," said Jamie Mahon who was a bit of a scholar, and they all chanted, "Buggerabo, buggerabis, buggerabit," and howled with laughter until they collapsed with the silent pain of it. "You'll have to confess that one," Tim Whosit had said. And he remembered now on the cold dune with the wind coming in off the sea smelling of ships and lost sails, of gulls and fish and landfalls found only in the horizon fulfillments of dreams; remembered Miss Trumper's protesting paws hitting him feebly and him saying I can't stop I'm sorry but I can't stop Miss Trumper.

"O Jesus," he whispered, and it was a prayer he whined into the stippled dark. "It's a mortal sin."

"What do you mean?" Keith asked curious. "Do you mean deathly?"

"I dunno. Mortal. Not venial. Big, I always thought it meant. Funny, y' know, the way they'd explain. There was an old Irish geezer came 'round one year to the Missions. 'Boys,' he said, 'eating meat on Fridays is a terrible thing. A mortal sin, boys. Imagine now, you were out say, and hungry. You hadn't had a bite all day. And there, boys, right under your nose you might say, was this darling pie. Ah, the smell of it! The gravy! The crust! And yer took one nibble, mark you, just one teeny nibble, y'd be damned for ever.'"

"He was kidding," Keith said.

"No, he wasn't. He meant it. And us kids shivered in the chapel and nudged each other because only the week before we'd seen Jamie Mahon munching a dirty big pie while we ate our tomater sandwiches. All drama, it was. . . ."

"Uh-huh." Drama, Keith thought. He didn't know his luck! Stuck with sterile church service for years till Bernard put his foot down and told Iris let the boy shop around if he wants and if he feels he'll get something from it. But then it was too late. He'd missed the bus, the poetic bus, the celestial omnibus, and though the incense and the Latin and the plainsong and the candelabra touched his heart, they did not touch his mind. Unexpectedly, desperately, he wanted to say aloud with Eliot, "I should be glad of another death," but instead stumbled sandily to his feet and pressed, waded, up over the dune to relieve himself in the darkened hollow on the other side.

There was a great lump of driftwood outlined by sea glow and he called back over his shoulder, over the hill.

"Hey, come here, Chook! We're a couple of idiots. Where's your matches?"

Chookie staggered up the loose and crumbling slope, a determined back-slider.

"What d'y'know!" he said. "How about that! I'll mosey about and gather some more sticks. There's sure to be a bit of bracken and stuff along the top."

"Thought you were the big bushman, the original first-type sundowner," Keith said maliciously.

"Well, I'm okay in me own territory," Chookie said defensively. "But all that water boxed me. And there weren't nothing back there but sand."

Half a dozen matches got the fire going at last, with a lot of dry leaves Keith fished up from the scrub behind the beach. Squatting before the blaze, they watched the salt burn green and blue, deep aquamarines hidden in the scarlet, while they held out their hands or stood or stomped and saw their shadows, huge as giants, career all over the white moon hillocks.

"She's right. She's a bit of all right." Chook stuck his ugly paws right over the main log which had caught and was burning steadily. "This'll keep us warm all night." He sat on his hunkers and squeezed the duffle coat hood around his mulberry-glowing jug ears. "Wish we had a few spuds."

The schoolboy hero! The survivor from *Treasure Island*! Some nasty part of Keith stood off and grinned and some other part was thrilled and responded to the desolation and the ancient fire-rite, so that he moved in closer until he could see the nimbused hair of the bigger boy catch light, trap fire.

"It should burn for an hour if we keep these smaller bits packed up close. Let's get some sleep while it's warm, and if it gets too bad later on we can head back to the highway."

Keith curled up with his head on his arm.

"Good night," he said, politely and crazily.

Chookie gurgled something.

"What's that? Did you say something?"

No answer.

"Hey! What did you say?" Keith persisted, propping his head and looking hard across the firelight into the fluid shadows.

"Nothin'." Chookie shut his lips tight. Despite himself, despite tight-panted, slick as hair-oil Mumberson, something still made him gabble a prayer in the dark. He clenched his fingers in traditional appeal and said the first words he could remember of the act of contrition. But he didn't get very far, not past "who art so deserving of all my love and I" something something. . . . He fought silently to finish it in the inner dark and the outer dark came up across the sea like the spread of an albatross's wing, like the crow in the *Looking Glass*, and he sniveled a bit in the privacy of his arm and went to sleep at last.

If I count this in pence, Keith calculated, as I did ten years ago, the wealth will seem immense, an infinity of winegums or licorice snakes or rainbow monsters or even those jelly babies with the starvation plumped bellies and the rudimentary navals poked in by some wit of a candy manufacturer. Or the four-a-penny conversation sweets, flat as plates with gimmick phrases flat as fate written in heavy pink cochineal: *Dig me Crazy, Surfie Man!* Two pounds four and eight made four hundred and eighty plus fifty-six pence, and the sum total stark. Even a pie was a shilling—and they had to eat.

Chookie looked a bit livelier. They'd wasted fourpence on a morning paper and there was no mention of rape or missing boys or stolen duffle coats.

"Consider," Keith said as they warmed up their dew-shrunk legs along Highway One, "where and what exactly is it we intend?"

"Ever smoked grass?" Chookie asked. "Dried out buff's beaut if you shred her up a bit."

"Oh, skip the folklore!" Keith said impatiently. "This morning, this bleary-eyed morning, I cannot see why we're doing this."

"You talk funny," Chook said.

"How do you mean funny?"

"Y' words. What y' say. Well, I dunno. I got my reasons."

"Maybe you have. But I haven't."

"Maybe."

"I feel like tossing it in and going back. I'm aching, cold, hungry, bored, and Bernard always said I knew which side my bread was buttered."

Chookie scowled at the rising sun across the water.

"Y' said y' wanted to get away. What was all that stuff you give me about wanting to get away? Said y' people gave y' a touch of them."

"Well, this seems pretty wet, stringing along the road with no money and no plans. Where do *you* want to go?"

"Sydney."

"Sydney? But that's precisely where they'll expect us to go."

"So what!" Chookie snarled.

"Well, we're certainly pointing the right way. There must be only five hundred miles to go by now. If you get there." Keith experienced a gush of despair. "And then you'll get hauled back, anyway. We both will, and you know it."

"There's no need," said the other defensively.

"Your family'll be on your tail. Mine must be half nuts by now." Keith smiled with pleasure at the thought. I shall see if Bernard cares. I shall see.

But Chookie was saying, "Listen, clunk, they'll be so glad I've gone they'll cover up for me, see? At least, the ole man will. I've never been his pride and joy. Never looked pretty like the girls. Never come top like Ken and Bert who's studyin' for an artiteck. No. No-good Mumbo he called me, an' shot me out on the paper-run when I was nine jus' after we came to live in Condamine, and the milk-run three years after that while in between times I come bottom. And then I struck out on me own doin' a spot of gardenin'. Never went much on the hard yakker, but I seemed to have a bit of a way with plants an' things. Liked them, anyway, though I had trouble with the proper names."

"What's that plant outside the Town Hall?" Keith asked promptly and bitchily.

"Which Town Hall?"

"Brisbane, of course."

"I don't think I ever noticed. You mean them big green-leaved things creepin' up the front?"

"Uh-huh."

"Them? Them's monsterio delicioso."

"That's it," Keith said, triumphant. "Everyone says that wrong."

"Ah, yer silly poof!" Chookie said. "Whassit matter? I worked in a nursery for near three months getting the hang of it like, but like you they thought I was too dumb mixin' up the leptospermum with the pittostrum."

Again, Keith felt the incomprehensible surge of shame. The other boy's face was lumpy in the morning heat and scowled a little in protest against what he was.

"Sorry," he said. "I'm sorry."

"That's okay," said Chookie briefly. "Skip it."

A semi-trailer was rocking down the gradient behind them, happy as a roller-coaster, so they gave it a whirl with their thumbs hitching thattaway, but the driver snorted and grinned and shoved his up at them as he screamed past.

"Swine!" Keith said.

The tried for half the morning. Around eleven a utility truck with an empty carrier and two men in front pulled out of a side road and turned south, hesitated for a doomed second, and was trapped by young Leverson's ready eye.

"Going to Sydney?" he asked.

The driver nodded, inspecting them for loutishness. "Not quite. Coff's," one of them said. "Okay. Hop up back. How far?"

Keith was opening his mouth to explode this kindness when Chookie hacked him sharply on the ankle bone.

"We're on a walking marathon. Student thing, you know." Yielding, Keith explained in his best polite student voice. "We don't mind how far."

"All right," the driver said. "Pull a coupla sacks over yerselves and get a snooze. We're not stopping this side of the Harbor if we can help it. We're running behind time."

The dust jived in the corners of the platform; their bums crashed up and down as they jerked off, and then the truck got going smooth as custard, taking film snaps of moving tree turbulence that closed over, became cocoon womb and then sleep in the rhythm, the swing-sway rhythm.

Mum, Chookie begged in his sleep. Mum, where's me pitcher money? And she said you're not going again. Your dad said you wasn't to and I say you're not sitting down in the bleachers with girls and carrying on then reading your missal on Sunday. You should be ashamed. I don't do nothin' he whined in his sleep, true. Nothin'! And she slapped his face hard and said she didn't mind the lie, but hadn't he no respect for God's holy house and he'd better get Father Lingard to hear his confession in the Sacristy before Mass started. Do you really know what a state of grace is, Chookie? Father Lingard had asked, grave as God, standing under the stained glass and the Crucifix behind him on the lockers. It's not—? No, Chookie, you don't really understand, do you? Well, you told us—Chook, a state of grace is being free from Miss Trumper paddling her hands at you on the living-room sofa. It was striped—blue with brownish thread—and there was a stain near the arm that his unseeing eyes had fastened on unconsciously so that his soul now bore a duplicate Rorschach blot like a couple hard at it. Or—no, Father, he whined. Mum! And he whimpered and pleaded in his sleep for the mum of farther back who made cookies with currant eyes or dabbed stingy stuff on his toes or wiped his behind and praised him and hugged him hard and touched his bony knees with plaster.

He half woke, half slept, and lay there with his head cuddled into the crook of his arm, hearing the kids giggle behind him when he got the add-ups wrong and Sister Bernadette ("Bumface," he used to call her in the playground) red as hell-fire, shrieking at him to come out and towering over him with the blackboard pointer. Hold out your hand, she ordered, bigger than Mother Church. And he'd spat on his corny little palm first and rubbed it hard on the seat of his pants and grinned at Tony Mason in the back row. Don't you dare smile, she cried, and down came the strap. There was a split in one corner and he could spot the sawdust through it as she raised it again and he was so frightened he giggled aloud and couldn't stop and the pain made him wet his pants. Under the ashamed lids of his eyes he saw a few spots dabble the floor and she saw them, too, and her virtue seemed assaulted, for she turned away and began working furiously at a long tot that stretched like Jacob's ladder from Condamine to Heaven.

But he was bully-cock of the yard later.

I peed meself laughing, he lied. And the others took it up and passed it on. Did you hear? they asked. Good ole Chookie peed hisself laughing. Good ole Chook! And he grew away from Mum in that moment so that there was no one to turn to for hot cake in the afternoon or for the pressed football jacket. He pressed it himself and stitched his own number on with his big rawboned twenty thumbs tangling the thread and making strides of tacks while with a terrible desolation inside he heard his mother say that Arch seemed to be getting a bit of sense at last, growing up a bit and doing things for himself. Grew away and rubbed his own muddy rings around his eyes and grew beyond that and didn't even cry at all much, hard and bold in class and dumb as they come—but brazen. Chewed gum through Confirmation classes and during the Sacrament itself, not game enough to pop a piece in his gob, kept a plug at the ready in his pressed-down best.

"You have no sense of or, Mumberson," Father Lingard

said, passing him out and handing him his altar boy's dismissal. "No sense of or. Of what is fitting." Or what? Chookie wanted frantically to ask and excused himself later to the gang. Ole L's been at the altar wine. Kept on saying no sense of or like a nut or something.

So that was that. And after he told Mum and all the thunder and lightning cleared a bit and she'd put on her wounded look for a change, he got into tighter pants and left school with some queer sort of storm in his stomach as he took a last look round the familiar yard, the pepper trees and the slab seats like those where little Sister Teresa had coached them in Catechism for their First Communion. He remembered her sweet, delicate face, melting with trust and belief. "It is the most important moment of your lives, children," she had said. And Chookie had believed her with all his ginger seven-year-old heart. "At that moment your whole lives will change. God will be within you."

But it hadn't been a bit like that, not for him. He'd prayed like mad all through the Offertory, keeping his eyes closed tight like fists and his fists closed tight like eyes and he'd gone up to the altar rails behind the other blue-serge boys and white flouncy little girls. He'd opened his mouth and put out his tongue ever so gently for God and then it was all over and he was walking back to his seat, shuffling and edging past the other kids. And nothing happened. The sky didn't burst like a cracker or flare like a Roman candle—although next day Barbie Jazz Garters told everyone she had seen a vision. He had trouble swallowing and after, at the breakfast, he got a bellyache looking at the cold ham sandwiches. Breakfast was bacon and eggs and that was what he'd expected and what he wanted. You'll love the Communion breakfast afterward they'd all said. They'd all been saying it all his life. There's no bloody glory, Chookie mumbled into the hessian, and turned over and saw Mum walking him home in disgrace from the school hall where he'd howled because there wasn't bacon and eggs and taking him the angry way home shortcutting through the Methodist churchyard with her fingers like pincers on his muscleless arm. But Sister Teresa had meant it nice and he liked her and so he'd got this funny

184

feeling now when he looked around and saw the corner of the building where he split his eyebrow open and the old bougainvillea where they'd had their first cigarettes.

He could still remember the day that mad Joey Finn had climbed up fifteen feet into the branch tangle and sat there like a monkey peering down through the leaves at the class underneath. Sister Bernadette nearly burst trying to get him down to the rest of them who were having a tables lesson out in the open. But he stayed squatting on a branch, chanting after them mockingly, one table behind, and after a while ole Bumface said in her oiliest tones, "We will ignore him children, and pray for him." And they did. And then the mad blighter prayed back just one word behind like a litany and it was gorgeous and he wanted to laugh so much he nearly died hiding his face and pretending with the others it was terrible.

Good-by. So long. Bung-ho. The lump in the throat, in the stomach. And vaulting the fence from primary into the playing yard of the Brothers next door, down to the handball courts where some wit had managed to scrawl UP BROTHER SYLVESTER at the top of the concrete wall.

"How could the boy have got there?" grave saintly Brother Leopold had asked the assembled school when the outrage was discovered.

"Levitation, sir," a suave anonymous senior had suggested.

"Who said that? Come out the boy who said that!" But there was nothing except the discreet movement of laughter waving across the other three hundred faces.

So long, chapel. So long, brimstone missions and unspeaking unspeakable mystic retreats filled to the brim with spiritual reading and reluctant examination of conscience. So long. Hooroo. Hooroo to that sub-junior window through which he shot pellets at the infants, the littlies in their hot blue serge. So long.

"You do well to leave, Mumberson," Brother Leopold had said. "You do the best thing. I feel an academic career is not for you." He placed an indicting forefinger on the noncommittal reference he had just completed. "But there are many openings for your special abilities."

"What are they, sir?"

"What, my boy? Your special abilities?"

Chookie had smiled warily. "Well . . ." he said.

"Indeed there are many openings," Brother Leopold went on, avoiding mutual embarrassment. "Trust in God, lad. Ask and ye shall receive, remember. We have only to ask. God bless you now."

They were anxious to leave each other. Neither was quite sure what to say and although each knew that platitudes were in order, these did not soothe.

You ask, all right, Chookie thought, you ask and you end up on the back of a truck heading nowhere, with a mortal sin heavy as lead weighing you down on the tray. Groaning, he pushed the sin back but it rolled and crushed him and at last, like Keith, he and his sin fell asleep.

"Feeling better?" Miss Paradise asked, not nastily, but not sweetly either, as though she were jealous or had an unpleasant steel weapon to grind. Under the dry violet light of the trees in Kitty Trumper's garden, she sat beside the swing-hammock and knitted something shapeless and terrible in expensive wool.

"What's that called?" inquired Miss Trumper with the languor of the invalid.

"Mohair. Kitty, there's so much you've never been able to answer or seemed to be sure of, perhaps because you never really hear. Remember the time that colonel proposed?"

Kitty Trumper's sad orbs began to water. "Don't."

Her protest did not even ruffle the poise of the monster who clicked needles and occasionally teeth (in a moment I shall run you through, Kitty dear!). But—"I'm sorry, darling," she said leaving a snail-trail of reference. "What I can't understand, though, is why you didn't report this to the right authorities."

Rock, rock. The hammock wobbled uncertainly its striped but split chrysalis, on the brink of discarding the dried-out pupa.

"Has there been any word?" nagged Miss Paradise. "About him?"

"I don't know."

"He seems to have vanished. I've made a few discreet, very discreet inquiries, you know. Father Lingard. I saw him at the library. In the Westerns. Isn't that funny, dear? He said, by the way, 'I'm doing a thesis on the Western for a higher degree.' Do you think he meant it?"

Miss Trumper closed her eyes gently so that even that might not disturb her companion.

"It seems strange his family does nothing."

"They don't care," said Kitty Trumper, still with her eyes closed.

The burning center of the sun fired a black pit through her lids. She preferred dull rainy days when blotting-paper skies soaked up the guilts of weather and soul, not letting the sun expose. The stained sky was washed with self but concealed by the bruises of thunder.

"Poor old Chookie." She expelled her sadness. "Poor old Chookie."

Miss Paradise was exasperated. "Oh Kitty, really!" she said. "You baffle me. Truly you do. Two days ago you were hysterical with what we all presumed to be shock." She let that one sink in. "And hate. Now it's 'poor old Chookie'!"

"Poor old Chookie and poor old Kitty. Verna, what has happened to that strange little nun I met in the convent garden?"

"Who was that?"

"I don't know. I couldn't see in the twilight. She ran from me after a moment. Someone pulled her away. She was trembling and so thin, even with all that heavy habit, those mounds and mounds of clothes. I was conscious of the bone."

Miss Paradise finished another row, stabbed her needles viciously into the ball of wool, and creaked upward.

"I'll make cocoa," she announced. It was like the pronouncement of one about to sacrifice all and enter the tropical jungles of the Congo.

"Do me a favor, Verna?" pleaded Kitty Trumper's voice.

Her eyes were still closed—perhaps against negation. "Only a teeny favor."

Angrily Miss Paradise swung about.

"You always did seem to think, Kitty, that teensy-weensy adjectives removed half the difficulty from the request. Modified it. Made it the teensy-weensiest of demands. Ach! You saints!"

"No, but—"

"No but about it! Lie there while I get the cocoa."

When she returns I shall broach the matter, Miss Trumper told herself, but when her friend returned with two angry cups clashing on their saucers and sat aloof and righteous in the winter garden where the concrete steps led up between succulents to a terrace of Rousseau green, she could not speak. One of the yuccas was in flower, with its proboscis a mass of bees and bloom, curving dangerously and sexually over the fish-pond's gold-finned water. All the trains, Miss Trumper thought, have gone out. I have missed the last train, and now, unlike Anna Karenina, I cannot even heave my grief to oblivion on the rails. The disappearing vans, but the guard leaning out waving a last-halt flag had the familiar face of a dream or an acquaintance one cannot place—the ubiquitous traveler in half a dozen European towns or chartered buses; on paddle-wheels or Rhine steamers, or in cafés on terraces; passed along escalators (you riding up, he down— but always away). You saw him on the liner coming back six tables away at second sitting and once in Colombo rickshaw whirled; and after in a smoky goods grinding up the Gap; but never never. . . .

She cried openly into the cocoa and the white drops widened and thinned a mixture of grief and chocolate.

"Verna, I shall ring Father Lingard."

Miss Paradise expressed her doubt with the faintest grimace, the shadow of a shadow.

"Do you think he can help you now? Really? I mean— you've been over and over it with me and where did it ever get you? Sometimes I think you'd do better never to discuss it at all. Every time you do you only remind yourself. Haven't you thought of that?"

I'm very humble, Miss Trumper hoped, and knew she would say yes . . . but, "No," she said. "I want to. I have to. Please, could you do it for me?"

"My dear," Miss Paradise, said, superiorly Christian, "he likes Protestants a great deal. More than they ever care for him, I'm positive."

"Don't shame me," begged the other. "I'm not very well at all."

The hammock creaked in duet with its sobbing burden and the branches, gripped by ropes, moaned and tugged to get free, then capitulated, sagging with her.

"Bikky?" Miss Paradise asked, chirrupy to the end.

Father Lake was crooning softly in the presbytery garden as he polished the entire range of priestly footwear—a self-imposed penance—especially as the lumpy leather brogues of the Mons were nicked and cracked.

Caint use yer cors yer feet's too big! he sobbed over-slowly. *Caint luv yer cause yer feet's too big!* Except for that tiny section of his spiritual page, one bottom corner turned whimsically over like those small ears in the autograph books of teen-age girls ("Don't look" on the outside and "Sticky-beak!" on the inside), he was sonorously happy.

Happy as Monsignor asleep in unsafely green vales, padding past Clongowes, not rich enough to go there; seeing Mourne on a trippers' holiday with the other goggling Dubliners, leaving it all for God and coming here now to this rolling brown land of flat voices and beer and dust and sins dry as overbaked scones. He snored untidily and dreamt the Virgin was scolding him about something and he clutched the wheel and spun it and spun it. "Pray for us now," he mumbled.

Father Lingard came out from the telephone, dangling a collar on one finger.

"Don't wake the Mons," he said into the sunny air of polish. "I've got to go on a call."

"Someone sick?"

"No. A Miss Trumper up near the convent."

"Not the old lady who ran across there the other night?"

"That's the one. Don't worry about mine. I'll do them."

"No, sorry. I have to. Hang on a moment. Do you think she knows something about Sister Matthew? Why she went? I must confess, Doug, the excitement of the scandal has done me a world of good."

"That proves what I've always said; we feed on each other's misfortunes."

"Shouldn't I fight?"

Lingard laughed. "You're honest. That's the main thing. I cannot bear the long sanctimonious clucking face. See you in about an hour. God bless."

If He could be bothered, he would have added.

Yet he himself bothered now, about some fragile plea through a courtesy he could not shake off, no matter how his soul corroded within, and each hour, of which each action seemed a deadly explicable second, rusted, piled up its uselessness. Out of courtesy, too, he thought, I turn in the gate, gently reclasp the latch, pad down between hydrangea bushes to the front elkhorned veranda as much a stereotype of colonial living as steep galvanized roofing and ornamental timbering on gables.

Something scrubbed, something painful about the house hesitated with him as he heard Japanese wind-bells make glistening sounds above the plop-plop of an end tap weeping into a pot of maiden-hair. The door opened on Miss Trumper buckled into the armor of a Sunday suit, backing away, but still in control. He examined her face with interest. It was narrow and nervous and in the eyes was that frightening honesty that preludes disaster. Her hair was badly tinted and could not make up its mind to be one thing or the other, though it had settled largely for copper, a startling eruption above her pale washed-out face and faded blue eyes.

"Father Lingard," she said, "come in, please." And put one hand upon his sleeve as if he mightn't.

They faced each other in the haunted living room packed with dozens of Miss Trumpers who observed them from the protective frames of glass and gilt.

But she did not seem to know how to go about starting and could hear the priest making flattering remarks about the garden and the garden and the garden.

Garden meant Chookie.

Miss Trumper flinched.

"No," she said. "No."

"I thought it quite lovely," he persisted out of ignorance, but wondering at the agitation that made her hands journey for rest along the seams of the aseptic settee cushions with their fragrance of disinfectant and lavender.

"I have to tell you something," she gasped suddenly. "Something that has worried me for years."

"Yes?" he prompted, in a familiar situation at last.

She could not look at him across the surface of this great lake in which she was sure she must drown. Help, a small voice cried a long way away. Heeeeelp.

She looked at him. He was aloof and not especially reassuring, although there was a despair about his mouth that had familiarity, that suggested he might not only understand but, forgive. Putting off the deadly moment, she managed to pack a teatray, to fuss about helping him to sugar before she should offer the bitter pill of her guilt, struggling with the biscuits. Observing her antics with a milk jug, Lingard was at once aware. God help her, he prayed. God help. And his own automatic appeal registered within his prayer-dry soul and gave him a pleasure he had not now had for years. He smiled.

The smile jogged her. She put down her cup, rattling it lopsidedly upon its saucer.

"It was years ago"—as if time excused or absolved—"I did something . . . I have never ceased . . . regretting."

He did not say anything for a minute while she fought a strange battle with the corners of her mouth that threatened to become that other mask, the one in planetary opposition to the grinner.

Lingard had heard too many confessions to make a mistake. Bowing his head, he prompted gently, "Go on."

"It was the war, you understand. We were all silly."

"We were," he agreed consolingly and gravely.

"Yes"—eagerly—"I thought I was in love. Oh, I was really—and—well—you understand?" These lacunae, the moral lapses for which one supplied the hard fact!

"Yes," he said.

"And so I was expecting his child. And suddenly he went off. I never heard another word. I tried. I don't think he was killed. Or married either." She cried a little at that stage. "He just got tired of me, I suppose." She picked carefully at a thread on her skirt. Something would unravel. "Anyway, I couldn't face it—the baby—I didn't know what to do. I went to a doctor and—"

"Yes?" he asked, for she must confess it herself.

"I had an abortion."

Father Lingard remained entirely still.

"It—that—" she began to cry again. "It worries me all the time. I've never forgotten or forgiven myself."

"Of course, that is the hardest thing of all," he said gently, "to forgive oneself. It's easy enough to forgive others, I know. But never oneself.

"Don't cry," he said. "I do believe God forgives you. You have only to be sorry for that. And you are sorry. You've proved it by suffering for the last fifteen years."

The rain of this particular charity felt warm. He had moved away neither in shock nor horror.

"You must try to forgive yourself," she heard him saying, "if God can. Otherwise you will be at war with yourself forever."

"Oh, I am," she said. "I am. . . . But there is something else . . . something."

He nodded, a trick of the confessional that prompted without a word.

"That boy." She went scarlet with shame. "That lad who gardened for me." She was dying within. "I . . . he . . . I caused him to come in . . . I made him. . . ."

"Here," Father Lingard said at this juncture, "let me pour you another cup." He put it gently before her shaking body.

"Can't you see," she cried, "that is another unforgivable thing? I caused him to sin. He's only a baby. If only I could tell him I'm sorry. Or ask him to forgive. But he has run away."

"Run away?"

"Yes. I suppose he thinks he is to blame. Oh, if he only knew!"

"Perhaps he is sorry, too."

"Oh, could he be?" Miss Trumper leapt pathetically at this, longing that she be able to pardon also. It could be her salvation to restore hope in another.

"I'm sure he is," Father Lingard said. "Very, very sure. And if he ever does come back or tell you he is sorry, in some way, you must accept. Accept his sorrow before you insist on burdening him with your own. For that will be the much harder thing. I'm not excusing, you understand. Or even saying you should not still be sorry. But what is done is done, and the worst thing of all, my dear, is to feel no shame and no sorrow. After all, you have suffered intensely for the wrong you did and now you have a duty to God. To yourself, really, too, to try to live as He would want."

"But how is that?"

He consoled her as best he could. He drank tea. He asked for a pelargonium clipping and borrowed a paperback as insurance against another visit and a proof that he did not find her corrupt beyond redemption. It was this last gesture that helped most of all. And as she tottered with him to the front gate he said unexpectedly, "If one saw behind the faces into the hearts, one would die."

They had slept through the bumping night and in the morning the truck pulled up somewhere at a town that was still rubbing the sleep from its eyes. Sunburned timber houses straggled out along the main street which led directly to a river of sorts. But the east was the town's pillow, dirty dunes rumpled along the gray sky. Weak pink filtered upward.

Keith rolled over and sat up, each vertebra throbbing, his bladder uncomfortable. Somewhere in front of the truck he could hear Chookie arguing with the driver, who was keeping the engine running. Over the backboard Keith observed a ritzy motel, crab-lazy, sprawled on the opposite side of the water, with its snoozing cars drawn up blindly before each blind door, shuttered across family units and the sinning couples who made love to synthetic music that trickled through speakers above the wall-lamps. There was a lot of plate glass on the river side of the building, a dining room and bar sumptuous beyond the detached appearance of this fly-speckled town.

Slinging his legs over the side, Keith slid to the roadway and walked around to the front.

"Where are we?" He yawned. The sky opened up a little to allow some dim light to seep through.

The driver tended to be whining. "Yers was asleep. So I never woke yer. Anyway, I tole yer we had no time to stop, we was going through."

"It's just outside Coff's. A place called Moonee Beach," Chook said. "We slept straight through."

Damn, thought Keith. Oh, damnation! He felt like howling with irritation.

"Sorry," the driver said. "I gotter put you off here. I live near by and then we're goin' straight through to Sydney."

"That's okay," Chookie said. "It don't matter. We're on a walking tour, anyway. We'll soon hit the big smoke, but."

"Yeah," agreed the man. "Y'll see it okay."

They watched him go. Keith excused himself, vanishing behind a tree near the bridge, then came back scowling.

Across the river, curtains had been twitched from the plate glass and, as if it were some fantastic theater, waitresses could be seen moving around tables with such vigor he imagined he could smell the bacon.

"There's nothin' open yet," Chookie said. "She's only just on six."

"Well, what do we do now, traveler?" Keith held his crankiness carefully, allowing none to spill over, for at the first opportunity he would toss this clod off and get a train back. "Do we merely keep walking? Are we going to keep dodging south with no point in it? No point at all? It's ludicrous, isn't it?"

"No sense in standin'," Chookie said placatingly.

And they set off again along the dew-gray road, past the School of Arts and a church hall and a closed all-night diner that had been shut for months. Slow as remorse the sun crawled up the sky; the cars kept on passing them and they felt the sea pressing in on the land as they sought the next township. It was four miles and took them nearly two hours before they came down the highway to its neglected outskirts.

"I've got a quid after this," Keith said, chipping congealed yolk from his late breakfast plate and wiping a bread crust across. "That won't take both of us back." He felt secure in his nastiness with the warmth of food settling down inside.

Chookie shrugged and grinned, knowing he wasn't wanted but unable to accept. "Here's my five bob," he said, sliding the coins across the counter. "Can I have that last chip if y' don't want it?"

Keith nodded sourly, thinking of his parents. Would it be worth it if he did go back or would the cold war go on and on and on? Really, they didn't give a hoot about him—only themselves and what he reflected of them like a vaguely distorting mirror in which they chose to see only the glamorized reflection, never the fat man or the skinny lady or the dwarf hedged in by autumnal circumstance.

"Your parents get on?" he asked.

"Now and again. Every Saturdee!"

"My mother has a lover."

"A what?"

"Another man. She sleeps with another man."

"So what?"

"What do you mean 'so what?' Don't you think it matters?"

"Not much."

Keith was sorry he'd opened his mouth. He poured himself more treacly tea, tipping the pot till the lid flapped down and the overworked leaves began dropping out.

"Why should you care? Does your old man care?"

"Oh, skip it!" Keith snapped.

"But does he?"

"Oh, I don't know. No. I don't think he does."

"Well, then, that's all that matters, isn't it? I mean his feelings are worth more'n yours, aren't they? Mine fought, sometimes. There was too many of us ever to care more about one than the other really, not that they ever did care much about

195

me. But the ole man, he only played up once. He uster say if he was offered a sheila or a schooner he'd sooner take half a schooner."

Keith giggled. "My dad would say 'neither just now thanks.'"

In the street the sun grappled with them. Chookie took off the duffle coat and carried it untidily on his ginger arm, looking slightly puzzled, his lashless lids pulled together in thought, his free paw cracking two pennies in his pocket. I'll write to the ole girl, he thought. I gotter do it. Don't care if they find me and pin me. She wasn't a bad ole kook. Tell her I'm sorry like. I pinched her biscuits, too, he remembered. But that ain't the main thing. It was the main thing, that gripped him and squeezed and squeezed.

"Half a mo," he said. "I gotta find a paper shop. I wanter send a card."

"Who to?"

"Y'd never guess."

He went into the news agent's and thumbed through a pile while Keith, clutching his money greedily, glanced over the paperback titles. One of the cards sported impossible flowers. It said, "Thinking of you," in Gothic gilt. Chookie paid for it and its envelope, said he wouldn't be a minute, and went back fifty yards to the post office where he scratched clumsily on the card with a government nib: "Dear Miss Trumper. I'm sorry. I hope your alright. I thought I was helping you first then when I saw I wasn't it was too late. I'm sorry. Chookie." He printed her address and licked the stamp thoughtfully. On the top righthand corner of the envelope, tiny as ants, he printed S.A.G. and gummed the stamp down over this abbreviation of his prayer to St. Anthony, and then the red lips of a postal bin claimed it quickly and cusped over his secret.

Dim, distant, disturbing, the kneeling penitent bent forward in Chookie's brain as he slipped the letter into the right hole, and he found his left hand clutching the coat so hard there was sweat on his clammy freckled skin and a stain on the fabric.

Keith had come up. "You're a mug."

"Why?"

"They'll see where it was sent from."

"Aw, I don't seem to care this morning. I feel better now."

"What was it? A public confession?"

"You might call it that," swanked Chookie, who now was confident enough to tell the other boy to bugger off. "I'm goin' across to the sea for a cool-off." Water holes and creek reaches he'd ploughed across with his heavy untrained stroke, gulping, gasping, loutish, yelling, blowing his nose between his fingers, diving from half-sunk logs, swinging from motor-tires, doing a Tarzan on a rope that pranced above the water. He'd never argued with a bright blue biting stretch like this before, that vast blue and white moving plain that caught his eye and enraptured him.

Keith should have grabbed the chance. He couldn't analyze the reasons that impeded his traveling limbs.

"Listen—" he began. "Listen."

But some tide had turned within Chookie this morning and he was off down the branch dirt road to the thin line of blue, striding steadily into heat and dust with Keith pattering after him. I'm going back, he wanted to yell. I'm hitching to the next station and I'm going back. Do you hear? But he didn't yell. He kept on after him, jog-trotting to catch up past the dance hall and the corner store and the bum houses split at the seams that hung on with the windiness of men on cliff edges. Someone a week before, maybe, had dropped a cigarette carton and a chocolate wrapper, and this link he perceived in the incandescence of such moments as he skipped over the truck ruts and cried hopelessly to the not-looking-back figure, "Hang on. Wait, can't you? Wait. I'm coming."

Chookie had peeled off down to his underpants, revealing the coin-spotted shoulders of the red-head. All his clothes he had dumped untidily on the sand when he remembered the harmonica. Fishing it out of his trouser pocket, he shook it, then, unable to resist, capered and sucked a tune from the cheap reeds, brassy, cheeky, while the sun worked pinkly on his bony shoulders and back as he made love to the instrument, playing nothing in particular but something he intended to be the purple sea nibbling the shore rind, putting its cold tongues into bays and caves. All the loneliness of the wild plains which he saw merely as the brown shimmer of the west penetrated his mournful insolent tune as he cradled the tiny mouth-organ, rocking it in his knuckly hands, his thighs swaying.

"What's that?" Keith asked, spoiling it, the silly bastard, and coming up like a mug.

Chookie shook the moisture out, wiped it across his under-pants, and wrapped it up carefully in a hanky.

"Y' never know," he said. "I might be another Adler."

"Did you learn? Take lessons I mean?"

"Don't be crazy."

"You taught yourself?"

"Who else? It ain't hard. Catch Mum and Dad givin' me lessons! The ole man was always tryin' to knock me off it like, but it was me hobby and sometimes I used to get with a mate from school who played the piano a bit by ear and we had terrific times. Used to sneak up to the School of Arts on a Sunday afternoon when nobody was around—all at church—and we'd set the joint jumpin'."

Chookie folded his pants up into a gray jam roll that he wedged under a lump of driftwood and, turning his back abruptly on Keith, sprinted across the loose sand to the rocking coast. He didn't know what to do with this fierce blueness that played with him gently near the beach, but showed violence and impatience the deeper he went. Shading his eyes he saw that Keith had stripped and was wading through the sand as if it were water. This loneliness was palpable. Miles away, headlands lay under haze that became cloud that became upper sky. There were only the two of them and the world, circular, ultramarine, and lost.

"I'll show you, if you like," Keith offered, coming up beside him and panting from the cold of sinewy water. They swam out beyond the shore-break.

"How do you like it?" blond bobbing head asked red.

"Way out!" Chookie trod water madly. He was frightened

as well as excited. Keith showed him how to wait for the clean line of the rising wave, how to rise with it, hanging suspended above the trough, how to swim in ahead furiously to be caught just as it broke and then how, swinging his arms flat back by his side, he could take the wave, be absorbed by it and ride it right up the shingle till chest, belly, thighs grated on sand and the sea sucked your legs trying to lug you back.

It took him half a dozen rides to get the hang of it, because he was too tense to offer himself blindly to the water-pull and pluck. But all at once he found himself coming in smoothly as a gull and he staggered to his feet on the beach, rubbing his salt-stung eyes and coughing.

"Geez, it's marvelous! Marvelous!"

"Boards are better," Keith said. "That's what I was down the coast for this weekend, gunning with a couple of pals."

"Gunning?"

"Riding. It's just a term."

"Nothin' could be much better than that."

"You've never done it."

"Okay. I believe you. Come on. Let's try again."

Keith hesitated. "I've had it, a bit," he said. "Think I'll rest up by the dunes and get a shirt on my back. I can feel the burn starting."

This is it, he decided. I'll slip off and get a ride into the railway. No good telling this character, he's so naïve. He'll simply tag along like an omen, wanting meals and fares. He lay down for a while to disarm Chookie, but the other was wrestling the surf, was locking flesh-muscle in water-muscle and being flung in and down and drawn back farther and tossed in, in a surge of foam and blind eyes and choking. Keith slipped into his shirt and slumped once more on his stomach, feeling the wet clinging cotton of his underwear gradually dry and loosen its hold. Darkness exploded into millions of microscopic fireworks as the sun split under his closed pressed lids like a gorgeous fruit, and before he knew it he was drowsing steadily, deaf when Chookie came dripping up the beach until the minute of defeat as he flopped on the sand beside him.

The hour lengthened. Skin tautened like rubber of an over-distended toy when, drunk on heat and light, they trudged back through lunchtime and sand-hummocks to the town road. Here Keith suddenly became practical and provident, buying a loaf of bread and dates and a packet of sliced cheese, and sitting by the road they shared sandwiches but not their thoughts. Across the way was a pub, noisy as a cicada-mad tree. "Hang about a bit," Chookie said, his mouth bulging with crammed bread and date. "We might get a lift."

They hung. They slammed more sandwiches roughly together and watched for half an hour, but no one else came and no one went away, and to pass time Chookie told a funny story about an organist until at last Keith, sensing him washed and unsmelling, drawn down the long line of this inevitability and wild doom, stopped hating him. Them, cried the secret voice. Hate them. Bernard. Iris. Registering, he substituted Gerald, Iris, and they were destroyed in mental effigy dragged down the unending channels of childhood where he threw with them the blood alleys and the Christmas bike and the first pantomime. See, the fat man said, the fat guy with the features all crowded in the middle of his face. See. I put this long long scarf in here. See . . . tapping an urn made of silver . . . and see, everybody, it's just a straight straight bit of cloth like Mum or Dad or Bernard or Iris might use. Isn't it? Isn't it? Isn't it now? And I pop the lid on and knock like this round and round the bowl. See? Knock knock knock. And then I lift the lid and what do we have? What do we have here? Why! It's . . . knotted! See! Knot after knot. Just like Mum or Dad or Bernard or Iris might have tied it. Oh, he clapped and clapped that funny trick and then there was another funny trick with glass balls and then another.

All chromium and zoom, a cream convertible slithered to a vulgar pause in the snapping gravel, wretching Chookie and Keith from their separate kingdoms to this present which revealed a phony athlete in trunks racing pubwards and returning with half a dozen bottles that he stacked behind the front seat.

"Excuse," Keith said, sauntering and putting on the dog, "I wonder if we could trouble you for a lift?"

The athlete had plenty of brachial muscle. His shining

breasts were wide as car tires. His forehead was low. Only dimly did he mistrust them, for the elasticity of his body responses had not failed him yet.

"What way you going?" he asked.

"Next town," Keith said cunningly, hoping to goodness it was north.

"Brisbane," the athlete said. "But you'll have to squeeze in together in the front."

Chookie was reluctant. His postcard, like a giant flag, would wave him in, no hero, but scoundrel draped across the city. He pulled at Keith's arm, ineffectually, for the boy was already swinging into the front of the car and grinning back insolently. Okay, bastard, thought Chookie, okay. You got me. No dough. No job. He scowled his hopelessness at them, went back to the grass margin where he had left the duffle coat and tried to put a happy face on.

"Here's y' book," he called to Keith.

"Okay," the other said, not glancing, but gluttoning on the complicated dashboard of the car. "Okay."

Chookie squeezed in beside and the driver gave him a special investigating glance that frightened the hell out of him. He decided to disarm.

"What a beaut!" Chookie admired, his eyes running over the car's form. "Could you let her out a bit?"

The athlete's simplicity constantly sought these sunny spots and in them expanded and glowed. Matily they squashed together, beside his cigarette-ad profile and watched his large, confident, and cruel brown hands twiddle about along the dashboard. It had as many gadgets as a computer.

"Music?" the joy-boy asked and did not stay for an answer as they bucketed jazzily back to the highway in a flurry of calypso and small stones. The sudden wind scalped them, the trees became a forty-foot hedge and, "Jeepers!" Chookie cried, but the pace forced the word back down his throat as the speedometer registered ninety on the straight strip running north.

"What you kids do?" the driver asked. They could not see his eyes behind protectively dark lenses and waited a little for him to answer his own question. "Holidays?"

They agreed. They'd come up from Sydney, they said, and were on their way home, they explained with touching omission of detail.

"You staying there?" asked the driver. "Whereabouts?"

"Strathfield," Keith said instantly—who had an aunt there. "We both did. Chook works with my dad."

"Oh?" The driver managed a side glance. "You haven't much luggage on you. What've you been doing?"

"Sleeping out. Just for fun. My buddy plays the harmonica. We worked the surf pavilions."

"Izzat so?" Dark eyes was impressed. They were on the fringe of the next town and the car slowed down.

"I'll take you on a bit," the driver said. "To my next stop." One hand patted Keith's plump knee and removed itself before the knee could either respond or withdraw. "How would that be? We could stick around a little."

The boys' eyes slid together fraternally while physical comfort softened Keith's acceptance of the situation.

"Okay," they said. "Kind of you."

"Forget it!" said the big boy. And, "Zoom zoom!" he cried playfully as they passed the de-restricting sign and roared loutishly north.

They tagged along all afternoon, bumming food and Cokes with an expertise that gave them both a thrill until, 'round above five, the big fellow slung off to the pub, and the boys, in the amity of outcasts, sensed each other's body warmth there in the slanting sun. Lean and singular, Chookie rubbed an impractical hand across his nose.

"Chow?" Chookie asked unbelievably.

"You've had plenty. It's too early, anyway."

"But I've got gut-ache. Me belly's aching like hell."

"It was the way you gulped that bread down this morning. Too much bread, you great gutser!" And he tapped the other lightly on the stomach. "Let's have a malted. That'll fill the spaces and settle your ulcer."

"What ulcer?"

"Oh, no ulcer. It's just a phrase. Bernard has one. He's always sipping the stuff for his ulcer, so he says."

"Who's Bernard?"

"My father."

"You call him by his first name?"

"Yes. Two chocolate malteds, please." Keith pressed an unexpected surge of feeling against the counter to diminish it and watched a fly crawl lingeringly over a plate of cakes. "They wanted me to, Bernard and Iris. They thought it was treating me like an adult."

"Cripes," Chookie said. "Mine woulder walloped me if I'd come that at him."

I never wanted to, Keith stopped himself from admitting. Not really. I didn't want to be an adult as fast as that. And not that sort of adult. He thought longingly of the other homes he had visited where there were limitations imposed, where language was minded before children, reading matter vetted, and soft drinks the only ones offering.

"He should learn to drink wine with his dinner," Iris had announced with maddening suburban liberalism when he turned thirteen. "He must appreciate the normal complements of living." At least she didn't say "gracious!" "I don't like it much," he complained after the first few mouthfuls of a rather terrible wine. "I'd just as soon not."

"You'll get used to it," Iris reassured him, no longer all mother. But he pined for a big bosom and hips and pumpkin pies and Yorkshire puddings instead of this dried-out version of society hostess who lived it up with bulk liquors (Bernard, bring flagons!), brass costume jewelry and a lot of hair rinse. But he'd persevered. He'd played it along with them. And after he'd got used to the game and the scoring rules, took over and laid down a few rules himself, and appalled them finally with his sudden monstrous unchildishness. If they had peeled away the grotesqueries of the puppet-work they would have found a frightened small boy working the glove and somewhere there would have been tears.

Chookie made disgusting noises as his straw probed the froth dregs. He was recollecting also, not pleasantly, and he was seven—or was it eight? Just after they'd come in from Dirranbandi and there'd been all them rows over some bit the ole man had been chasing after. One evening when they was all in bed he'd heard 'em goin' hammer and tongs in the kitchen and suddenly his dad had shoved his mum through the back door and burst its hinges. The police had come and all after that and the ole man had been bound over and his mum had gone about victorious and injured and Pop never had a beer for months. But he'd liked his dad in those days, and with a few bob he'd saved working on the paper run he'd managed to give him on Father's Day a bottle of beer wrapped in paper with blue moustaches and red walking sticks all over.

"Howju get that, Arch?" his dad had asked. "That's mighty nice of y'. Howju get it, hay?"

Mum had come in. She was like an empress those days, swollen and mighty and about to have her fourth.

"Where did yer get it, Arch?" she asked. "I won't have no boy of mine going into pubs. Understand that now. I'll have a word with Grogan about this, see if I don't."

But the ole man had been opening the bottle and was rummaging about for a glass. "Real nice of y' boy," he had said smiling. "Best present I've had in years, savin' yer mum!"

"No yer don't!" Mum said, lunging across. "He can take it right back. I won't have no child going into any pub. Just tell me where yer got it, Arch, and I'll take it meself." Her voice rose.

"Too late," Dad said, calm like. "I've poured meself one!" And he lifted the glass and jerked it upward at her. Toastin', he explained later.

But Mum ground down like a great tank, grabbed the bottle and poured it into the sink before either of them was properly ready to stop her.

"Why you lousy old bitch!" his dad had roared. "You filthy rotten wowser of a bitch!" And then he had drunk the rest of his glass extra slow and mocking and his mum had slammed into the front bedroom and later, just a little later, they could hear her sniveling and blowing her nose. The ole man had crept up beside the door and hissed through it, "I hope y' know y' stink. I'm glad."

For some unknown reason, the next day Chookie had gone

down to an old apple tree in the backyard by the fowl run and had spent half an hour carving his initials: A M 1897. It looked beaut. He forgot the tree was only a youngster. Someone, some day, seeing that . . . what? During the year he remembered adding a few other initials and dates and things like DIG HERE, rubbing a chunk of dirt in to take away the newness, to take away the now of it all.

"Finished?" Keith was asking. Delicately he blotted his moustache on a filthy linen square.

"Swank!" sneered Chook good-naturedly. "There useter to be an ole bloke up at Condo who smarmed about in suit and sandshoes and every Fridee he'd come up Fitzherbert Street to the pubs pullin' on a pair of ole knitted gloves. And his fingers'd stick straight through the ends. He carried a sort of cane, too."

"Was he mad or something?"

"Yeah. Just a nut. A Queensland nut." He giggled away.

"One and four, please," Keith said, holding out a paw.

"Geez! You don't forget nothin', do you? Okay, here." He counted it in threepences and pennies, rattling a lot, taking his mouth-organ out and giving it another shake, a testing happy trill and a scrupulous rewrap.

"Let's pick up the big boy again," Keith said. "For kicks. We'll ride right in to town!"

10

Stubbornly Bernard refused to take any action.

"No," he said to Iris. "No. He has to work this one out himself. He's alive, not far away, and in no trouble, thank God. He'll be home. If anything were wrong we would have heard."

Iris tantrumed for three insane hours while Bernard, far more anxious than he would for one tremblingly satisfying moment have revealed, made several pots of tea and continued to speak with a quiet reasonableness that only served to stimulate her rage.

"Why!" she screamed. "Why."

"I simply forbid it," Bernard explained, exerting moth-eaten authority.

Iris said, "But you hate me, you bastard! You're only doing this because you hate me. Because it makes me sick with worry. You're attacking me through him. Don't you feel anything for your own child?"

After two hours of it, he lost his temper.

"Shut up, you madwoman," he said, "or I'll say a few things you won't like."

She narrowed her bloodshot eyes and challenged him.

"Go on! Say the worst. You've never been a proper father to him, I mean a normal father, stuck in there with your music, your books."

"At least I am his father," Bernard said carefully. "But if we had a child now I wouldn't be so sure."

The blood paused in Iris's face. "What do you mean?"

"You know exactly what I mean. And, my dear Iris, so does Keith. And that is partly the cause of this bother. Oh, don't cry. If you do that I'll want to hit you. You entered on your whole little romance dry-eyed—and I knew—yes! Don't be surprised. I was the willing cuckold. And don't deny. I thought it might brighten your life. After all, we didn't seem to be going anywhere. What had I to lose—that I hadn't already lost?"

Now that he exposed his indifference to her she hated him, perversely, longing for him to want what he gave away so readily.

"No," he went outrageously on. "You had my blessing for what it was worth. Gerald was a clean, dull bore. But clean, Iris. I did like that clean bit. And I felt sorry for him, too, you know. It's no good being hurt when I say that. Only another man understands what I mean. After all, what was he depriving me of?"

"You go on about it now quite a lot for a man who didn't care."

"But I didn't, Iris. Rest assured. That was a nice comfy cliché, wasn't it? But there was someone who did. Keith cared."

"He never knew."

"Ah yes. But he did."

"How do you know?"

"In half a dozen ways that if you had been a more observant mother you might have noticed. The chief clue was his sudden aversion to you. Poor old Keith. He'd always missed out on something parental—father-love, you say. Yes. And then . . . boom! Mother virtue collapses."

"I don't believe you. You're only saying it to cover neglect."

"No? Well, we can always ask him."

Iris really wept then. "You couldn't do that."

"My dear, there is no need. Have you never watched young Seabrook and Keith together? Didn't you ask yourself why they developed this unexpected attachment? They never used to be great friends, if you recall. Surely you asked yourself. Do you think for a minute that they haven't spent days talking about it? Perhaps young Tom was speculating on you as a step-mamma."

Iris went into the bathroom and began to vomit while Bernard, in between heartbeats and sips of tea, went out to the front porch and watched the long road to the bridge down which his son must come. Early afternoon traffic. The gardens beyond the river. Everything was in its set place, with accustomed attitudes to reassure him. Asphalt walks and cut lawns, the roly-poly slope that somersaulted straight over the retaining wall to the river flats. Fifteen years up here, Bernard moaned within, is too long. And yet when he first moved into his domestic nook, nothing was capable of being long enough, and he had been, he recalled, afraid to examine the gyrating circumference of mortality that spun, flashing ominous light-shafts. Turning aside, he had imagined some infinity of material bliss, but found he had peered into the shifting nebulae that clouded a desperate unknown, that his tolerance of for ever and ever was sickeningly limited to the duration, say, of a hire-purchase span or Iris's plans for the Christmas holidays or the quartet he was always half-way through writing: the end was never really in sight, yet one had an idea of the whole that had all the muted prismatic colors melting into one shimmering, elusive, incomplete thing. I do not hate you, Iris, he discovered in that moment. Not at all now. Whatever it was that scorched or burned I have expelled in my last fire-breathings upon you. All I want, all I will ever want, is the warmth of my son, our mutual toleration, for his running away has at last convinced me of his love.

When he inspected the sky-shadow above him, the somber quality of trees along River Terrace, when he calculated that although there might be no general rain ever again, he was yet aware that in this particularly secret and tantalizing acre the drought had broken and he could see Keith clearly through the·glass that had divided them from each other, clearly as if he had only to reach out to touch with father fingers the firm arm, and still straight shoulder. They faced each other through the transparent barrier and each was mouthing something at the other, was crying, "Come in," was answering, "I want to, I want to." Boy, he shouted silently, rubbing his soft musician hands through his straggling hair, boy. You were right all those years ago when you lusted after denial. He began to smile, a smile that overpowered him, brought him back from the lost country to definite decisions in his own well-charted landscape. He walked slowly back to the house.

"I'm sorry," he was just starting to say to Iris, when the telephone began to ring.

At four Mr. Varga left his Wednesday rooms stone cold sober and drove out toward the coast road, nagged by conscience, the silence of the Leverson family, and a sense of doom. Searching seemed pointless, but a night at the shack might drag off the fog that settled, sticky, oppressive, each time he attempted to think. His own peculiar neurosis, he had discovered, was an inability to sort out problems even after hours of extensive analysis. In fact, the lengthier the probing, the hazier, the more autumn-toned the solution. I will not think of this at all as I drive, he rationalized, and in this way I shall eventually bring a sharper mind to the whole matter. He was glad Leverson had avoided police action. And he especially refused to analyze this gladness. Taste the moment, Leo would advise gaily. It may be your last.

He drove with *brio*, with the elegance of a man confident of his dress and the condition of his bank account and bowels. There were times when he barely remembered being a child, and that was the impression he created wherever he went—a circumfusion of permanent gecko-faced adulthood, the eyes blinking against the secret sins; the thick hide of the rationalizer, horny and coated with the self-induced imperviousness he must maintain to preserve his balance.

He coffeed and sandwiched along the highway. He wiped a fastidious mouth. He selected his favorite menthol-flavored cigarette, and he drove doomwards through early summer languors, the somnolence of rising sap and heat coming and the eye-burning blueness of the coastal road.

Eheu, sighed his classical fly-screen door as he pulled it back.

Eheu. The room hooded its eyes, and yawned in his face while he pottered, plugged in an electric jug to hear the purring and final bubbling with the gratitude of one who has clung to a raft in a never-ending desert of water. Keith would have gone south, he supposed. Anything else was ridiculous. He could visualize young Leverson charming the haulers all the way to Sydney until the city's skin drum was before him ready to be tapped by the most sensitive of fibrillating fingers.

His big male muscular pin-ups flexed continually from the walls, giving an illusion of crowdedness with all those impassive, unaccusing but commemoratory figures. What was it Julia Geoghegan had said?—"Beef patties, darling?" Of course she was an amusing bitch, he knew; but there was probably something awry with her own sexual drive. They had all been squatting about the fire last winter at the Seabrooks. Julia was dazzling despite her age, with heavy green-blue lids and a lot of fake rings that she wore with her own special flair together with shockingly expensive clothes that never quite fitted. The skirt had ridden up above her bony knees so that he caught a glimpse of nylons held up by old chewed garters and then a mass of white thigh blotched with networks of varicose veins. Every gesture was dramatized and underlined by her ring-cluttered hands as she talked swiftly, intelligently, and breathlessly, holding them all on lines which she twitched.

"We were never teen-agers," she was saying. "Nevernevernever. Tobralco prints of animals and flowers or the gathered crêpe suitable for forty-year-olds. There was never this cult. Fashion designers left us alone because we were at the awkward age. Now the only awkward age is ours."

"The menopause," suggested snaky Leo.

"My dear, you flatter me. I'm way past. But no. That's really what I meant, you know. The forty-five plus group nobody wants." Her husband laughed into his Scotch like something demented.

"There's an enormous wasted labor force there," Julia said, "rotting away at bowls or in front of the telly or going on to quiz shows to be insulted by pup announcers and nearly win things they don't really want."

"But they think that's their reward," Kathleen Seabrook

said, "after years of baby-minding and getting up at night. It's a well-earned rest."

"It might be," agreed Dr. Geoghegan, "for those who have had four or five children, but hardly for those with one or none." She could not be bothered being kind to Kathleen, whom she thought a fool. "That's what puzzles me. How on earth do you fill in your time?"

And then, of course, Leo had made the one remark that no one could ever forget—now that the facts were established: "Oh, there's reading and shows and a little adultery on the side."

"The back, surely," Dr. Geoghegan had suggested quick as birth-pangs. But they had all looked at each other, not diverted, and they knew.

Varga locked the house up on the savory traces of his meal. The shack was like a false heart which he entered and set vibrating. Tick. Tick. He regarded its plumb square glassy walls with the despair of one who has tried for years to achieve an intimacy with another and failed. "I'll sell you, you Judas," he snarled at it in the darkness. "But for three times what you cost me." The restlessness that poisoned him drove him out again in dissatisfaction. He was forever driving to and then away, the attained proving empty and desolate. Perhaps he had half expected the boy would have been there making use of the place. But there was no sign at all that anyone had trodden for one moment on his seagrass matting. Even the cushions were still lying where Tommy Seabrook had pitched them. The car sounded angry as he, snarling on the U-turn, while his radio throbbed savagely and he sang with it in a kind of tuneless rage that augmented his arrogance, his defeat, his emptiness. He was tired of these purposeless high-speed excursions that like drugs became so necessary he was constantly haring down highways at dangerous speeds while the inner distortion took over and the outside world streamed by in a joyless scuttling of pedestrian or lurching of oncoming car. His technique was startling, but the eyes did not see. Instinct guided the twisting wheels and so, raging, singing, he was three-quarters of the way back to the city when a new night-club beckoned with glittering eye from a side road.

It was the biggest, glassiest purveyor of no-joy he had seen for weeks. Sea Urchins, said a sign, flashing on and off provocatively. The shrimps were drawn up in shoals and had been sucked in by a blare of youth and jazz. Speakers screeched across the car park and falsely green lawns, across the fountain that fell like flowers, across the no-man's land of footpath. Leo drove into a narrow space near a side wall and swam up the stream of light and noise.

Couples, untouching, gyrated to the pulsations that came from a small platform where five young men, wielding guitars like submachine guns, thrust phrases over and over at the tumescent mob. Polo necks and beards became confused. Girls in cotton sweatshirts and tight jeans waggled their behinds and flung their manes of hair forward with screams. The foyer cage of glass looked in on this tank of trapped fish, and shark Leo prowled up and down the black and white tiles until a pink-sequined girl sidled out of a pouf booth and attended to him. There were mobiles of harmless artiness, unframed nudes, lots of potted cotton palms and rubber plants, and a whole wall of hand-printed anemone, mollusk, stone-fish (hoped Varga), trochus, nautilus and conch.

Moodily he sat at a side table and forked up oysters, stirred up an entrée of mussels in a thin wine sauce. No one looked at him. He was too old. There raged about him adolescence with its hair bleached, straightened, thudding and thumping to the music. The guitarists vanished. A spaghetti-tube pianist hit the stage while the girls went mad, screaming before and after he began to play, stroking imperfect minor chords in beguine time. Cameo faces swayed behind curtains of hair. Surfie boys moved with the undulating ease of those who have been on top of the world. Leo attempted to hook onto one submissive eye, but they glazed, swept past, and under his fishy breath Leo cursed.

I've got you under my skin, the pianist crooned in a rich fruitcake voice. *I got you deep in the heart of me* . . . somewhere close by in the pearl-gray smoke fuzz a girl-kid squealed. Lordy, thought Varga half-turning and seeing the face, the jeans. Not here. Not again. . . . *simply a part of me*. . . .

Drool, drool, and another squeal from the rear and half a dozen swaying youngsters let loose, pushing through the late fad bead-craze curtains.

"Mister?" someone said behind. "Mister?" And there was an Ajax boy, blond as a starlet, bunched over a chair at the next table, and making gimme gestures with his cigarette-lusting fingers. Leo looked this bird over—who winked and smiled very cutely and said thanks and turned away so that all Varga could see was a tight little bottom, and a spread of muscular back and a bigger man, a real muscle-man with a low forehead and behind that . . . behind that, two straining kids in grubby clothes. One of them moved off up near the stage where the guitarists had reappeared, together with a youth in a sprayed-on glitter suit of sinuous silver that rippled with every thrust of his pelvis. Girls went mad. "Twist and shout," hummed the kid at the next table, pounding with his foot. Twist and shout. And above the riot and the racket the high operating thrust of a mouth-organ swung away with the tune and the rhythm and there was chaos as the player got shoved up, dirty jeans and all, with the jerking quintet on stage. "Woweeeeeee!" screamed the girls. Woweeeeeee! *Now you got me going like I knew you would.* . . . Take it away, kid! Take it away, pianner. And they took it away in a series of vibrating chords while the singer and the organist reeled off into space above the rhythm line, pursuing each other with wild improvisation that touched the essence of jazz. The squealers moved forward and among them, Keith, distant, sound-borne, waved at by Ajax and athlete, but unhearing, was tensed forward, forward, to the stage where Chookie curved and grinned above his instrument.

Leo let excitement take over and the impulsiveness that all his life created intolerable situations jogged him by the shoulder to make him lean forward to the next couple, smiling like a crocodile above his beard.

"Coffee with me?"

But this was not his lucky night. During a measuring pause of insolent length, the sandpiper inspected as much of Mr.

Varga as was visible, noting with an expert tiny eye the texture of fabric, the heavy case of a watch, and, inhaling with the merest twitch of his nose an expensive aromatic aftershave lotion, consented. "We're all together." He turned to the athlete, who was beating the table with a closed fist, and said something softly. There was a nod. Mr. Varga accepted, set out to be charming while the orgy out by the piano filled in the gaps. Leo beat time, too, with his plump, black-haired hand, and was alert for the slightest sign. He never missed a nuance. But he talked too much. He messed things up for himself by rattling on, not in a good-natured or simple way, but with the angry compulsiveness of one who has something to hide and sets up a smoke-screen of wit and false wisdom that is all give-away. The surfie boy watched him carefully. He didn't go much on middle-aged types with their jowl folds and their receding hair. Leo's went out like the tide and broke in a smother of black curls on the crisp edge of his collar.

"Ride?" Leo asked, longing to inquire about Keith, but withholding the impulse for a judicious moment.

"What?" asked the boy coolly.

"Boards."

The kid grinned. "I'm fussy," he said.

"You're good at double-talk, too," Leo said. "I mean surf."

Surfie boy couldn't be bothered answering. He turned away rudely and said something to the big man at his side. Leo created a hiatus by calling the waitress and ordering more coffee. "Sweets, perhaps?" he insisted, forcing them to acknowledge. And when the breaking-down process was under way, he leaned over to the older man and said as casually as he could, "That blond lad you waved to—happen to know him?"

"Only casually."

"Oh?"

"I gave them a lift. They're coming up to town with us."

"Them?"

"Him and that other kid. The one playing the mouth-organ up there."

Leo was silent, inspecting the stage.

"Do you know him?" asked the athlete.

"I'd hardly be inquiring, would I?"

"Wouldn't you?"

"What the hell do you mean by that?"

"What you mean, probably."

Surfie boy was grinning wildly, sucking his coffee up through a lump that filtered from his spoon. He giggled. "You sound like an underwater gun," he said.

"What do you mean?" Leo asked. Something dangerous swelled inside him.

"Oh, come off it! Gun. Everyone knows what that is."

"I think you've got me wrong," Leo said, knowing he hadn't. He was afraid to say more.

"Have I?" The kid exchanged a glance with his companion. "I don't think we have, though. This place is packed with 'em."

"Packed with what?"

"Oh, for God's sake! Stop kidding! You're wasting your time with us, I tell you." He scraped the last of the cream noisily from his dish.

"Tell me," Leo said softly and with menace, leaning dangerously across the table so that their faces could almost have touched, "if I've got you all wrong as you say, why do you accept my coffee? Are you a couple of gold-diggers? Stinking little gold-diggers?"

"Manners," the boy said. "Watch it, mister. I could make it nasty for you. It's an offense to solicit."

Leo stood up sharply, so abruptly the table rocked and some of the coffee slopped hotly on the boy's thigh.

"Jesus!" he said. "Watch it, will you, you great ape?"

Just as Leo tried to apologize the words banked up inside and unexpectedly the big man swung at him and gave him a shove. Behind him the music had stopped. Keith was winding back through voices. "Keith!" cried Leo uselessly. "Keith!"

Athlete pushed his fist into Leo's calling mouth and instinctively the two of them grappled and rocked between the tables, belting each other about the chest and face while furniture quaked and toppled. Keith began to run forward. He had seen the great black flag of Leo's beard and behind him Chookie had leaped from the stage, flailing the mob so that in a minute it seemed everyone was running and hitting without reason, slashing between the screams and squeals of the girls and the shoving onlookers. Two waiters had come forward and had each grabbed one of the fighters around the waist, tugging and dragging them apart. Crazily Keith began to laugh and laugh. Leo's nose was bleeding and blood was trickling down messily into the dark hair of his beard, while from the dizzy corner of his eye he saw Keith laughing and the snarl in him built up like an enormous growth, so that he shouted, "Get outside, you little bitch. Get out into the car and wait for me." Then he was punched again and subsided under a pile of rolling men who had him down and pinioned.

"Quick!" Chookie hissed, coming up behind Keith in the crowd. "If y' don't hurry the cops'll be here."

They pushed through the glass doors just as the manager began to shout that no one was to leave.

In the cool eclipse of the car park they ran between the vehicles, bending low and looking back along the glossy hoods to see if they were being followed. But between the impassive cars nothing else moved, though in a minute they heard the scream of a siren coming along the main road.

"This way," Chookie whispered. "This way. The mug left the key in it. He was so pissed he didn't notice what he was doin'."

The athlete's lone chrome job smiled through the blackness at them. Come in, stranger, it too was saying, and before they knew it they were inside and Chookie was fiddling with the dashboard knobs.

"Can you drive?" Keith found himself obliged to know.

"Yup!" Chookie grinned confidently. "I am the original twelve-year-old milk-boy champ!"

Their frightened eyes inspected each other and each was unwilling to give that final order.

"Should we wait?" Keith asked, only an amateur at that.

"The police . . ." His voice wobbled away. "Go on," he said urgently. "Turn her over."

It started as sweetly as forgotten childhood, and in half a minute Arch Mumberson had her backed out of the park, swung about, and was rocketing north.

Shrimps in a can, Iris and Bernard lay implacable in bed. Bernard's parrot profile projected an enormous dada parrot on to the wall, a shadow Iris tried to avoid seeing. But she was turned that way with her back to him. After this, she was thinking, I shall be able to cartoon him at parties, tear him out of newspaper, make masks, do anything at all that will involve me with him, and still we shall be as separate as paper dolls. There's nothing now—husband, lover, son. A few tears of self-pity rolled down.

Ringing violently, the telephone throbbed like an important cardiac muscle in the heart of the house and made these two at last to confront each other.

"I'll take it this time," Bernard said, and he struggled out with his aging white legs and went, closing the bedroom door behind him so that she might not hear.

"Yes?" he asked the black cavern.

"Mr. Leverson?"

"Yes." Hearing the stranger voice identify itself with city police headquarters he felt his heart stop as if it too had been picked up by a listener. Had he a son? the voice demanded. Have I a son? Bernard pondered. He had indeed only just discovered his son, discovered with complete warmth and love the troubled eye, the sulking lip, the helplessness, emptiness and need that was his son.

"Yes," he said heavily. "I have."

Could he tell them where the lad was now? the voice went on. Bernard paused. No, he said at last, he couldn't do that. The lad had been gone from home for some days. Had he sought police aid? the voice, censuring, inquired. No, Bernard was guiltily forced to admit, he hadn't. He had his reasons. Need he explain now? No, the voice said then, more kindly.

No. That could be gone into later. The voice went on for some time, making statements that spelled doom and from which he extracted only one thing.

"Where?" he asked heavily after a while. "Where did you say?"

"Just outside Brisbane on the main highway."

"Anyone hurt?" Bernard asked, not wanting to know.

The barbaric simplicity of this question struck him as he said the words that had to be asked. Across the living room there was one of Iris's flower arrangements in a bowl of translucent green; three—three!—everlastings limped upward against an ivy-entwined rib of polished driftwood. There was a great deal more leaf than flower, but the discs of copper glowed tawnily through a complication of tendril. He saw this. He saw his left hand tremble as it played with the tassel of his dressing gown. He did not even hear the answer the first time and had to ask the voice to repeat it.

"I'm afraid so," said the small far voice. "A youth was killed. The other lad is in hospital. I think he'll be all right."

"I see." Bernard could not force himself to the next step of the game at once, but in a minute his voice came out high and dry. "Which lad was killed, can you tell me?" Keith he thought, Keith. Pink, warm, wet, scabby, peeing, jumping, giggling, pop-eyed, grinning, yowling, whining, arrogating. The voice was like a far star of which some rays might reach him millions of years from now.

"That's the trouble," the slow voice was explaining. "We're not sure. There were only a couple of things to go by. One of the boys must have been carrying a book. There was a name in it. Only a paperback, you know. But that's how we got on to you. We've been a while tracking you down. You see, the lad's still unconscious."

"I see." Bernard saw. He saw. Beneath his dressing gown his body felt as if it were weightless, yet the curve of thigh and arm were part of the nervous entity that was he. It might not be his boy, the voice was saying stupidly, might not. But if he could help, identify. . . . Bernard thought he was going to vomit there and then with apprehension, but he leaned against the wall and, holding to the acknowledged support of a room-divider he had always hated, agreed that whatever he could do he would.

Iris was paler than loss when he opened the bedroom door again and he told her what must be done. She did not answer but commenced dressing in silent frenzy, pulling on a skirt, dragging a sweater carelessly over her limp hair.

"Don't come," he said. "Please don't come. We are both guilty."

Without a word she pulled on stockings and shoes and walked out of the house to wait in the driveway for him to back the car. She waited there in the dark of the hedge as he finished dressing and thought how like tears the city lights looked, wetly splashed upon the air in the fine tropical weather. Dusk powdered with neon and the long spatterings of yellow across the outgoing tide where boats waited patiently for men to pasture them at sea. She wished she were going out with them to an unknown landfall.

"Please pray," she asked her husband when she slid in beside him, shivering on the cold leather. "Please pray." Her trembling filled him with pity and a trace of the old love which made him pat her knee and take her hand. Moved by the same need, she gripped his fingers so harshly he exclaimed. Where will we be, Bernard found himself wondering, if it is Keith? Or if it is not? Are we reuniting? Is some catalytic process at work? When we stand before whomever we stand before, must we become a couple or will we proceed as separately as we have been? Appalled, he was aware that at this moment that should not be the core problem, yet it was the original ache, the one from which all others had stemmed. His guilt ate away at him and was still probing and piercing when a starched woman said, "This way," and took them into an office that seemed crowded with men in blue or white uniforms.

The sense of unreality persisted. Once before, at an artists' ball, surrounded by fleshy Pierrettes, Cavalier bucks with the eyes of wine-merchants, he had this same sensation, as Iris and he had lived it up all night in borrowed costumes and personalities. Nothing of it was true. Yet now the voices addressed him, as then; eyes investigated, as then; but he could not focus and questions and eyes slid over and away into a mist through which Iris was saying yes and no and attempting to discipline her crumpling face.

". . . was wearing a duffle coat," he heard one voice say at last. "Did your son own such a coat?"

"No. No, certainly not. I never allowed him to get one," Bernard said. The first denial after years of indulgence, he lamented. The first.

"Mr. Leverson"—a big man with rimless glasses seemed to be questioning him and instructing at once—"it was in the pocket of this coat that we found the book."

"The book?"

"The book with your son's name in it."

Iris cried out loud, gabbling sounds of protest and outrage. He lent many books, Bernard argued inwardly. Over and over he would lend them and I always had to reprimand and say, Who does the paying?

"Perhaps it is one of my son's friends," he said stupidly.

"I'm terribly sorry," someone said inanely. "Terribly."

"Would you care to identify him, Mr. Leverson?" another gentle voice inquired.

Bernard could only nod. The muscles jerked. The brain willed it. He was hollowed out of time. Automaton feet followed authority. The hard polish of the corridor reflected the hard white of the aseptic walls harder than marriage, than anything either had ever known. Someone propelled them on, on, through mazes of especial agony and at last into another door, into an area of whiteness.

At the sight of the silent form on the bed Iris began to cry out loud as if she were alone.

"Please," Bernard said. "Please, Iris." They were terrified to look as the the nurse drew back the edge of the sheet from the still still face whose features were unlike any they had seen. And then Iris cried out once more and swayed and fell against her husband as she realized the red hair, the vulnerable ugly face upon the pillow were not those of her son.

Is relief always like this, sharp as knives? Without smile or word? People about them were apologizing for the unnecessary shock, sympathizing, but not congratulating, Bernard at last was aware, as they sat once more in a waiting room and obediently swallowed sedatives.

When at last they could turn to each other, alone for the moment in the organized neglect that is part of hospitals, Bernard reached for the words each wanted. "The other boy?" he asked. "The one with him?" Poor Iris, he thought. Poor dear Iris. Her hair hung desolate over the collar of her coat; she had forgotten make-up and he almost loved her for that, for a positive display of otherness, of concern, that aged but endeared. It could only be, Bernard realized. Thank God, he said. Thank God. He is safe and I have my miracle. Tonight, or tomorrow perhaps, for I feel too tired tonight, I will write to Doug Lingard and offer proof and display my cure like a leper with a dried-out scar. Proud as a leper supporting the stumps of the disease, but moving still, living, absorbing God in great doses. Then he too—he too may tell how and why to the little nun. A panacea of wider and wider application.

"When you feel a little better," a nurse was saying too brightly, "you'll be able to go up and see your boy."

"How is he?" Bernard asked. "How is he?"

"He's quite comfortable," she assured in hospital jargon. "Doctor's settled him down nicely."

The doctors had disappeared.

They waited and waited. After half an hour someone brought them cups of tea and plain biscuits. "Not long now," said the nurse. She smiled brilliantly, a flash that came, that went. Bernard and Iris sat close together for the first few minutes and then he rose and stood apart near a window that stared desolately down the concrete drive and past the flashy cars in the section reserved for staff only. Inwardly his heart prayed over and over, Let him be all right let him be. After this, he thought . . . and made all sorts of promises.

"You can go up now. Doctor's ready," another Sister said, coming from a side room. The little nurse bustled them into a lift that rose and rose toward heaven, led them through a swinging door, and took them to another man in a white coat who was standing beside the screened bed. The eyes were those of not-enemy and not-friend. They met Bernard's, that is all, with that impersonal curiosity that doctors perfect, giving nothing but waiting to extract. "Just a few minutes," he said gravely and held a wing of the screen aside for them.

They tiptoed forward, smiling foolishly and automatically upon this homonuclus that had survived for them, had survived with closed eyes and withdrawn mouth turned inward toward the pillow that supported the bandaged head. His arms lay outside the coverlet, alive, but not moving now, no longer fighting. Someone had called "Time!" and he was back in his corner and his parents were in theirs. The fight was over really, Bernard knew, over for a long while at least— and he was the loser.

"Keith," Iris whispered. But he did not move. His breathing went steadily; he was another person, they both saw now, for the first time perhaps since the umbilical cord had been cut! It is too late, Bernard thought, too late to give you the sort of discipline I now know you wanted more than anything in the world.

He bent his head down close to his son's cheek and whispered, "I'm sorry, feller."

"He's not out of it yet," the doctor explained. "Probably another fifteen minutes. He's been heavily sedated."

"Out of what?" Bernard asked, suddenly afraid.

The doctor held a finger to his lips. "Outside. I'll explain outside."

"It's nearly a week since I've seen him," Bernard said to the doctor. "It seems like five years."

He moved forward and gently touched the blankets that mounded across the breathing chest. The face remained aloof, the lips closed over the inner dream. The eyelids did not flicker, although they soon would. Bernard took in every detail of his face, his self-face, from the adolescent down above his upper lip, the curled lobe of the ear, the gentle pulsing of the artery within the neck. He absorbed all this and then looked down the length of him that seemed more than a week ago, down down to where he could see a cage supporting the bedclothes above the feet. And he realized instantly what had happened.

"How bad?" he asked the doctor, who had been bracing himself for this.

"Only one," he said. "Just below the knee. We couldn't avoid it. It had to be done at once."

Iris ran from the room. He could hear her struggling with the nurse in the corridor. But Bernard came back to the bed and bent down to touch his sleeping son's cheek. He was in a fisher hat and staggering along with a slopping bucket of sea-water, had cut his foot on an oyster shell, had run madly across the lawn to impale his tender sole on a half-concealed rake, had fallen from park trees and cut his knees, had opened up a shin on gravel, shale, rock, had worn plaster, lint, iodine, ointment of all kinds. Was thankfully put into long'uns and transferred accident proclivity to fingers, and then became overnight the sullen sophisticate who had forgotten what it was like to take a fall, only to pretend superciliousness in order to say, "Hey bop a re bop, Bernard!"

Bernard's love shook him with its surprise, beat down his shuddering, dawning blood so that he could apprehend nothing at all beyond his son restored. The four days were the five years of non-loving in which they had lost each other and now could only re-claim, re-assert by the tenderest mundanity. Understand? he begged the white-coated man beside him. Understand that beside my discovery this—this thing—is a bagatelle.

Bernard put his mouth to the discovered curve of his boy's cheek and found the most fatuous smile of delight on his own lips. With a gentle finger he traced a line written about the sleeping mouth, and looking up, the taste of his son still upon his tongue, made his last gesture.

"That's new," he said.